DARK INSIDE

JEYN ROBERTS

DARK INSIDE

SIMON & SCHUSTER BFYR

NEW YORK LONDON TORONTO SYDNEY NEW DELHI

To my parents, Don and Peggy Roberts.
Your love and support know no bounds.

SIMON & SCHUSTER BFYR

An imprint of Simon & Schuster Children's Publishing Division
1230 Avenue of the Americas, New York, New York 10020

SIMON & SCHUSTER BFYR is a trademark of Simon & Schuster, Inc.
For information about special discounts for bulk purchases, please
contact Simon & Schuster Special Sales at 1-866-506-1949 or
business@simonandschuster.com.
The Simon & Schuster Speakers Bureau can bring authors to your
live event. For more information or to book an event, contact the
Simon & Schuster Speakers Bureau at 1-866-248-3049 or visit our
website at www.simonspeakers.com.
Also available in a SIMON & SCHUSTER BFYR hardcover edition
Book design by Krista Vossen
The text for this book is set in Bembo Std.
Manufactured in the United States of America
First SIMON & SCHUSTER BFYR paperback edition September 2012
2 4 6 8 10 9 7 5 3 1
The Library of Congress has cataloged the hardcover edition as
follows:
Roberts, Jeyn.
Dark inside / Jeyn Roberts. — 1st ed.
p. cm.
Summary: After tremendous earthquakes destroy the Earth's major
cities, an ancient evil emerges, turning ordinary people into hunters,
killers, and insane monsters but a small group of teens comes
together in a fight for survival and safety.
ISBN 978-1-4424-2351-0 (hardcover : alk. paper)
[1. Science fiction. 2. Survival—Fiction. 3. Monsters—Fiction.
4. Good and evil—Fiction.] I. Title.
PZ7.R54317Dar 2011
[Fic]—dc22
2011008642
ISBN 978-1-4424-2352-7 (pbk)
ISBN 978-1-4424-2353-4 (eBook)

ACKNOWLEDGMENTS

Thanks to:

Alison Acheson for all her support and teaching skills. And to all the wonderful people in my writing for children class at the University of British Columbia.

Mimi Thebo at Bath Spa University for being my mentor and guide.

Kaliya Muntean and Fiona Lee, who are wonderful muses and great friends.

Matthew and Shauna Hooten for being such good support.

Ruth Alltimes at Macmillan for being an outstanding editor and having such patience.

David Gale and Navah Wolfe at Simon & Schuster for more fantastic editing skills.

And I'd like to thank my agents, Julia Churchill and Sarah Davies. Without them, none of this would have been possible.

NOTHING

I'm standing at the edge of existence. Behind me, a thousand monsters descend. Their disguises change with each stride.

When they look in a mirror do they see their true selves?

Arms open wide. In front of me is nothing. No one ever knew how existence would end. Sure, they made assumptions: fire, flood, plague, etc. They studied the skies for locusts and watched for rain. They built their cities, destroyed the forests, and poisoned the water. Warning signs left behind in the ruins of ancient civilizations have been misinterpreted. The sins of mankind are always to blame. But who would have guessed it would be so gray? So empty.

Is there really a way back?

Hello? Is there anyone there?

Sorry, wrong number.

There are too many thoughts to cover in such little time. I knew they would find me. I'm glowing in the moonlight. My darkness was too bright to hide forever. They find all of us eventually. They play the odds, and they're up a thousand to one.

In front of me is nothing. No bright lights, no darkness. No energy. Just nothing.

There is no future because we no longer have a past. Our present is devised of basic survival, and it's about to end.

They have made sure of that.

I am Nothing.

I am existence.

I am pain.

I kneel down in the dirt and write some of my last words. I'd speak them, but there is no one left to listen.

GAME OVER

MASON

"There's been an accident."

No words have ever been so terrifying.

It was a sunny day. Beautiful. Early September. He'd been laughing. School had just started. Someone told a joke. Mason had finished first period and returned to his locker when the principal found him. Pulled him aside and away from his friends and spoke those four words.

There's been an accident.

Twenty minutes later Mason arrived at Royal Hospital. They wouldn't let him drive. His car was back in the parking lot. Mr. Yan, the geology teacher, drove. He'd never even met Mr. Yan before. He'd never thought to study geology. Since when did any of that matter?

It was sunny outside. Bright. Hot. The days were getting shorter and girls were noticeably wearing fewer clothes. Warm light filtered through the Honda's window, warming Mason's jeans. He absently thought about removing his hoodie, but the consideration was too casual. Too normal. How could he think of being warm? How selfish was he?

The teacher offered to come in, but Mason shook his head.

No. His head bounced up and down when asked if he'd be all right. Yes. He'd be sure to call the school if he needed a ride home. Yes. As Mr. Yan drove off, Mason noticed that his white Honda Civic had a dent in the bumper.

Another car drove through a red light and hit her. Side collision. Your mother was the only one in the car. She's at the hospital. We'll take you there. You can't drive—you're in shock.

Shock? Was that what this was?

Somehow he made it inside. A woman in admitting told him where to go. She was eating a bagel. There was a coffee stain on her sleeve. A permanent frown tattooed into her forehead, her mouth drawn taut against her teeth. She pointed toward the main room and told him to wait. There were too many people around. More than the waiting room could hold. It seemed awfully busy for a Wednesday afternoon. He couldn't find a seat. So he squeezed his slender frame into a corner between a vending machine and the wall. From there he could see and hear everything.

Ambulance lights flickered through the windows. Paramedics rushed to bring stretchers through the emergency doors. Doctors shouted in the hallways and nurses ran with clipboards and medical supplies. People crowded the tiny waiting room's chairs. None were smiling. Most stared off into space while others spoke in hushed voices. A woman a few feet away kept opening and closing the clasp on her purse. Her eyes were red and puffy, and when she looked at Mason, tears welled up and rolled down her cheeks. She was holding a pink blanket in her lap; drops of blood stained the fabric.

Mason looked down at his feet. He didn't want to see any more. His shoelace was coming untied.

Eventually a doctor called his name.

"They're taking her into surgery," the doctor told him.

"There's nothing you can do except wait. We can call some-one if you'd like. Are there other family members you'd like us to contact?"

There was no one else. Just Mom and him. Mason's father had died five years ago, when he was twelve.

"Will she be okay?"

"We're doing the best we can."

Not an answer. That wasn't a good sign.

A nurse brought him coffee. The paper cup burned his fingers, but he didn't drop it. Instead he raised the liquid to his lips and took a large gulp. Burned his tongue. He barely noticed. He placed the cup on the waiting room table and promptly forgot about it.

His phone began to ring. People glared at him. A mother with two small children looked at him as if he were pure evil. There was a sign on the wall reminding people to turn off their cell phones. No electronics were allowed in the emer-gency room. Why hadn't he noticed it before? He hit the off button without taking the call. There was nothing to say, anyway.

More ambulances arrived, and stretchers and paramed-ics piled in through the doors. The waiting room went from being crowded to ridiculously out of control. Where were all these people coming from? They were beginning to overflow into the hallway. No one seemed to know what was going on.

There was a television mounted in a metal frame above the heads of a young Asian family who didn't speak a word of English. The grandmother was lying on a stretcher pushed up against the wall by the nurses' station. The orderlies didn't know what to do with her. Stretchers filled with people were lining the hallways. The hospital seemed to have run out of room.

The television was turned to a local channel and a talk-show host was interviewing someone about an upcoming movie. The volume was low, and very few people paid attention. Mason watched for a bit, a helpful distraction although he couldn't hear the words. He was still pressed up against the vending machine. Glancing at his watch, he discovered it was almost two. He'd been there for four hours and had no idea what was going on. Was his mother still in surgery? He thought about asking the nurse for an update but changed his mind quickly once he saw the line of twenty people screaming for attention. No one else was getting information, why should he be any different?

"Mason Dowell?"

The doctor had stopped in front of him and Mason hadn't even noticed. He was holding the same clipboard from before and his face was stern and unreadable. Blinking several times, he looked down at the paperwork with heavy eyes.

"Is she okay?" The words blurted out. He hated the sound of his voice. High-pitched. Breathy. Panicky.

"For now." The doctor wouldn't look at him. "We've managed to stop the internal bleeding, but she's still unconscious. All we can do is wait. I think it might be best if you go and get some rest. I can try and arrange for someone to take you home."

"Can I see her?"

"There's nothing to see. She's just resting. We're very busy right now. Go home and get something to eat. Make some phone calls. Come back later tonight and you can see her then."

Someone gasped.

Both of them turned to look. The waiting room had grown awfully quiet. Everyone stared at the television. Someone rushed over and turned up the volume.

It took Mason a few seconds to realize what he was looking

at. The talk show had been replaced by a news bulletin, some-where live on location. Fire trucks and police cars blocked the remains of a building. They were using hoses to control the flames that burst through the destroyed structure. Emergency lights flashed and people rushed about, but it was impossible to recognize them because of the smoke and dust.

"I repeat," the news reporter's voice said in the background. "Tragedy strikes at local Saskatoon High School. Channel Nine doesn't know all the details yet, but we believe that four men and three women entered the school around one thirty, armed with explosives. The bombs were ignited in the gymnasium, cafeteria, and about five classrooms. There is no word on who did this or if it's linked to a terrorist organiza-tion. We are not sure of the casualties yet, but estimates are in the hundreds. They're bringing some of the bodies out now."

The camera panned over to the building, where offi-cials were bringing out black bags. The glass entrance was destroyed and half the doorway had caved in. Mason had walked through those doors a few hours ago.

"That's my school," he said.

No one heard him.

"I've never seen anything like this," the reporter said. Her voice was shaking and constrained. She was no longer read-ing the script; the words leaving her lips were her own. "The whole school has been destroyed. It's all gone. What kind of monsters would do that?" Tears glistened in her eyes.

The camera panned over to the left as a police officer walked into the shot. His forced expression filled the screen. "If you or anyone you know has children attending the school, please do not come down here. I repeat: Do not come down. There is nothing you can do to help, but there is a number you can call." Local numbers came up on the screen. "I repeat: Do not come down. The authorities are busy and cannot help you."

The camera panned across the parking lot and the hundreds of cars that remained empty. Mason spotted his Toyota Corolla next to a smashed Ford truck covered in rubble. Funny, his car looked untouched. There didn't seem to be a single scratch.

"That's my school," he repeated.

"Son?" The doctor put his hand on Mason's shoulder. "You'd better go home."

"Yeah, okay." The weight of the entire hospital crushed down on Mason's back. He needed to get out of there and make some phone calls. Find out what happened.

"Let me get someone to take you." The doctor looked around the waiting room. "Stay here and I'll go see who's getting off duty. Give me twenty minutes."

"No, don't bother. I can go myself." Mason zipped up his hoodie. If he hurried, he could get to the school in less than half an hour.

"I don't think—"

"It's fine." Mason stepped backward. "I'm not that far away. I've got to go. I'll be back in a few hours. I'll—um—eat something like you said. Take a rest. Have a shower."

The doctor smiled. "Do what you've got to do. We'll see you this evening. Your mother is lucky to have you."

It was still bright and warm outside. Sunny. Beautiful. Shouldn't it be darker? Mason stumbled over the curb, nearly falling right into the path of an incoming ambulance. He stepped backward as red lights washed over him and the vehicle sped by. His cell phone bounced out of his hoodie pocket, but he managed to grab it before it hit the ground. Turning it on, he remembered that someone had called earlier. There was one new message.

"Dude!" The voice on the recording was his friend Tom. "I heard about your mom. I'm really sorry. Hope she's all right. I'll call you the second I'm done with class. Let me know if you're still in the hospital. I'll head down. Gotta go. Coach'll have me running laps if I'm late again."

There was a beep and a voice asking him if he wanted to replay the message, save it, or delete it.

Running laps. Gym.

Explosives.

Tom had been in the gym along with all the others. Kids he'd grown up with. They were all the friends who shared his life. He should have been in gym. He would have been if it hadn't been for those four horrible words. Had his mother just saved his life?

He scrolled through his phone until he found Tom's number. Pressed the button and held it against his ear. Waited for it to ring. Nothing happened. It didn't go straight to voice mail. Not even a recorded voice telling him to try again.

Ending the call, he looked though his list of numbers. Dozens of them, all friends, every single one had been at the school. If he called them, would he get nothing but dead air? He wasn't brave enough to try and find out.

Flagging down the first taxi, Mason climbed in and asked the driver to take him to the 7-Eleven a block from the school. He'd walk the rest. He nervously ran his fingers through his tousled brown hair, trying to distract himself; anything to keep him from kicking the backseat and screaming.

He needed to see. To make sure. He wouldn't allow himself to believe it was real until he saw it with his own eyes.

ARIES

The man on the bus had gone insane.

At least it seemed that way. He was rocking back and forth in the seat, muttering to himself in a language that Aries didn't understand. Twice he got up from his chair and wandered down the aisle, stopping every few steps to shake his head and cover his ears. Finally he plopped down in the seat right in front of her and rummaged through the pockets of his coat.

"What's wrong with him?" Sara hissed in her ear. Her eyes were wide and she was pressed back in her own seat as far as her body would allow. She twisted strands of hair between her fingers, something she did only when she was nervous.

"I think he's mentally ill," Aries whispered back. She glanced around, avoiding the stares of other people who were trying hard to pretend the insane man didn't exist. A few rows in front of her, a guy around her age watched her intently. A book was open in his hands, but he didn't appear to be reading. His eyes were dark and almost hidden behind his longish hair. He gave her a tiny smirk and she pulled her gaze away, her cheeks burning.

"They shouldn't allow those sorts of people on the bus in

the first place," Colin said from the seat behind them. He was the drama king of the school, and Sara thought he was the greatest thing in the world. Aries thought he was arrogant and liked himself a little too much. She put up with him because of Sara. Isn't that what friends did? They'd been permanently linked since they were little, and she'd walk across fire for Sara. Putting up with an obnoxious boyfriend like Colin was part of the best friend code. She knew she'd put Sara through worse during their years of friendship.

It was a beautiful Vancouver evening, one of the nice ones where it wasn't raining, and they were on their way back to Clayton Heights High School for rehearsals of *Alice in Wonderland*. Aries had the role of Alice, and Colin was still complaining about Ms. Darcy, the drama teacher's, choice of play. There was no male lead in *Alice in Wonderland* and Colin was determined to let the entire world know he'd been robbed.

"What if he attacks us?" Sara said. She was going to be the Queen of Hearts, a role, she joked, that had been created just for her. Sara didn't understand why little girls wanted to be princesses when they could be queens. Even her cell phone had a tiny dangling jewelled crown attached to it.

"He won't do anything," Colin said, and he wrapped his arms around Sara. "Not while I'm here."

The man suddenly let out a stream of cuss words that made almost everyone on the bus blush. Colin's cheeks reddened, and instantly he didn't look so sure of himself. Letting go of Sara, he leaned back in his own seat and looked up. Reading the bus ads suddenly seemed more important than reassuring Sara.

Aries rolled her eyes and pressed the buzzer. They were getting off at the next stop. Colin would be able to leave without his cowardice being properly revealed. The moment they got to school Colin would probably tell the story about how he'd been preparing to stand up to the crazy guy on the bus. Then Sara would smile and kiss him on the cheek and pretend he was the hero he wanted to be. Aries would politely join in, keeping the secret truth to herself. Boys could be ridiculously stupid sometimes.

She looked back at the strange guy. He was still watching her. He'd put the book away, but he wasn't getting up. One leg rested on the seat, slender fingers tapped absently at his knee. So intense-looking. She tried to place him; did he go to her school? She couldn't tell for sure.

Colin got up out of his seat, clinging to the safety rail. Sara joined him. Aries zipped up her backpack and was about to move when the insane man turned around and looked right at her. She froze, half off the seat, when he reached out and grabbed her arm. His fingers were icy cold.

"Pretty girlie," he said. "Brace yourself. It's about to open."

"Excuse me?"

"Couldn't keep it closed forever. Too much hate. They found a crack. Let it out again. Here we go. Ten, nine, eight." Spittle flung from the man's lips, and his grip tightened on her arm.

"Let go of me," Aries said. She pulled backward but it was useless. She grabbed hold of his filthy hand and tried to pry his fingers off. She didn't want to touch him; his gray skin was clammy. His clothing was filthy and he smelled faintly of spoiled milk. Crumbs were stuck in his beard, and his cheeks were pockmarked and scabbed. Her stomach lurched as she asked him again to let go.

"Hey!" Colin yelled out, but he didn't move to help. He was frozen. Sara stood beside him, her mouth wide-open, but no sounds came out.

"Seven, six, the cities are collapsing around us. Five!" the man said. "Game over! Four! Hear the screams. Feel the power! Three!"

The bus lurched, rising up over the top of something, and then crashed back to the ground. People fell forward in their seats. There were screams as several people slammed about in different directions. Colin staggered against Sara, sending her down the aisle and crashing against an old lady with groceries. Mandarin oranges rolled away, and a bottle of spaghetti sauce exploded. The strong smell of spiced tomatoes filled the air.

But Aries and the insane man didn't move. His eyes were fixed on her. She looked right into them.

She expected his eyes to be bloodshot. Crazy people always had bloodshot eyes in books and movies. It was the standard insanity cliché. But his weren't. They were something else.

The veins in his eyes were black.

"Two."

The bus lurched again, the driver slammed on the brakes, and more people screamed. They came to a sudden stop in the middle of an intersection, and other cars honked their horns in protest. A sophomore girl was thrown forward, her purse dangling from her shoulders. Her back cracked against the metal railings. People surged out of their seats and onto the floor, trying to get free. But the doors weren't opening. Men banged their fists against the glass windows.

Still Aries and the crazy man didn't move.

"One."

The ground exploded.

The bus staggered forward. The road beneath them began to break apart; pieces of concrete vibrated and scattered as if alive. A fire hydrant burst, and water surged upward, raining down into the intersection. Power lines swayed until wires tore and flayed violently. The lights from the businesses and street surged and went dark. Cars hit their brakes and crashed into one another. Through the window, Aries watched people trying to climb out of the wreckages, while others ran for the safety of the parking lot and sidewalks. Beside the intersection a grocery store rocked on its foundations. Glass shattered, sending tiny projectile missiles in all directions. People covered their heads with their hands to avoid being sliced apart. They fell over one another as they tried to keep their balance on the shaking ground.

A moment ago people were frantically trying to get off the bus. Now they turned and started pushing their way back in. The ground kept vibrating, and the bus groaned and heaved; a giant chunk of concrete smashed into it from behind, forcing the back of the bus up into the air several feet.

Aries could hear Sara calling her name, but she couldn't see her through the confusion. People were all around her, crawling along the floor, climbing over the seats, banging against the glass to try to save themselves.

"What's happening? What's happening?" Someone kept repeating the words over and over. Another person was calling for help. Others were screaming. Over the noise, the crazy man began shouting something that sounded foreign. She couldn't tell if he was laughing or crying.

Somewhere in the distance there was a loud explosion. The bus windows shattered, forcing Aries to cover her head and duck down between the seats. Bits of glass rained down on her, catching in her hair and bouncing off the backs of her hands. The crazy man had released his grip. She no longer heard him, but he was close. She could still smell the scent of sour milk.

A delivery truck sped through the intersection and crashed

into the side of the bus. The collision was powerful; it rocked the bus, which tilted over onto its side. Aries grabbed hold of the seat and held on tightly. Bodies crashed against her. For a brief second she saw Colin's face pressed up against her leg, but he disappeared quickly in the sea of struggling bodies.

The ground continued to shake.

Hours? Minutes?

And then it was over.

The bus was deathly quiet. Aries lay there, her back against the metal window frame and the broken cement, unable to think about anything. Her leg hurt but not enough to make her think it was broken. Liquid dribbled down her face, making her forehead itch insanely. She couldn't free her hand to scratch or check if it was blood. Was she bleeding? She wasn't sure. There was too much weight pressed against her chest. Her arms were stuck. Too many people were lying on top of her. Breathing deeply, she inhaled dust and started coughing. The taste of copper was heavy in the air.

Wiggling her fingers, she tried to pull her hand free. She had to yank hard; her arm was stuck underneath someone's back. She pushed against the body weighing her down, almost screaming when the head rolled toward her, showing the insane man's face. A tightness stretched across her chest, cold air filled her lungs, and she was positive she'd stopped breathing. The edge of her vision darkened into a tunnel. She was going to pass out.

What if he woke up? His lips were practically touching her cheek. The sour milk smell invaded her nose. If he moved she was going to have a heart attack on the spot. She looked straight up through the broken windows and at the sky. Pictured how good the fresh air would feel against her skin once she got free.

A hand reached out. "Here," a voice said. Fingers tightened around hers, giving them a soft squeeze. The hand was warm and soft. Firm. Reassuring. The dark-haired guy appeared in front of her. With his free arm, he grabbed hold of the crazy man's jacket, yanking the body backward and off of her.

"Is that better?"

She nodded. Somehow she managed to find her legs somewhere in all that clutter and she brought them up to her chest. The guy continued to hold her hand, helping her maintain balance while she struggled to her knees.

"Sara?" Her voice was loud and strained.

The bus was full of bodies, some of them moving, most of them still. Grabbing hold of a seat's metal railing, she pulled herself up until she was standing. The seats were still bolted to what was now the side of the bus, crowding the small amount of free space. Bits of glass quivered above her head, raining down the occasional shard.

There were so many bodies.

"Let's look for her," the guy said.

He was still holding her hand, and she allowed him to gently lead her toward the front. She stepped through the bodies, stopping to check the faces of everyone she passed. What had Sara been wearing? She couldn't remember. Her jacket? A hoodie? Which one? Other people started to get up, staggering and tripping as they tried to make their way off. Because the bus was lying on its side, they couldn't go through the door, so someone took one of the emergency hammers off the wall and smashed his way through the front window. A woman whose arm was bent awkwardly began to climb over the steering wheel to get outside. Other people searched around, looking for their friends and family members. She saw Colin step over the body of the elderly lady. His foot came down on one of the mandarin oranges, squishing it into a mushy pulp.

"Help me," she called out. "I can't find Sara."

But Colin ignored her. She could see in his eyes that he was set on getting free. Unfocused. Rattled. His hair was sticking up and his cheek was splotchy with grime. She'd never seen him look dirty before. Even his fingernails had been meticulously clean. He moved past her, never giving her a second glance.

She thought about calling after him, but it seemed pointless. Instead she concentrated on methodically moving among the bodies, desperately searching for her friend. Voices called out, pleading, asking for help. Someone screamed for his mother, begging her to come because he couldn't understand where he was. Everywhere was pain and death. A few hands reached out weakly for her, and she helped free a man from underneath an unconscious woman. The man's ankle was broken and beginning to swell but he still managed to crawl toward the front. She continued to look for Sara, but she wasn't there.

"Why don't we check outside?" the guy said. She nodded and allowed him to put his arm around her. It seemed like the right thing to do. His body was warm, and the muscles beneath his jacket pressed against her, drawing her in, comforting her.

Maybe Sara had already managed to get out?

An overly pregnant woman struggled to stand from between two crushed seats. "Please, help me," she said.

The stranger let go of Aries and they both put their arms around the stunned woman. Blood trickled down her forehead from where she'd smashed her face into the window. The three of them stumbled through the front window and onto the broken street. There were benches at the bus stop, and they helped the woman over and sat her down. Another woman came over to lend a hand. Blood seeped from a gash in her forehead, but she crouched down beside the expectant mother and began talking to her calmly.

The first thing that struck Aries was the lack of noise. There were so many people standing around, many of them covered in blood and injured. But they were quiet. They moved about, some helping one another, barely uttering a single word.

The street was destroyed. Most of the concrete was torn apart; it lay in piles, strewn across the ground. There was broken glass everywhere. It crunched beneath her feet. The sun was beginning to set; the sky was filled with pinks and purples. Long shadows spread out across the ground. Normally by now the street lamps would start to switch on, but with the power out, there would be no city glow. Soon everything would be pitch-black. Aries shuddered. The thought of being on the streets once the sun went down was enough to make her feel like she was five years old and terrified of closet monsters or things that hid under the bed.

The building on the corner had imploded. It used to be a grocery store. Now it was nothing but a pile of debris. Shopping carts lay on their sides where the parking lot used to be. Some of the wheels were still spinning. How many people were trapped inside? There were dozens of cars in the lot, many of them rolled over on their sides. The smell of gasoline was strong.

Walking the length of the bus, she studied the faces of everyone around her. She moved between the groups, bending down to check people lying on the ground. There were a lot of dazed and pained expressions, but none of them were familiar. None of them were Sara.

One of the drivers had a first aid kit in his trunk. He

opened it and began handing out supplies. The stranger from the bus came over holding a sterile white bandage. "You're bleeding." He brought the gauze up to Aries's forehead and pressed gently against her skin. "Hold this. Are you all right?"

She put her hand up, fingers touching against his as she took control of the bandage. She pressed carefully against her own skin but there was no pain. When she pulled the cloth away there was dark blood. "I don't think it's mine," she said. "I'm not hurt."

"Good. Did you find your friend?"

She shook her head.

"Well, let's try the bus again. We'll keep looking for her." The guy turned back toward the wreckage, and she followed. She liked his calmness, the way he carried his body when he walked. It made her feel safe. Stronger. She saw Colin standing in the road and thought about calling out to him but then changed her mind. He'd ignored her before; she doubted he'd be much help now.

"What happened?" she asked as they climbed back on the bus.

"Earthquake," the guy said. His eyes flickered in the dying sunlight. "It's like the ground just opened up and swallowed us whole."

Brace yourself. It's about to open.

The crazy man had said that just before he started his countdown.

But how was that possible? No one could predict earthquakes—could they?

"Sara has to be in here," Aries said, her voice sounding heavy and strange in her ears. "She's blond. Wears glasses. I need to find her."

"We'll find her."

"I can't remember what she's wearing."

"I saw her sitting with you. I know what she looks like."

"Isn't that weird that I can't remember? I should know. She's my best friend. Oh, God. What if she's dead? I've got to tell her mom."

The guy turned and placed a hand on her shoulder. She looked into his eyes, wondering how they could be dark and piercing but friendly and soft at the same time. She tried to recall if she knew his face. He seemed familiar in a vague sort of way. Did they go to school together?

"We'll find her," he repeated.

And they did. But by then it was too late.

CLEMENTINE

Outside, the wind pressed against the small town hall, shaking the windows and seeping through the cracks. A major draft blew across the floor, numbing the noses and ears of everyone seated. The room had been built more than a hundred years ago when the town of Glenmore was first established. Wonderful inventions such as insulation didn't exist back then. No wonder the people looked sad and depressed in the black-and-white pictures decorating the walls.

Clementine sat squished between her mother and father, second row from the back and right by the aisle and entrance. The meeting was for seven, but they'd arrived late; Mom had been desperately trying to reach Heath on the phone, but all the lines were down. Heath was in Seattle getting a degree in computer programming.

A lot of people were dead in Seattle. The earthquake had destroyed most of the West Coast, from California to Alaska.

Clementine didn't believe for a second that Heath was dead. Mom had one of those built-in sensor detectors that went off whenever her children were in trouble. She'd known immediately when Clementine fell from the pyramid during cheerleading practice and sprained her ankle. When Heath got into a car accident, she'd called him less than a minute after to make sure he wasn't hurt. Her spider senses tingled when her family was in trouble. If Heath was dead, she'd know.

When Washington got their phone lines working again, they'd receive a phone call or e-mail from Heath, joking about how he was shaking things up in the city and telling them not to worry.

But there was always the possibility that wasn't true. Who knew how these mother/child instincts worked? Maybe there was some sort of time-zone limitation?

"If we don't reach him by tomorrow morning, I'm driving to Seattle myself," Mom said just before they left for the town meeting.

"Come on, honey," Dad said. "I'm sure Heath is fine. They'll get the lines fixed and he'll call. Just give it a few more days. You'll see."

But Dad wasn't confident with his words. As he'd spoken, he'd stared at the ceiling and hadn't taken Mom's hand as he normally did when he was trying to be reassuring. So Clementine knew that tomorrow morning Mom would load up the SUV and take the two-day trip to Seattle. She decided now that she'd go too. She'd miss the big game on Friday, but that wasn't nearly as important as making sure her brother was alive. Part of her was excited about the journey. She'd never taken a road trip west before. The other part of her was terrified and guilt ridden.

Dear Heath, you'd better be okay. You promised me that if I ever made it west to Seattle you'd take me sightseeing. I guess that's out of the question. In all honesty, knowing you're safe is more important than getting the chance to see the rock 'n' roll museum.

The town hall was crowded. Almost everyone was there.

Glenmore was small, just under a thousand people, but none-theless, the tiny building could barely fit all of them. Craig Strathmore, the linebacker, was five rows up from her. He'd waved to her when they'd walked in, a gesture that warmed her stomach. As far as farm boys went, he was one nice piece of cowboy. Up toward the front, Clementine saw Jan and Imogene, other cheerleaders she hung out with. They were sitting with their parents too. It was obvious that neither of them had come willingly. Jan played with a strand of her hair, lazily scanning the crowd with a bored frown on her face. She turned and spotted Clementine, than made a big show of rolling her eyes and shrugging her shoulders. Clementine grinned back.

She was about to ask Dad if she could go and sit with them when the mayor took the podium.

"Attention. Call to order."

The room immediately went quiet. Eyes forward, people waited for him to speak. It was the first emergency meeting in over thirty years. Although everyone knew what the mayor would talk about, people were still curious to know what the town of Glenmore was going to do. Clementine was already envisioning the multitude of bake sales and potluck dinners in the church parking lot.

"As you know, there's been a plea from the president for all Americans to help out in this time of trouble," the mayor said. Someone must have set the sound system wrong, because there was a sudden screech of feedback. An assistant immedi-ately ran up to play around with the buttons, and the mayor tapped the microphone a few times before he continued. Some of the older folks in the front rows took out their hear-ing aids. "We've been asked to send supplies to the coast and any people who might be willing to volunteer with cleanup.

They've got a lot of missing people over there, some of whom are from this very town."

Although they weren't rude enough to turn around and stare, Clementine could feel hundreds of pairs of invisible eyes focus on her family. No one else had people on the West Coast.

She caught Craig giving her a sympathy glance before his father whispered angrily in his ear, forcing him to turn around and face the front again. The whole scene struck her as funny, and she found herself struggling not to giggle.

Dear Heath, if you die, then I'd better get your car.

No, it wouldn't do her any good to laugh.

The discussion carried on with a lot of uproar. What about all the violence—those rumors about people killing each other for no reason? How long would it take before that sort of behavior found its way over to Glenmore? How would they protect themselves if half the men left to go help on the coast?

"We need all able bodies here," someone shouted in the crowd. "We don't need them off where God knows what might be happening. That's a death order if I've ever heard one."

"It wouldn't be very Christian of us to not help," another said. "The orders came from the president himself."

"How dare you say I'm not Christian, Hank. Where were you last Sunday? Watching the game on TV?"

"Order! Order!"

Clementine knew the exact moment the door opened, because a gust of wind blew up against her neck, sending icy shivers down her spine. She should have worn her warmer jacket, but it was September. Isn't it still supposed to be relatively warm in September?

She turned her head to look at the latecomers. Henry and James Tills had entered the town hall. They were both smiling, but neither looked happy.

Something was wrong with Henry's eyes. If she hadn't known him as well as she did she might have thought he was wearing contacts. But Henry wasn't the type.

"Evening, boys," the mayor said. A squeal of feedback went through the microphone again, causing several people to cover their ears. "Little early for that kind of protection, don't you think? No need to be arming ourselves just yet."

Murmurs broke out among the people in the hall, and many of them turned in their seats to watch the door. It wasn't until Henry and James passed them in the aisle that Clementine noticed the weapons. Mom immediately reached out and squeezed her hand.

"Clem," she whispered. "You need to leave. Get up."

"What?"

"Leave now," Mom yanked her forward in her seat, pushing her right onto the floor. Clementine's knees scraped against the cement. One of her shoes slipped off her heel, but she didn't get a chance to search for it before Mom shoved her again, forcing her into the aisle.

She was about to open her mouth to protest, but she saw the look on her mother's face. So instead she pulled herself up to her feet and brushed the blond hair back from her face.

The town hall had grown awfully quiet.

She took a few steps backward toward the hall doors. Henry and James Tills had already passed her. They were making their way down toward the center of the room. Neither of them looked back at her as she stood stupidly with her hands at her sides. She glanced over at Mom, but she wasn't looking. She was staring straight ahead as if concerned that any unexpected movement might cause the wrong kind of attention.

Clementine focused again on the only other two people standing in the room.

James held the weapon in his arms, but there was something wrong with the way he was standing. His back was twitching as if he were having a seizure. Muscles rippled against the tightness of his shirt. There was blood on his pants. His leg made a sickening squelching noise every time he placed weight on it. She stared at James's jeans, watching the movement of his ankle. She couldn't stop looking at the way his foot dragged against the ground when he stepped forward.

Mom reached out and grabbed her arm, breaking her paralysis. She looked into her mother's eyes and saw something she'd never seen in sixteen years. Her strong, confident, stubborn mom was freaked. That wasn't right. Mom was the one who always kept everyone together. She never fell apart. She was too solid that way. Strong. Clementine opened her mouth to speak, but Mom brought a finger to her lips. Her hands were trembling.

"Go," she mouthed silently. Beside her, Dad motioned with his hands. Shooing her away like an annoying fly. His eyes never met hers; they were focused on the backs of Henry and James. There was no mistaking the concern on his face either.

Clementine shook her head. "Come with me," she mouthed back.

Mom grabbed her arm a second time, pushing her away from the chairs. Clementine began slowly moving toward the entrance, walking backward, afraid to take her eyes off the two men. She'd known both Henry and James since she was a toddler. These men were liked. They were served coffee and pie at the diner and helped out with the town festivals. Henry played Santa every year for the church Christmas party.

But panic filled the room like an electric charge. Everyone was frozen in their seats, waiting for the proverbial pin to drop. Even the few people in the back row who could see Clementine silently sneaking away seemed to ignore her completely. What would happen once Henry and James reached the front of the room?

She didn't find out. Her shoulders brushed against the doorframe and her fingers found the handle. Looking back at her parents, she saw that her father had risen from his seat along with a few of the other men. Her mother was staring at her hands. Clementine pushed down on the latch, letting the door open a few inches, worried that the sound might draw attention to her actions. What if the wind knocked the door right out of her hands? Another foot and soon there was enough space to squeeze her body through. There was a second of panic when she turned her back to the men to make her escape.

Once outside, the wind whipped ferociously at her neck. She closed the door as quietly as she could. What if the noise made everyone turn and look? Even worse, what if it locked and her parents couldn't get free? It felt like a betrayal, turning the handle till the latch clicked. She was leaving them all behind. Her mother and father. Her friends. She didn't know what fate she was giving them. So far nothing had happened. This was a small town. Things didn't happen. Her mother was probably overreacting, but something inside her was also telling her to run.

To leave everyone behind, though? That seemed cowardly.

She decided to wait on the steps until everyone came back out. They'd laugh about it later on the ride home. Tomorrow they'd pack their bags and drive west to Seattle to check on Heath. It would be a good story to tell him.

A car's engine roared to life and headlights switched on, bathing her in blinding white light.

"Well, well, well, we've got ourselves an escapee."

She knew that voice. It belonged to her neighbor Sam Anselm. She took a few steps forward until she could see through the headlights' glare.

The town hall was surrounded.

There were at least twenty men and women, armed and ready to ambush. They had positioned their cars around the building so that no one would be getting out. Clementine took another step, painfully aware that Sam had his gun tracking her movements.

"What's going on, Sam?" Her voice sounded taut and strange in her throat. She swallowed hard but it didn't help.

"I think you need to go back inside, young missy," Sam said. "That is, if you really want to know."

"And if I don't?"

"Then we'll have a little party out here. Just the two of us."

Sam was on her before she had time to react. Grabbing hold of her arm, he dragged her away from the town hall and toward his truck. She yanked hard, trying to break free, but his grip was too strong.

"Sam. Sam, stop it, please," she said. The others were beginning to descend on the town hall with their weapons raised. "Don't do this."

"But I enjoy it," he said.

She stumbled over the walkway and almost fell, eyes filling with tears from the pain of him dragging her along. The muscles in her arm flared, and she was afraid he might tear the ligaments if she continued to fight. So she allowed him to pull her a few more feet, until he stopped at the edge of the parking lot.

His hand abruptly let go of her arm, and he stared at her as if he didn't know who she was. His eyes grew wide and confused.

"Clem?"

"Sam?"

"I didn't hurt you, did I? Please say I didn't hurt you." His hands reached out and grabbed her shoulders.

"No, I'm fine. I—"

"You've got to get out of here. Now! Before I go back. I go in and out. My brain. The voices. White noise. They're so loud. I can't stop them. They're telling me to do things."

"What are you talking about, Sam? I can't go. My parents are inside."

"Leave. You have to go or they'll kill you. I'll kill you. Once it takes over I can't stop it."

"What? What takes over?"

"I don't know. The voices. The things inside my head. They're real. Curled up against my brain. Fighting me."

He gave her a shove backward and she thought about how her mother had done the same thing moments ago. Everyone kept telling her to run, but no one was saying where they wanted her to go.

Gunshots fired against the night. They came from inside the town hall. Someone screamed.

Everyone she knew was inside that building.

"Run," Sam said, reading her mind. "You can't save them. Don't go home. That's the first place they'll look for you."

"But where will I go?"

Sam dropped to his knees, clutching at his ears and screaming. His gun dropped to the earth beside him, and she thought about trying to grab it. But she didn't know anything about weapons; it would be useless in her hands.

When Sam raised his head, his eyes were clouded and there was no recognition when he looked right at her. He'd bitten his lip or cheek when he fell. He smiled; she could see the blood on his teeth. Her heart pounded and skipped a beat.

Sam no longer appeared to be home.

She decided to do what she was told. She turned and ran.

MICHAEL

"I can't take this anymore. Toss in some music or something; I'm sick of the news."

They were driving in Joe's truck. Not anywhere in particular, just wasting time. Something they did every afternoon after school let out. They'd been doing this ritual since they both got their driver's licenses last year. Michael rolled the window down, enjoying the way the wind caught his long brown hair.

"What do you want to hear?"

"I don't care. Anything except this crap. Who cares about an earthquake?"

Michael cared, but he didn't bother admitting it. Besides, Joe was right, the news hadn't broadcast anything original in hours. Just the same old stuff since the initial reports started coming in last night. Most of the information played on a loop. No one seemed to know anything. Searching through the music, he settled on Green Day, the only CD that wasn't scratched beyond recognition. Joe didn't take good care of his things.

"So you heard about Sasquatch?" That was Joe's pet name

for Mr. Petrov, the crazy old Vietnam veteran who lived down the street from the school. He was known for screaming at teenagers who came too close to his front lawn. He also had one of the only houses that was toilet papered on a regular basis.

"Yeah, he attacked the mailman or something yesterday."

"Bit his earlobe off," Joe said. "Clear right off. Chewed on it for a while too before the police hit him with a Taser. I mean, how messed up is that?"

"What did they do with him?"

"Heard they hauled him off to the nuthouse. About time, too. It's not like it's news. He's been loopy for years."

Michael tapped his fingers gently on the car door in time to the music. It was strange to think of Mr. Petrov's house as being empty. He'd been a bit of a shut-in, rarely leaving his yard except to buy groceries every single Monday at the Safeway. He was a local attraction. There wasn't much else going on in Whitefish.

"Do you think they'll put his house up for sale?" he asked. "He doesn't have any family, right? I wonder what will happen to his stuff?"

Joe didn't answer. Tapping the brakes, he slowed the truck and swerved slightly to the right. "What the hell is that guy doing?"

Michael looked. Ahead of them, the drivers of a motor-cycle and a car appeared to be in an argument. The car driver, with his head clear out the window, was screaming obscenities at the guy on the bike. Honking his horn several times, he hit the gas pedal as the biker tried to speed away. His license plates were out-of-state—Idaho.

"That's some serious road rage," Michael said.

Joe leaned his head out the window. "Just say no, dude," he screamed. "It's all about the love."

"I don't think you're helping."

The car honked its horn again, the red brake lights glowing as the driver slowed down to keep the same speed as the motorcycle.

The biker decided he'd had enough. He revved the engine, and the motorcycle gained speed, edging ahead until he'd almost passed the car.

"Oh my God."

The driver swerved his car straight into the motorcycle's path, front fender meeting with back tire. The biker lost control; the machine spun sideways and into the path of a Mack truck. Both rider and bike were propelled toward Joe's car. The guy's body twisted and turned, doing airborne cartwheels, a rag doll tossed through the air. Joe slammed the brakes while spinning the steering wheel, sending them into the ditch.

Over the sound of Green Day, Michael heard the body as it smashed against the pavement. There was a squelching noise, like a water balloon exploding upon impact.

The truck came to a stop right at the base of the tree line. Michael's body jerked against the seat belt, shooting pain along his chest and up into his shoulder.

"Oh my God, did you see that? Did you see that?" Joe's voice raised several octaves. "I'm gonna hurl." He barely managed to get the door open before the contents of his lunch forced their way up.

There had to be something wrong with his eyes. Michael knew he couldn't have just witnessed that. Had the driver done it on purpose? It sure looked that way. What kind of person would do such a thing? He had to be wrong. People don't do things like that.

Michael opened his own door and jumped out before Joe's vomit smell overpowered him enough to attack his own churning stomach. Scrambling up the ditch, he joined the group of onlookers surrounding the crash scene.

Several cars had stopped in the middle of the highway, including the Mack truck and the enraged driver. People got out of their vehicles, but they didn't know what to do. Most of them stood around with bewildered expressions on their faces. Someone brought out a camera and started taking pictures.

The biker was dead. His body was sprawled in the road, leaving a thick trail of blood from where he'd skidded across the pavement. His helmet was still protecting his face, and Michael was glad he didn't have to look at the guy's eyes. Turning his gaze away, he searched for the driver of the car. If Michael had been the one to do something like this, he'd be a complete mess. Probably ready to go toss himself off the nearest overpass. A few months ago he'd hit a deer by accident and he still had nightmares about it. Hitting an animal was one thing; he couldn't imagine the guilt of hurting a human.

The road-raged driver had parked his car a ways down the road. He moved back toward the crowd, his face bright red and breathing heavily. Talking to himself, he paused once to scream at an elderly couple cowering by their car.

The guy walked past the crowd of stunned onlookers, side-stepping the ruined motorcycle, and stopped in front of the body. He began to scream at the dead man, hurling a wrath of insults, while kicking at the motorcycle helmet.

The crowd froze. No one knew what to do. Someone started to cry, whimpering sounds mixing in with thudding sneaker kicks. Finally the trucker stepped forward, grabbing the guy by the back of his jacket and pulling him away. He spoke calmly considering the situation, but his words had little results. The enraged man turned his focus on the Mack guy and began attacking, scratching at the trucker's face as if he wanted to rip the poor guy's eyes right out of their sockets.

It was enough to make Michael jump into action. He caught the attention of another man several feet away. The older guy, with a receding hairline, nodded at him. Both of them stepped forward. Michael pushed the insane man backward while the other grabbed him by the arms to try and stop his advances.

But the guy wasn't going down without a fight. In the end, it took six of them to get him on his stomach, with both the trucker and a burly guy sitting on top of him. The enraged guy continued to scream, spittle flying from his lips as he cursed at anyone who got too close.

"Don't move," the balding man said. "I've got a phone in my car. I'll call the police."

Michael glanced over at Joe, who was sitting on a rock by the side of his truck, his face pasty. A few other people had joined him, mostly women and the elderly couple. Everyone was making an effort to stay as far away from the insane man as possible. Although he was momentarily subdued, Michael didn't blame them.

"Phone's out," the guy said, returning to the scene. He was holding an iPhone. "I'm getting a signal, but I can't get through. Anyone else have one that works?"

"It doesn't matter," the trucker said. He nodded back in the direction behind them. "Cops are coming. I can see the flashers."

In the distance, Michael could see the red and blue lights as the police car tried to make its way through the group of onlookers. It seemed a little strange; the accident covered all four lanes of traffic, but there were fewer than a dozen cars stopped along the road. Shouldn't there be more? Where was everyone? Had the police already diverted traffic?

Someone pulled a blanket from their car and covered the dead man. Only, his body was too long, leaving the bottom part of his calves and his feet sticking out from under the plaid fabric. It couldn't cover all the blood, either.

The police finally worked their way through the small crowd. Michael knew one of them, Clive Templeton, who had graduated from his high school only a few years earlier. Clive was the first to reach the scene. The other, Officer Burke, stopped to talk to the hyperventilating elderly couple.

"Everyone stand back," Clive said. He talked with the balding guy and the trucker for a while. Michael didn't get involved; he hadn't seen anything different from the others. After a few minutes, Clive and Burke handcuffed the still-screaming man, grabbed him by the arms, and brought him up to his feet.

"Everyone can return to their cars," Burke said. "There's nothing more to see here."

That didn't seem right. Shouldn't they be gathering information from the other bystanders? Michael was no criminal expert, but shouldn't they have witness accounts for when this went to court? What if the guy pleaded not guilty? Stepping forward, he decided to offer up his phone number or something in case they needed him.

But the cops were ignoring him, pushing people back and away from the scene. The trucker got back in his cab and started up his engine. The balding guy came over to stand next to him.

"This is wrong," Michael said.

"It's strange all right," the guy said.

"Shouldn't they be doing more? I mean, there's not even an ambulance here yet. What are they supposed to do with the body? Put it by the side of the road and hope the wild animals don't eat it?"

The guy snorted. "Maybe they've got one on the way."

"I hope so." He turned to hold out his hand to the balding man. "I'm Michael."

"Evans." They shook hands. Evans handed him a business card with his name on it. "Just in case. You never know if you might need it."

Clive wandered over to where they stood. "I said back to your car," he snapped. He was wearing sunglasses, the mirrored kind; it was impossible to read his expression. "Don't make me kick your ass, Mikey boy. School's out."

Michael put the card in his back pocket, nodded at Clive, and backed away. There was something creepy about not being able to see the man's eyes. Evans appeared to be thinking the same thing; he turned and headed back to his car without so much as a wave of his hand.

Back at the truck, Joe was inside, twisting the key, but the engine wasn't roaring to life.

"I don't know what happened," he said. "Musta broke something when we hit the ditch. It ain't starting."

"Great." Michael looked back at the officers. What would their reactions be? Most of the crowd had dispersed; a few people were putting their cars in gear and pulling back onto the highway. The trucker was gone, the tail end of his cargo disappearing around the bend. Evans waited at the side of the road, sitting behind the wheel, watching the officers. They were holding on to the enraged man, speaking to him in low voices. The guy didn't look so angry anymore. His complexion was pale, eyes wide. He was trembling.

"I said, get back in your vehicles," Burke said, walking over to the truck. He swung his weapon around until it was aimed right at Michael's head. "Don't think I won't shoot you, kid."

Michael's legs quivered as his body temperature dropped. He didn't know how to respond. What words could he use to get that gun away from his face? He opened his mouth twice, but nothing came out. "Our truck's not working," he finally muttered, pointing a hand over in Joe's direction. He didn't dare take his eyes off the gun.

"That's not my problem," Burke said.

Evans's car pulled up beside them. "Come with me," the balding man said. "I'll give you both a ride home."

Burke nodded toward Evans, signaling that they should take the offer. Lowering his weapon, he turned his back and returned to where Clive held the handcuffed man. Michael glanced at Joe, who wasn't waiting to be asked twice. They both climbed into the car, Joe stuffing his lanky body into the backseat.

"Thanks." Michael rolled down his window as Evans started to pull away from the scene. As they distanced themselves, he watched the scene gradually growing smaller in the side mirror. They got only about fifty feet away when it happened.

Officer Burke was holding on to the driver one moment; the next he simply let go. The handcuffed man stood there for a few seconds, looking between the cops and the woods. Michael saw Clive give him a hard push.

"What the hell?" Michael turned in his seat. Evans slammed on the brakes as the motorcycle killer ran, hands still cuffed behind his back, straight for the tree line.

He never got a chance. Burke raised his gun, aimed, and shot the man before his feet left the pavement. The guy flew forward, hitting the ground and rolling several times before coming to a stop at the bottom of the ditch.

"He just shot that guy," Joe blurted.

"Get us out of here, now," Michael said to Evans, surprised

at how calm his voice sounded. Inside, his thoughts were screaming. From behind them, Clive turned his gun toward them and pulled the trigger.

"Get down," Evans shouted as he slammed his foot on the gas.

The rear window shattered, spraying Joe with glass. He ducked, even as Evans pulled away, spinning tires and leaving smoking black marks on the pavement.

They spent the next five minutes driving at top speed, but it didn't look like the police officers were going to give chase. Eventually Evans slowed the car down to a reasonable pace.

Michael found his phone in his pocket but paused when he realized he had no idea who he should call. If he dialed 911 would anyone believe them? He'd just witnessed the entire thing and he couldn't quite understand what happened. He punched the numbers into the phone anyway, but all he got was a busy signal. He tried a second time. Then a third. This time he got a recording: There are too many people trying to get through—please dial again. What the hell was going on? He'd never heard of 911 being busy before. Who else was there? Dad was in Denver on business, and he couldn't think of any reason for actually calling him except he was terrified. Finally he dialed Dad's number regardless, but the call didn't go through. He didn't even get an out-of-service message.

"Phone's not working," he said.

"Radio's out too," Evans said. "I can't get any of the stations. I can't even get dead air. It's weird. Maybe the trees?"

"We always get radio here," Joe said. "There's a broadcasting tower not too far away."

"Then it's something else," Evans said.

They drove along in silence for a bit. Joe kept busy picking bits of glass off the backseat and tossing them out the window. Finally he raised his head and looked around bewilderedly. "I need to get home," he said. "Mom's gonna pitch a fit when she finds out I left the truck behind."

"We're sure as hell not going back to get it," Michael said.

"It's our only car, too," Joe said. "The Jeep's in the shop. Dad took it in this morning for a brake job. I'm supposed to drive him back there tonight to pick it up."

"They'll understand."

"I don't know. Dad was in a real pissy mood this morning. He was acting weird."

"Let's just worry about getting home in one piece."

"I can drop you off," Evans said. "Where are you from?"

"Whitefish," Michael said.

"I know where that is. I'm staying at the hotel there."

"Thanks."

It didn't take long to get back to town. Michael gave Evans directions, and they pulled up to Joe's house first. He got out without saying a word and headed up the steps to his front porch. He was in shock. Michael didn't blame him. Had they really just witnessed both a murder and an execution?

When Evans pulled into the driveway in front of Michael's apartment, the building was quiet. What had he been expecting? Flashing blue and red lights? Would Clive and Burke come back for him? He didn't want to think about it. He didn't think they knew where he lived, but that didn't really mean much. They were cops, after all. They'd find him if they wanted to.

Evans must have read his mind. "If they come back for you, I'm staying at the Super Eight. Room six-fourteen. Come and find me if you need help."

Michael nodded and got out of the car. As he watched the balding man drive off, his hand closed around the business card in his back pocket.

ARIES

The stranger was less squeamish about moving among the dead. As he worked his way across the bus, he stopped every few feet to reposition the bodies in order to see their faces. Aries struggled along behind him, trying to keep her balance. There weren't many free spots to put her feet. She didn't want to accidentally step on anyone's arm or fingers—or, even worse, someone's face—and the thought that one wrong movement might send her tumbling down onto the pile of bodies terrified her. So she followed the stranger carefully, stepping where he stepped, and held on to the seat frames as tightly as possible.

He picked up someone by his jacket and shoved him aside. Underneath were more bodies. They were piled on top of one another like a collapsed cheerleading pyramid. He reached out his hand and checked the pulse on someone's wrist. "This one's still alive."

Aries strained to see who the hand belonged to, but she couldn't tell in the mass of clothing and bodies. Her hopes were dashed when the stranger moved aside someone's backpack and revealed the face of a middle-aged woman.

"Should we carry her outside?" She'd taken first aid years ago in school but couldn't remember the proper steps. You weren't supposed to move people in case they had neck injuries, but wasn't staying there worse? It was dangerous leaving them in the middle of the road where another car might hit them. What if a gas leak happened and the bus exploded? Aren't you supposed to get them out of harm's way?

"No," he said. "We'll leave her here."

"When do you think the ambulance will come?"

The stranger climbed to his feet and brushed his hands against his jeans, leaving behind a smear of blood. Continuing forward, he avoided looking at her. "There won't be an ambulance."

Aries froze. "What do you mean?"

"The entire city was just destroyed. The roads are torn apart. Thousands of people are dead or dying. Do you really believe help will come?"

"But they've got to come."

"*They* don't have to do anything."

"These people will die."

The stranger glanced back at her over his shoulder. "And so will millions of others. What's a few more?"

"What do you mean millions?"

"This went farther than just Vancouver. Seattle, Los Angeles, Mexico. Even Alaska if we look in the other direction. A lot of people live on the West Coast. But it's not just North America. An earthquake of this magnitude probably reached Asia."

"Oh."

The stranger continued on, shuffling bodies aside, checking the occasional pulse. He was several feet away, almost to the back of the bus.

Aries knelt at the feet of the middle-aged woman, who

was barely alive. She placed her hand against the lady's forehead, trying to think about what she could do to save her life. The small amount of training she'd received years ago was not enough to help her in such a situation. She knew how to do mouth-to-mouth resuscitation, and that was it. She picked up the woman's limp hand and squeezed it gently, seeking something comforting to say. Even in her unconscious state, the lady still might be able to hear.

"I think I found your friend."

He was standing at the back of the bus and she couldn't see where he was looking. Getting to her feet, she loosened her fingers, allowing the hand of the dying woman to drop to the ground, and went for Sara instead.

"Is she dead?"

The stranger looked away too quickly. That was all the answer she needed. Her bottom lip began to quiver and she breathed in deeply to try and hold back the sobs. Holding tightly to the mangled seat, she focused on maintaining balance and blinked several times to keep the tears from blurring her vision. She was determined to remain calm. She would not fall apart on the bus in front of this stranger. There would be plenty of time later once she was alone. She would be brave.

"You don't have to look," he said, seeing through her facade. His eyes softened. "If you've got a picture, I can identify her for you."

She almost accepted, but she knew if she didn't look she'd regret it. "No, I'm fine." She took another deep breath, closed her eyes, and counted to three inside her head. Opening her eyes, she focused on the image before her.

The person lying on the ground, her neck shoved awkwardly against the mangled seats, was Sara. Her eyes were open, staring at the ads for résumé building and continuing education. One hand rested gently on her chest, the other disappeared beneath her body. Legs splayed in different directions. Blood dribbled from her mouth, already starting to cake and dry. Her neck twisted and unnatural, bits of blond hair stuck against her bloodied face.

Why did her eyes have to be open?

"That's her," she whispered.

"I'm sorry," the stranger said.

How long would it be before someone could take Sara away? She would have to call Sara's parents. Maybe they could find a way to come and get her if they were okay. They didn't live that far away. She took her cell phone from her pocket, but there was no service. That didn't really surprise her; the earthquake would have temporarily destroyed all means of communication.

She'd have to walk, then. If she left now she could get there in a few hours. But was it safe to leave Sara alone? What if someone did something to her body? She caught the dead glaze of her friend's eyes, accusing her, begging her not to leave.

"Can you close her eyes?"

She was thankful that he didn't smirk or give her a look. Instead he reached over and ran the tips of his fingers against Sara's skin, closing those beautiful gray eyes forever.

"Thank you."

"We should go. It's not safe to stay here."

"Can we cover her up with something?" She felt stupid the moment the words left her lips. "I mean, it just seems wrong leaving her like that."

The stranger unzipped his jacket. Carefully he placed the clothing over her deceased friend. It covered only her face and shoulders, but it made Aries feel better. At the same time she worried about the guy. He had on only a shirt now, and although it was still September it was starting to get chilly. She could see his muscles against the tight fabric. His arms were pale and bare; she wanted to feel them around her again. Comforting. The thought warmed her cheeks and she looked away in embarrassment.

"You don't have to do that," she said.

"I know."

"You'll be cold."

"I'll be fine."

There were a few more bodies to check, but in the end, Aries and the stranger got off the bus by themselves. Everyone there was dead, dying, or unable to move. There was nothing they could do to help, so they left. It seemed wrong, but there weren't any right answers to hand in.

The first thing she noticed when they got back outside was how different the air smelled. There was no brisk night air smelling faintly like leaves and car exhaust. There was a sickening acrid flavor that stuck to the insides of her nostrils, threatening to make her gag. In the distance, the skyline was orange and red from where a fire raged. Monstrous black clouds of smoke rapidly spread through the night, pushed by the wind. Bits of ash fell from above and stuck to their hair. Gray snowflakes.

"Can you hear it?" the stranger asked. He stood, arms at his side, eyes closed, face pointed up toward the sky.

"Hear what?" She strained her ears but there was no unusual noise.

"The nothingness. No fire trucks, ambulances, police cars. No people, cars, stereos, televisions, computers. All the things we use to replace the silence of loneliness. All the distractions we buy that fill up the empty voids inside our souls. It's all gone."

"Are you saying our souls are empty?"

"No, I'm saying they've been filled."

"With what?"

The stranger smiled at her. "Humanity has found a cure to a disease they never knew existed."

"You sound just like the crazy man on the bus."

The smile faltered. "Sorry. I was just thinking out loud."

She gave him a long look but couldn't really see anything wrong with him. He didn't look like he was crazy, not in the way the guy on the bus was. He was clean and dressed nicely. His black hair was freshly washed and shiny. There was a seriousness about him and he moved gracefully. He reminded her of some of the others she knew from drama class. He probably read a lot of literary fiction, maybe wrote stories while reciting Dylan Thomas poetry from heart.

"I don't know your name," she finally said. It was lame, but she couldn't think of anything else to ask.

"Daniel."

She wasn't surprised. He looked just like she'd expect a Daniel to look.

"I'm Aries. You know, like the horoscope. But I'm actually a Gemini." It was the standard speech she gave people when introducing herself. Normally she thought it was rather witty, but tonight it sounded stupid. It wasn't the right time to try and make little jokes.

"How ironic."

She couldn't tell if he was mocking her or being clever himself. It was hard to read his expression. His face was unmoving; he didn't seem to have any emotions at all.

A thought occurred to her. There was no one else around. Alive at least. Who knew where Colin ran off to? Probably cowering somewhere, he'd be useless if she needed him any-way. Suddenly she was aware of just how unsafe the situation was. Though she wasn't scared. For some reason her body remained strangely calm. Somehow Daniel made her feel safe even though she knew he could be a threat himself. Maybe it was because he'd already pulled her out from the mountain of bodies. He'd been there for her when she needed it. He seemed truly concerned for her.

The thought made her realize there were others probably worrying about her. Her parents. She reached inside her jacket and clenched her fingers around her useless phone. Were they frantically trying to call her right now? Were they hurt? What if the house hadn't survived the earthquake?

"I should get home and check on my parents," she said. "I need to contact Sara's mom too."

"Do you live far from here?"

"About five miles. But I can walk."

"You'll never make it."

She involuntarily took a step backward.

Daniel was fast. He reached out and grabbed her before she could defend herself. She didn't even get a chance to scream.

"Listen to me, Aries. Something bad is about to happen. Worse than this." He waved his arm around at all the destruc-tion. "It'll make this look like a walk in the park. Don't ask me how I know, I just do. If you don't take cover now, you won't live to see morning. Hell, you probably won't live to see midnight."

"How do you know—"

"Didn't I just tell you not to ask?" He shook his head slightly. "A lot of people are going to die, and it's only the beginning."

Somewhere off in the distance there were screams. Daniel

stiffened and Aries turned around to try and see where the sound was coming from. The sun had almost completely disappeared into the west. The roads were dark; there were no streetlights. Through the twilight she could make out the shapes of people running. They were several blocks away. There were more screams, the sounds of people in agony. One of the shadows stumbled and hit the cement. Others descended on it in a frenzy.

"They're attacking that person."

"They'll come after you, too."

"What? Can't we do something? Call the police?"

"The police can't stop it. No one can. It's too late for that."

"But—"

"Enough. I need you to trust me. I know that's asking for a lot, but you'll have to take a leap of faith. Let me help you."

"Why?"

"Why not?"

"That's not enough of a reason."

"We're beyond reasoning."

"That's not an answer."

Daniel frowned at her. Turning on his heels, he walked a few feet away and then promptly came back. "You're infuriating. Did you know that? Can't you just stop thinking for one second and let me help?"

"Why are you telling me all this?"

"Because I have to tell someone. I can't keep it inside of me. I may not get a second chance."

She almost made a sharp retort but paused. He was scared. Why didn't she see that before? The wideness of his eyes frightened her too, at least enough to stop talking. Behind her, another scream rang out, loud and angry, almost a weird victory shriek. The group of attackers was getting closer. How long before they reached her? She nodded at him, dumbly. She would go along with him for now, while it was still dark and unsafe. She could give him the slip later if she needed to. It might take a few extra hours to get home, but it wasn't like anyone was going anywhere. Hopefully her parents were at home and waiting for her. Mom had told her they had nothing planned. When she didn't show up, surely they'd assume she'd contact them as soon as she could, and at least wait for a while before going out to search for her. If only she could call them. Maybe the landlines were still working. She'd have to find a phone and try.

"Okay." He reached out and took her hand. "Let's find you someplace to hide."

They checked the grocery store first but quickly agreed that it wasn't viable. The front doors were caved in, leaving splinters of glass and rubble. Anyone inside was probably dead or trapped. Even if she did manage to crawl in, she might not be able to get back out. The thought was enough to drive her into a panic.

"There's not much else here," he said. "You need someplace with shelter and food. You might be there for a while."

"We could try the school," she offered.

"Where?"

"A block away," she said. "We were headed there. We had rehearsal. *Alice in Wonderland*. Sara was the Queen of Hearts. She was so excited about it."

A loud bang made her yelp. Gunshots. The group of attackers had reached the accident. They had circled the bus, outnumbering those too injured to run. Through the dimming light, Aries could see the remaining victims trying to get free. One of the men—the bus driver, she thought but wasn't too sure—had a gun. He waved it blindly, sending shots into the air. Two men came at him from behind, bringing him to the ground. Even at a distance she could hear the sound as his head smashed into the pavement. Beyond that, the pregnant woman tried to crawl away until she was dragged back by her hair.

"They're killing them."

Daniel ignored her. "It's time to go." He grabbed her arm. "Show me where the school is."

"It's a block over. That way." She pointed toward the alley behind the grocery store. "But those people need help."

"If you try to help them, you'll die too."

The path before them was pitch-black. Reaching into her bag, she pulled out the miniature flashlight Dad gave her to put on her key chain.

"Here." She removed it and handed it over. "Maybe this will help."

He accepted the tiny metal object, turning it over in his hands before testing the light on the ground between them. "Thanks, but we'd still better stick to the shadows."

Easy enough directions.

The school was dark. She'd never seen it without any lights before. The building rose before them, three stories of eerie silence. She could smell the freshly cut grass; earlier that day she'd seen the gardener riding the mower.

It remained miraculously intact—a bit surprising considering the store beside it was a pile of rubble and the road looked like a construction crew had taken several jackhammers to it. There were five cars in the parking lot, all of them with shattered windows. Whoever owned them wouldn't be driving away anytime soon.

"Why didn't it get destroyed?" she wondered out loud.

"Is it new?" Daniel's voice was calmer than before. Even the tenseness in his shoulders had eased up a bit.

"The school? Yeah, about ten years, I think."

"Earthquake regulations. It's probably reinforced."

"Still. It's creepy."

"But it'll keep you safe. Come on."

They crossed the lawn and headed over to the side where Aries knew the entrance would be unlocked. Just around the corner were the doors that led to the theater. They were supposed to be having rehearsals. There was a good chance that some of her friends would be there. Right about now she could use a familiar face.

As they moved closer she could see that some of the windows were shattered. Bits of grass lay in the flower beds below. Still, there was very little damage considering the quake was so massive.

"Maybe we'll find Colin," she said. "I wouldn't be surprised if the coward came here. I hope he did. I really want to have a word with him."

"You'd be better off if it's empty," Daniel said. "Groups are bad. People do stupid things when they're together."

"But you're here," she said.

"Not for long."

She paused, her hand on the door. "What do you mean? Are you taking off?"

"You'll be safer without me."

Her stomach lurched and ice shot up along her spine. The thought of being alone in the school was enough to bring tears to her eyes. She didn't want to be on her own. She'd freak out. She grabbed hold of his arm, holding on tightly.

"You can't leave me. I need you."

She peered into his eyes, but it was impossible to read his expression in the darkness. Did he really think his being there was going to be dangerous? She couldn't imagine why he believed this. People worked better in pairs, didn't they? Two sets of eyes were better than one. She thought of being alone in the school, in the darkness where anyone would be able to effortlessly sneak up on her. The same panic she'd felt outside the grocery store coated her body, forcing her to shudder involuntarily.

"Please don't leave me," she finally said.

"Fine," he said.

"Promise?"

"Sure."

The school was dark and the silence was heavy in the air. Up ahead she could see that the emergency lights were on in the hallways, so at least there would be a small amount of light. It would help; at least they wouldn't be groping at the walls blindly to try and find the theater.

"It's so quiet," she said.

"That's a good sign," Daniel said.

"We should check the theater first," she said. "There might be people there."

"Where is it?"

"Just down the hall on the right. Follow me."

As they walked, Aries continued to talk. She'd never experienced the school so quiet before, and it creeped her out. At least by talking she could almost block out the eerie silence that was louder than any of the words that escaped her lips.

"Maybe Ms. Darcy will be there," she said. "She's really cool for a teacher. I get good marks in her class. She's the one who's directing *Alice in Wonderland*. Colin was against it, but that's only because there's no male lead. He always wants to be the center of attention. You'll like her. She'll probably know what to do. Not because she's an adult but because she's pretty smart."

She paused when she realized she could hear her own footsteps on the tiled floor but nothing else.

Turning around quickly, she saw nothing but empty hallway.

Daniel was gone.

NOTHING

They know we're here. They're coming for us. What lies beneath has pushed its way to the surface once again. Time to get away while there is still air left in our lungs.

But they will still come.

No matter how much we run and jump and hide.

They've known all along.

It's a game, you see. A simple ploy. If they were to get rid of all of us, then it would be Game Over for all eternity. What fun would that be?

So they will keep some of us alive. Let us breathe and eat and hide. Every now and then they will even let us breed. Then they hunt us anyway. But make no mistake, this is a calculated plot. They will take the ones they need for their future and destroy those they see as worthless.

They have plans for us.

They've already won.

They will remain smart during the annihilation their rage brings.

They walk the riverbed in their fancy clothes and diamond rings. They slouch through the streets with their shopping carts and mismatched shoes. They walk among us, which makes them especially hard to find. A family member perhaps. A lover. A child. This is how they survive and we die out. They are much cleverer than us.

They've been here for a very long time.

Just like animals can sense an earthquake, they felt it coming. They could taste the fear on their lips. It ignited a spark inside of them. Chaos. Perfect, lovable, candy-coated, goes-down-oh-so-sweet anarchy. A time to surge forth. Arrange their massacre. Send out their messengers. Plenty of time for preparation. They gathered their numbers and organized their attack. They didn't even need to RSVP.

It was the perfect plan, and they are the weapons that our leaders keep warning us about. They are the things that hide in your closet and fuel your fear. They lurk in both alleyways and living rooms. They sit across from you at restaurants and push past you to ride the bus.

They are the dark thoughts inside of us we pretend we don't hear. We ignored them but they didn't go away. They grew stronger. Louder. They began to make sense.

I can feel them inside me. The voices are tonguing secrets in my ears that travel down my vertebrae. A thousand squirming insects are chewing on my stomach lining. Mice crawl around inside my intestines. Cockroaches pick at the veins behind my eyes. The voices scream inside my head, but yet they never say more than a whisper. I can't breathe. I can't think.

I'm being eaten alive.

I look forward to death. It will be peaceful compared to this.

MASON

Sometime after two in the morning, Mason's mother drew her last breath. No one noticed or bothered to come. They probably wouldn't know what to do anyway; the morgue was filled to maximum capacity. He hadn't seen a doctor or even an orderly in over six hours. The hospital was in chaos.

Mason was holding her hand when she went. He'd been sitting by her bedside all night, unable to do anything except watch the rise and fall of her chest as the machines helped her breathe.

Thousands of people had died in the past twenty-four hours. Maybe even more—he'd heard nurses talking in the halls about the earthquakes. But he didn't know anyone on the West Coast. Besides, there were more important things on his mind. Hearing about the deaths of strangers didn't fill him with a lot of sadness.

But the bottom dropped out of his world when his mother joined them.

Earlier he'd had the television on to try to gain some understanding. The media was reporting that 123 schools had been bombed. People were screaming words like "terrorism," "mass suicide," and "organized plots," but so far there was nothing to show that the attacks were anything but random.

Then there were the earthquakes, six of them all over the world. Each of them measured at least 9.5 on the Richter scale. The West Coast was utterly destroyed. The quakes caused tsunamis. Rumor had it that most of Hawaii was gone and the casualties in Asia were in the millions.

The television networks were no longer scheduling regular programming. A thousand channels around the world were broadcasting nothing but news.

None of that mattered to Mason as he clung tightly to the cooling hand of his mother.

His friends were all dead. Only a handful had made it out of the school alive. His teachers were dead, even Mr. Yan with his dented Honda Civic.

Something horrible was happening, but Mason was too numb to truly care.

Earlier the taxi dropped him off by the 7-Eleven and he walked over to the school. The situation was surreal; he spent a bit of time wondering if he'd stumbled into someone else's dream. The sky overhead was thick and dark. Above his school was a continuous murky mountain of ash and smoke that sucked up all the scenery. The air burned his throat when he inhaled. It made him light-headed and he tripped over the sidewalk twice until his lungs and brain grew accustomed to the lack of oxygen.

The remains of his high school lay out before him, a pile of rubble and fire. No one even noticed as he crossed over the barriers set out for crowd control and moved toward the gymnasium. The firemen were busy and the police officers were over by the growing crowd of panicky parents and curious onlookers. Ambulances and paramedics rushed about, but there didn't seem to be many survivors left to take to the overcrowded hospital.

Chaos.

There was already a memorial section, and he moved among the lit candles, flowers, and pictures of his former fellow students and friends. He saw Tom's dad talking to another parent while his mother sobbed uncontrollably. Quickly, he moved on before anyone noticed him. He didn't want to have to explain why he was still alive.

The gymnasium was at the rear of the building, and Mason slipped away from the noise, ignoring the heat waves cascading from the destruction. What was he looking for? He couldn't answer that. Maybe there was some tiny bit of hope that a few of his friends might have escaped. But was he really expecting to see them being pulled, miraculously alive, from the rubble?

"I just need to see," he spoke out loud.

The parking lot at the back of the building was eerily empty of people. Hundreds of cars, his own somewhere in that sea of metal and concrete. If someone stopped him he'd say he was there to pick it up. Holding his car keys in the open for evidence, he moved as close to the school as possible, searching for any signs of life.

There were no bloodstains on the sidewalks. No bodies piled on one another for morgue removal. No half-burned books or personal items that might have been thrown through the air during the explosion. Had he been expecting that?

There was nothing to suggest that beneath the debris, hundreds of bodies waited. No proof at all that his school had become a tomb.

He methodically checked around the gymnasium doors to see if there might be a way to slip inside and take a look. But the entire back wall had collapsed, and the only way in were a few cracks big enough for a small animal. Heat poured off the building, burning his face, and the back of his neck grew wet with sweat. Getting down on his knees, he poked through the remains, hoping to find something that might have belonged to one of his friends. Eventually he found a pencil case, bright blue with pink flowers, that looked familiar. Inside were a few pens, an eraser, and a folded note. He opened it.

SEE YOU AT THE MALL AT FIVE.

Yeah, nope.

No one was meeting anyone at five.

He held the note tightly and reread it several times. *I must be in shock,* he thought. *I've lost all feeling in my body. This is what they mean when they say we go numb inside. Everyone's dead and I don't feel a thing. Mom's dying and all I can do is come down to the school and pick up a pencil case? What the hell's wrong with me? It's like they never existed.*

There it was again, that feeling as if he were in someone else's dream.

"Hey, you." A voice broke through his daze. Off in the distance a fireman was moving steadily toward him. "This is a restricted area. Get the hell away from here."

Mason turned and sprinted toward the parking lot. He found his car exactly where he left it that morning, right beside the blue truck with the broken window. Less than a day had passed, but it felt more like weeks. He'd been happy this morning. Hadn't Tom told him that great joke and made him laugh? They'd been planning a camping trip to Chestnut Lake for the weekend. Swimming, camp fires, some hiking—the kind of stuff he and his friends loved doing.

How did the world change so quickly?

He knew he probably shouldn't be driving in such a weird condition, but it didn't stop him from starting the ignition and pulling the car into reverse. Wheels squealing, he tore out of the parking lot, putting on the sunglasses he'd left on the passenger seat a few hours ago.

He didn't go home. Instead he drove around until his gas tank was nothing but fumes. Stopping to refill, he grabbed a bag of chips that he ate but didn't taste. Glancing at the clock, he decided he'd spent enough time away as the doctor ordered. He headed back to the hospital because there was nothing else he could do.

His mother's hand was so cold. Her body was relaxed; most of the wrinkles she fussed about had disappeared from her motionless face. Her hair fanned the pillow, dark brown like his own, thick and shiny, only a few gray hairs showing her age. She was beautiful, his mother, the woman who'd always been there for him. Two weeks ago he'd given her roses for her birthday and she'd been so happy. They'd gone out for dinner together, but she'd paid the bill. She wouldn't let him treat her when she knew he was saving his money for college.

Gently he touched her cheek and pulled the covers up to her shoulders before he turned off the light and left the hospital.

It was quiet outside. The night air was cool on his face and the moon was half a sliver in the sky. He got into his car and was surprised to see the cashier booth unmanned, with the barrier open. He'd been at the hospital for several hours and probably owed at least twenty bucks for parking. But since no one was there, he left without paying a dime.

There were very few cars on the streets. Everyone was inside, glued to their television or on the phone, desperately trying to reach foreign relatives in faraway places. Hadn't he heard something on television about the phone lines being down in several countries? Could the earthquakes really have caused all that? How many people were out there dialing and getting nothing but dead air? Hundreds or thousands must be desperate for news on their loved ones. Lucky them, at least they still had hope.

Diefenbaker Park was dark and silent. Normally there would be dozens of cars filled with teenagers drinking beers and having a good time. There would be couples parked in the lot that overlooked the river, sharing intimate moments before curfews called them home. Mason came here often with his friends; it seemed natural to him to be there now, and that's why he'd pointed the car in its direction. He hadn't even realized it until he pulled through the gates. Good thing his subconscious was paying attention to the roads. At least he'd put on his seat belt. His life might be over, and everyone he knew might be dead, but at least he didn't seem to have a desire to join them yet.

That had to be a good sign. Right?

He parked the car over by the train bridge and turned the key. The silence filled the car. He had to roll down the window to let some of it out. Is this what going insane felt like?

Eventually his eyes adjusted to the darkness, and the outlines of the trees became less blurry. He wished he had something to drink; something strong that would burn a hole in his stomach and shut down his brain. Back at the house he knew where his mother kept a bottle of whiskey. Why hadn't he thought to bring it with him? It's not like he had to worry about her catching him anymore.

Freeing himself from the seat belt, he got out of the car, slamming the door behind him as hard as he could. The noise echoed across the park, and in the distance an owl hooted.

A few feet away from the car was a garbage can. Mason approached it and kicked it hard. It toppled over, lid rolling away, trash flying. He kicked it again, sending it pivoting, lop-sided, into the middle of the parking lot. Again and again his foot met with plastic, leaving scuff marks and dents against the smooth surface. It emptied quickly, and cans, chocolate wrappers, and bags of dog crap scattered across the ground. He stomped on the cans, crushing them underneath his shoes, spreading bits of gravel, and creating dust clouds.

When he was finished he looked around at the clutter and destruction he'd created but it didn't make him feel better. His car was a few feet away, silent and dark against the night. He moved over toward it and kicked a tire several times in rapid succession. White heat flared through his leg and into his brain. But the pain didn't work the way he wanted it to.

The numbness was still there.

He wanted to feel. Something. Anything. The emptiness inside was worse than anything he'd ever experienced.

He could almost hear Tom's voice taunting him about turning emo. How he wished his friend were there to share his grief, but he was also thankful he was alone. Telling people his mother was dead would make it real. He could almost pretend it wasn't so if he didn't say it out loud.

Gravel crunched behind him and he spun around, half expecting to see a police car. Would they arrest him for destroying the trash can? He'd never vandalized anything before. Sorry, Officer—didn't mean for all that destruction, but my mother and all my friends died today. Isn't that worth a Get Out of Jail Free card?

But it wasn't a cop, just some guy walking across the parking lot toward him. Normally Mason would have turned back to his car without giving the guy a second glance. A lot of people walked throughout Diefenbaker Park late at night, and even the homeless people sometimes curled up on the benches.

But the guy was carrying a baseball bat, and that made Mason take notice.

And he was coming straight for him.

He didn't have time to react properly. The guy crossed the remaining few feet in three strides, raised the bat, and brought it down toward Mason's head. Luckily, Mason instinctively stepped backward, the weapon missing him by inches.

"What the hell?"

The stranger didn't answer. His response was to raise the bat again. Mason took a good look at his face. His lips curled and his eyes burned with hatred, although Mason was positive he'd never seen this person before. Why on earth was he trying to bash in his brains?

Mason moved again but not as quickly. The bat met with his shoulder, the impact vibrating through his entire body. Endorphins flooded to his brain, sending waves of nausea straight to his stomach. All rational thought died. The edge of his vision went blurry and then dark. His arm went instantly limp, dangling uselessly at his side as he swallowed twice, trying to keep the bile from rising in his throat and pouring from his lips.

Mason's knees hit the ground and the stranger raised the bat again. Thoughts jumped through his brain, popping out at him between the pain and dizziness. He was going to die. The nut job with the baseball bat was going to take him down in a matter of seconds and it would be over.

The thought sobered him enough to make him push forward on his legs and slam his body into his opponent. The baseball guy grunted, the first sound he'd made since the attack started, and he took a few steps backward before the weight of Mason's body brought him down. He didn't let go of the weapon, though, and he brought it back up in the air as the two of them struggled.

Mason picked up a handful of dirt and threw it in the guy's eyes. It didn't even make him blink. Using his good hand, Mason reached out and grabbed hold of the baseball bat, desperately trying to keep the guy from using it. A second blow and he'd be done, especially if he took a shot to the head. Shoving forward, he tried to get the upper hand by pressing all his body weight on top of the guy's arm. If he could get him to drop the bat, he'd have a better chance. His car was just five feet away. All he needed to do was get inside and lock the doors. A tiny bit of hope quelled the queasiness in his stomach. He might just get through this.

He didn't want to die.

He was a little surprised to realize this.

But the guy wasn't letting go of the bat without a fight. Mason shifted his leg over until his foot pressed up against the guy's wrist. He managed to bring himself up to his knees and press all his body weight against it, but the weapon stayed firm in the stranger's hand. It was an awkward position, and in a matter of seconds the guy bucked Mason off himself. Falling backward, Mason hit his shoulder against the pavement and white stars filled his vision, bringing with them a wave of dizziness. Rolling over onto his back, he gazed at the guy as he straightened, bat in hand, and situated himself right beside Mason's head.

"What do you want?" Mason mumbled.

The guy didn't say a word. Instead he brought the bat down.

Mason rolled to the left, grabbing the guy's ankle and dragging him down a second time. This time the guy dropped the bat and it bounced against the pavement, making a hollow sound as the aluminum hit the rocky surface. It didn't roll far enough away, though; it was still within reach. Mason managed to bring up his leg and kick out wildly. His foot met with the stranger's nose, and he could actually feel the cartilage breaking beneath his shoe.

Grabbing hold of the guy's jean jacket, Mason pulled himself up against him, like climbing a sideways ladder. His hands caught hair and he didn't stop to think.

He reacted.

The vibration spread up his fingers and into his arms as the head met with concrete. The guy immediately stopped moving.

Mason shoved himself off the body and crab walked backward, stumbling and falling when he tried to put weight on his bad arm. He shuffled along the ground until his head met with his car. Leaning against the smooth metal, he waited apprehensively for the man's body to move.

It didn't.

He lasted about ten seconds before the bile in his stomach pushed its way to the surface. Crawling to his knees, Mason heaved into the dirt. As he puked helplessly, his body tensed, waiting for the moment when the baseball bat would crack against his skull.

Nothing happened.

When it was over and his head had cleared enough to look, he saw that the man was still lying on the ground. Even through the darkness Mason could see the pool of blood spreading from underneath his head.

Had he killed him? Using the car as a crutch, Mason

managed to climb to his feet and stumble the few feet back until he was standing over the stranger. The man faced the sky and his eyes were closed. Mason couldn't tell if he was breathing or not, and he didn't want to lean in closer to get a better look. Picking up the baseball bat, he tossed it as hard as he could. It cleared the parking lot and landed a few feet away in the bushes.

He staggered back to his car and got in. Starting the engine, he winced as he placed his injured arm on the steering wheel. He backed out carefully. Even if the guy was dead, he didn't want to drive over him.

He made it only to the edge of the park before he had to pull over. His hands were shaking so badly he could barely hold on to the wheel. Turning off the car, he waited for the panic to subside.

Had he really just killed a man? Was he a murderer? No, it was done in self-defense. There's no way any court would convict him. But he'd left the scene of the crime. Should he have kept the baseball bat as proof that the guy had a weapon? What if someone came along and took it? A small cry escaped his lips. A man might be dead and the only thing that worried him was whether or not he was going to be arrested?

Shouldn't he be worried about the stranger's family? Should he try and find them? Wouldn't they be worried?

He realized he didn't care. There was no empathy in his brain.

Was he that dead inside?

He knew he should go to the police, but it was the last thing in the world he wanted to do. He made sure the doors were locked before he closed his eyes and leaned his head back.

He'd be better once he slept for a bit.

CLEMENTINE

There had been screams.

Begging. Pleading.

Agony.

Then silence.

Around four in the morning the gunshots finally ended. Shortly after that the screaming winded down and soon there was silence. No more voices. The only sounds were the crickets and wind echoing through the rafters.

Clementine was hiding in the barn. She had run the mile to her house, but when she'd arrived, she'd known immediately it wasn't safe. Whatever had happened to her parents and the folks at the town hall was happening to all the citizens of Glenmore. And Sam let her go free. He warned her specifically not to go home. Her house would be the first place they'd search if they came for her.

Scratch that. *When* they came for her.

It was just a matter of time.

Dear Heath, I promised myself I wouldn't think about them until I'm safe. Help me find a way out of this and then I'll allow myself to fall apart.

She had stood outside her house wondering what to do. It didn't take long to decide to hide in the barn. She had plenty of time afterward to regret that decision. She could have grabbed her cell phone and called someone. She should have taken the keys to the truck. If she had done that she'd be on the road and halfway to Des Moines by now. She could have gotten help. She could have run into the fields and taken cover in the corn. It would have provided better shelter in the long run.

Because she knew that the second they finished searching the house they'd come and check the barn.

Stupid! Stupid! Stupid!

She was trapped. The time to run had been hours ago while they were still busy at the town hall. Her parents' farm was right on the edge of town. They'd be getting close by now.

How many of them were there? She'd been too panicky to count. There had to be at least a dozen, maybe more. These were people she'd grown up with. Sam. He'd helped her dad repair a fence less than a week ago. He'd been in a good mood and she'd given him lemonade and some of her mother's cookies.

All these people she thought she knew. There were memories attached to all of them. Good memories. What happened to change them into killers?

She needed to get into the house. She didn't even have to go that far. The keys were in the fruit basket on the kitchen table, ten feet from the back door. She could be in and out in less than thirty seconds.

But every time she tried to convince her brain of the logic of moving, her legs refused to participate.

Dear Heath, remember last summer, before you went off to college? You told me if there was ever an issue with guys I could call you and you'd come instantly and rough them up. Well, I've got some problems and could use a bodyguard right about now. Your tough baby sister isn't as strong as she thought she was. In fact, she's turning out to be quite the marshmallow. People keep telling her to run and she goes the distance. Should have signed up for cross-country this year. I'd be heading for the Olympics in no time. Do they have a gold medal for being cowardly?

If only telepathy worked.

What was that stupid mantra that Imogene was always chanting? *I'm a strong and beautiful woman. Everything I touch will turn to gold.*

Yeah, and *I must, I must, I must increase my bust.*

A cracking noise outside the barn, and her heart instantly doubled up. Someone was standing outside the doors. They'd found her.

No, they hadn't found her. *Stop overreacting.* She needed to get control of herself; otherwise she'd jump up the minute they walked through. Hey! Here I am! Over here!

Remain calm. Count backward from twenty to try to slow her breathing. Push her heart back down her throat and force it into submission. She could do this. Her hiding spot in the corner was good. She'd managed to cover herself adequately with hay and an old horse blanket. On first glance she probably looked like a big lump of nothing. Didn't the heroine always go up into the rafters in the horror movies? Staying on the ground would give her leverage. When the killer went up to search the dead end, she would slip quietly out the door. She would run into the house and grab the keys and be on her way before the killer even knew she was gone. She'd go to the police in Des Moines and they'd send out the army or the FBI, and Sam, Henry, James, and the rest of the not-so-God-fearing nutcases of Glenmore would be arrested.

And for Christmas she'd get a pony and a Porsche.

They had guns. She may be fast, but there was no way she could outrun a bullet.

The noise came again. She'd been so busy fantasizing that she barely heard it. But it was there, a tiny scratching sound. Footsteps crunching in the dirt. A small cough. She covered her mouth with her hands.

There was a loud noise as someone grabbed hold of the doors and slid them open. More footsteps. She couldn't tell if it was one person or two and she wasn't stupid enough to pop her head up and check. It had to be just one. If there were two they'd be talking to each other. But who was it?

From her hiding spot under the blanket, she could just make out the five feet of flooring in front of her. Why hadn't she thought to try to reposition herself where she could get a better view of the door? She waited, her ears perked for what might be coming.

The person began moving toward the middle of the barn. They were taking their time, small unrushed steps, obviously in no hurry to kill her. They had to know she was there. Maybe they could smell her fear?

The person began to whistle. *Oh my darling, oh my darling, oh my darling, Clementine.* How she hated that song. Heath used to sing it to her whenever he wanted to annoy her.

She should have grabbed a weapon. Anything. There were so many other courses of action she could have taken. Instead she'd managed to pretty much serve herself up on a platter. She sure was living up to that blond-cheerleader stereotype.

A few weeks ago someone e-mailed a joke questionnaire on how to survive a zombie attack. She'd scored pretty high. Of course she'd stated she'd head down to the local weapons store and arm herself before holing up in an isolated cabin in the north. Okay, so it wasn't the best thing to use as a comparison to how well she could do in a real-life emergency situation, but the whole concept kept creeping into her mind. What a joke. She couldn't even survive a few hours up against psychotic humans.

The whistler moved slowly and steadily across the barn. At least she'd been smart enough to hide in a corner close to the door. As he passed her she fought the urge to move. She was like a mouse being hunted by an eagle. She needed to stay still and not jump and flee. Running blind never served the mouse justice, and it probably wouldn't work for her.

Funny how her legs had refused to work earlier, and now they were itching to kick.

Dear Heath, you were right. If I get out of this alive I'll take those tae kwon do lessons you said I needed. Just promise me you'll be here to help me get those punches right. Give me a sign to let me know you're not just a figment of my imagination and are still alive and well in Seattle. It'll give me the courage to kick ass. I promise.

She needed to stop this. Talking to her maybe/more-than-likely dead brother wasn't going to help the situation.

Meanwhile the whistler had grown quiet. She strained her ears, listening. Was he gone? Had he slipped back out the door while she was making all her imaginary resolutions?

No, there it was again—the sound of a boot scraping against wood from across the barn. Her assailant was climbing the ladder to the rafters. All she had to do was wait until he reached the top and she could get out. Moving as slowly as she could, she pushed the blanket off her head to get a better view. The doors to the barn were wide-open. She could slip out without making a sound.

Her assailant swung his foot up onto the beams. The creaking noise above was the signal she was waiting for. It was now or never. Carefully she pulled back the blanket and scanned the area. The barn floor was empty. She didn't even look at the rafters. She forced herself to walk quietly instead of run, fully aware that her back was like one giant target. There were no shouts or sudden footfalls. No one rushed toward her. She moved quickly but cautiously. One misplaced step, one creaky board, could end it.

Outside the air was cool on her face. She had forgotten to breathe. She inhaled heavily, and her wobbly legs continued to hold her weight. Avoiding the urge to lean against the barn and rest, she forced herself to keep moving. She would get the keys. The truck was hidden on the other side of the house. Whoever was in the barn would probably be there for at least ten more minutes. With a little luck she'd be able to start the car and be halfway down the lane before he got out of the rafters.

It was one hundred feet from the barn to the house. She could see the porch light burning. Turning it on was the last thing her mother had done before they left for the town hall. She always left it on no matter how much her father grumbled over the electric bill. They would never wait up for her again.

Dear Heath, I've really gone and messed things up. It's not like an exam where I can take notes. I don't get a chance to repeat this if I fail. Help me reach the truck. Give me strength, brother.

One hundred feet. Not far at all. But it was similar to crossing the open sea, and she didn't have any shark repellent.

It was time to go. No time like the present. If she waited too long it would be game over. She began to run, silently cursing herself every time her foot hit the grass. She couldn't be making that much noise. She was light enough to always be on the top of the cheerleading pyramid, and her mother was constantly complaining that she needed to gain a few pounds to fill out properly.

When she reached the safety of the house, she was overcome with such relief that she almost broke down in tears. Instead she forced herself onward, making her way around the side to the back.

Her hands were shaking as she unlocked the back door. The interior of the house was dark. Mom may have left the porch light on, but Dad had the sense to make sure the house wasn't burning any extra electricity. Leaving the key in the lock, she crossed the kitchen in three strides. She reached blindly into the fruit basket until she felt the leather key chain. Mom's address book was open on the table. She ripped Heath's address out as quietly as possible, folded the piece of paper, and stuck it in her pocket. Now all she had to do was get back out to the truck.

"Clem?"

She nearly peed herself.

Craig Strathmore stepped out from the shadows beside the fridge. His eyes were wide and unsure. His hands were clasped together and pressed against his stomach, white-knuckled in an awkward prayer. There was a small gash under his right eye; blood was smeared across his cheek from where he'd wiped it.

"Thank God it's you," he said. "I was looking for you."

"Craig? What happened? Why are you here?"

He looked down at his feet before taking another step forward. "Town hall. They're all dead. I don't understand. Henry Tills killed my parents. Shot them down. I mean, I've known him my entire life. My dad bowled with him. How could he do that?"

"I don't know."

"I slipped. Henry raised the gun at me and I slipped. Wet floor. Fell. The shot missed me by inches. He would have gotten a second chance, too, but he got distracted by my mother. Killed her. Right in front of my eyes."

"I'm sorry."

"I saw you sneak out the doors. I didn't know where else to go. I hoped maybe I could find you. I don't understand. Why are they doing this?"

"I don't know. But we've got to get out of here."

"Okay. Where are we gonna go?"

"Des Moines. The police will know what to do. We have to hurry. Someone's in the barn looking for me. You're lucky they didn't find you first."

"I'm scared," he whispered. His voice shuddered, and he closed his eyes tightly, his forehead crinkling into tiny lines. He'd aged twenty years in the course of a single evening. He opened his arms and waited, looking like a small child awakened from a bad dream.

There were dark stains on his letterman jacket, and it took her a few moments to realize it was blood. He was covered in it.

She didn't know what to do. How much time did they have?

Holding out her arms, she embraced him. She couldn't do anything else. She was helpless. His hands wrapped around her, resting on the small of her back, fingers cold and stiff on top of her jacket.

They rocked back and forth on the linoleum floor. He held her tight, desperately; she could feel the tautness of his chest pressing against her. Muscular arms gripping, pressing weight against her body. His head dropped down to rest against the curve of her neck. He exhaled into her hair; lips puckered and tasted her skin.

"Craig?"

"Yes?"

"You need to let go now."

"And if I don't?"

She tried to pull back. Fingernails dug into her jacket, gouging her back. He drew her in closer than she would have believed possible, lips pressed against her ear. He began to whistle.

Oh my darling, oh my darling, oh my darling Clementine.

She would have liked to scream but her throat closed. All the air inside her lungs was vacuumed out of her body.

"What's the matter, darling Clementine?"

She twisted her body, let her legs go slack, tried to worm her way out from his grasp. But he wasn't letting go. She clawed at the back of his jacket, his arms; she couldn't reach high enough to scratch at his face. He had made her his prisoner and she'd welcomed the embrace.

Stupid! Stupid! Stupid!

"You should have heard your mother's screams," Craig whispered in her ear. "They were exquisite. How she cried."

This was not Craig. This person holding her was not the guy she knew. Two months ago they'd been driving and hit a raccoon. The Craig she'd grown up with had pulled over to the side of the road and gotten misty-eyed. He may have been a football star, but he loved animals and was a vegetarian. The boy she knew would never get off on trying to scare her like this.

"Who are you?" she asked. There was something odd about his eyes. They were darker. At first she thought the shadows were playing tricks on her. But that wasn't it. The veins were black.

"I'm Craig."

"No, you're not."

"I'm the darkest corner of his soul. I'm all the things he

75

wanted to be, everything he dared to think when no one else was around. I'm the real Craig Strathmore. I'm his evolution. His true self."

"No. You're. Not." Raising her foot, she slammed her heel down onto the side of his leg. Craig grunted and loosened his grip just enough for her to slide out of his grasp. She dropped to the floor, reached out, and grabbed the first thing she found, which happened to be the paperweight her mother used to keep the kitchen door open. She brought it up and drove it straight into his knee.

Craig grunted both in surprise and pain. She climbed to her feet and started for the door, but he grabbed her ankle, bringing her back to the floor and cracking her knee on the linoleum. Her cartilage made an awful thunking noise, but she stumbled on, ignoring the pain and kicking out at him with her uninjured leg. He brought his arms up to defend his face, freeing her for one quick moment.

It took her a total of three seconds to get outside. Pressing the unlock button on the key chain, she threw open the car door and climbed into the cab. The engine came to life on the first try, and she turned on the headlights before putting the truck into gear.

The driveway to her parents' house was filled with people. There were at least a dozen of them, standing completely still and staring back at her. She recognized Henry and James Tills, Sam Anselm, and some of the others she'd seen earlier at the parking lot. Their clothing was wet with blood, black and shiny in the moonlight.

They were blocking the road.

Craig Strathmore, or whoever he was now, came out onto the front porch, limping, his eyes blazing, and heading directly toward her.

She didn't need a road. She hadn't been raised on a farm for nothing. Putting the car into first gear, she pressed hard on the gas, spun the wheel, and drove directly into the cornfields. It was a bumpy ride but the truck had four-wheel drive for a reason.

She didn't look in the rearview mirror to see if they were following her.

It was two miles to the road through the fields. She made it in record time. Her tires crunched as they spun up onto the highway. She pointed the car in the direction leading away from Glenmore.

She drove for an hour before finally pulling over to the side. There was no other traffic. She hadn't seen a single vehicle.

Dear Heath, there's something weird going on. The earthquakes were scary enough, but then the news started reporting all this violence. I didn't really believe it until tonight. It's everywhere, isn't it? Whatever it is, once I'm done in Des Moines I'm coming to find you. It was what Mom wanted, and I'll grant her that last wish. So you'd better not be dead. I'll be there as soon as I can. I'll be mad if you go on without me. Don't leave me alone like this.

She turned on the radio but couldn't find a station. Nothing but static. She played with the dials for about ten minutes, even climbed out of the truck to check the antenna.

It was as if she were the last person on earth.

MICHAEL

He awoke to the last rays of the western sun warming his pillow. Sweat covered his body, enough to soak the hairs behind his ears, and his upper body felt slightly damp. He hadn't meant to fall asleep; in fact he was shocked he'd done it. A few hours ago he didn't think he'd ever close his eyes again. After Evans dropped him off, he couldn't stop pacing. Every few minutes he'd look out the window, heart pounding, muscles stiff enough to shatter. After an hour or so, he didn't know what else to do so he lay down for a bit to try and clear his head.

Getting up off the bed, he stumbled into the living room, tripping over the bag of garbage he'd placed by the door but forgot to take out that morning.

The television still wasn't broadcasting, and he didn't even bother to check the Internet. In the kitchen he turned on the coffeepot and then went over to the window to take a look. A part of him still believed that the two officers were going to show up at his doorstep any minute, ready to finish him off because of the crimes he'd witnessed.

But the street was empty. Whitefish seemed to have shut down early.

They hadn't gone straight home after dropping Joe off. Instead, he and Evans had driven to the police department and found it empty. No cars in the parking lot. The front doors were locked. They'd banged on the glass, but no one came.

Since when was a police department allowed to shut down?

Michael had tried his phone again, but still nothing. Evans said he'd talked to several people and they all repeated the same thing. Nothing electronic had been working properly since the earthquakes. Phones, Internet, television, and even the radio. All forms of communication were erratic or on the blink.

"It's like something's making things and people go crazy," Evans said. "I was out by Great Falls yesterday. It's happening there, too. A bunch of idiots killed each other during a bar brawl."

"You think so? Is that even possible?"

"Dunno," Evans said. He smacked his fist against the car radio, but there was nothing but static. "We need information. Didn't you notice? There weren't any updates today. Just the same prerecorded crap on a constant loop. You know it's scary when the reporters stop broadcasting."

Michael was surprised.

"How can there be no news?" he asked.

"I don't know," Evans said. "But it's bad. We're being kept in the dark. My guess is what happened back there on the road isn't isolated. I think a hell of a lot more people are going to die."

Michael played the conversation over in his mind as he looked out the window. At the time he'd thought it was a bit overdramatic. Now he wasn't so sure. Normally, this time of evening there would be people walking around on the street. But he couldn't see anyone.

Definitely odd.

From the apartment below him, he heard the muffled sound of their door buzzer. No accompanying footsteps followed it. He poured some coffee and added a lot of sugar. There was no milk in the fridge. He would have to remember to buy some tomorrow.

Heading back to his bedroom, he paused at the front door when he heard another door buzzer, this time from his neighbor's apartment. He checked through the peephole to make sure no one was there before unlocking the door and stepping out into the hallway. His apartment faced the back, so there was no way to know who was at the front door unless he checked the window at the end of the hallway. Another buzzer went off; this time the muffled noise came from his neighbor in 415. Still no one answered. He began to think he was the only one left in the building.

He wasn't so sure he wanted to know who was out there. Stepping back inside his apartment, he double locked the door. Crossing the floor, he put his coffee mug down on the table. He turned and stared at his own intercom.

BBBUUUUZZZZZZ

He almost screamed like a girl. Recoiling back from the door, he tripped over the garbage a second time, falling backward and landing on his backside. The sheer terror of the situation caused him to bray loudly, like some sort of deranged donkey.

"Ohcrapohcrapohcrapohcrap."

Pulling himself up to his feet, he moved over toward the intercom, part of him desperately wanting to push the button. But the other half of him screamed, because wasn't it better to let them think he wasn't home? The receiver stuck out at him like it had a great big Don't Touch sign on it.

BBBUUUUZZZZZ

He couldn't help himself. He had to know.

Fingers pressing, he could hear the sound of outside air come through the tiny speakers. He didn't say anything; he didn't know how to respond.

"Hello?" The voice was slightly gargled. "I'm looking for someone. Michael. He lives in this building."

Evans.

"Hey," Michael said. "It's me. I'll let you in. Four-twelve."

He could hear the weird vibrating sound as the door unlocked. Evans muttered something, but he didn't catch it. A few minutes later when the knock came at his door, he peeked through the eyehole to make sure Evans was alone.

He was.

"What's wrong?" Michael opened the door, and Evans brushed past him as if he couldn't get inside fast enough. Michael closed the door and locked it. Whatever was chasing him might not be that far behind.

"Have you been outside?" Evans asked.

Michael shook his head. "I've been home since you dropped me off. Why? What's going on?"

"The entire town's gone crazy. They've blocked the roads. People in cars. They're not letting anyone in or out of town. They're shooting anyone who tries. Those cops we saw earlier. They're dead. Someone lynched them."

"What?"

"They're all dead," Evans continued. "They're pulling people out of their homes. Chasing them down in the streets. A group of them torched the supermarket. It started about an hour ago. I was at the gas station trying to call my wife from a pay phone. Some guy came after me with a crowbar."

"But . . ."

"I think I killed him. Don't look at me like that. What was I supposed to do? Gray-haired or not, he had a crowbar. Tried to splatter my brains across the walls. I had no other choice."

"Okay." Michael kept his mouth open, but nothing else came out. Instead he went back over to the door and double-checked the lock.

"Look." Evans started pacing around the cramped living room. "I've been driving around. I didn't know where else to go. My wife. I can't get ahold of her. I've got a little girl, too. You've gotta help me. I need to get home to them. I don't know what to do. They've barricaded the roads. I can't get out."

"Okay. Where's your wife?"

"Somers. Right on the lake."

Michael nodded. "I've been there. That's not very far."

"How are we supposed to get there? We can't go by car."

"There's got to be a way," Michael said. "There are other roads. They can't have barricaded them all."

"You don't get it, kid." Evans stomped over to the window and pointed out at the street. "It's psycho out there. They're killing everyone. It's only a matter of time till they find us.

"It's the earthquakes," Evans said. "Something happened that's . . ." He paused. "Something's turned people."

"But we're both fine," Michael said.

"For how long?"

Michael went over to the phone and picked it up. Tried calling his mother's number. Nothing. Suddenly, more than anything else in the world he wanted to hear her voice. He'd be satisfied with a recorded message saying she wasn't home. But he couldn't even get that.

What about Dad? Was he okay? He was supposed to get back from Denver in a few days. They were going to the football game this weekend. The tickets were on his dresser.

"I need to get home," Evans said. "My wife. My daughter. She's only two."

"Maybe I can help you," he said. He looked over at the fishing rods leaning against the couch.

He didn't want to go outside. More than anything he wanted to crawl into bed, pull up the covers, and wait for this whole thing to blow over. The lock on their door was strong and there was more than enough food to keep him alive for several weeks. But he knew Dad would be disappointed in him if he took the cowardly way out. Especially when there were children involved who needed help.

He took a deep breath. "I know a way out of here. We can walk." Michael went over to the window and saw that the street below was still empty. "There are trails not too far from here. I know of a few that loop around back to the highway. They'll take us about five miles from town. There are ski resorts out that way. We might be able to find a working phone or even someone who can give us a ride."

Evans nodded.

"Just let me get some stuff. I think we've got a flashlight kicking around. Not sure about batteries. There's water in the fridge. Why don't you grab it and whatever else you can find in the cupboard?"

Michael was surprised at how calm he felt. He went into the den, where he was pretty sure he'd last seen the flashlights. Sure enough, he found two of them in the back of the closet. Both of them worked.

Evans had reached out for him and Michael had found the solution. The fact that the older man needed help was the very thing that was keeping Michael from falling apart. His mother was like that, always the one to take control in serious situations. Although he hadn't seen her in years, he couldn't help but think she'd be proud of him for helping this man in his time of need.

Back in the living room, Evans seemed much better. He'd grabbed the water and shoved it into the backpack Michael gave him.

"We don't need much," he said. "There's tons of gas stations along the road. We'll be able to find what we need. It shouldn't take us more than a few days tops, even less if we can catch a ride with someone."

"You sure you won't get us lost?" Evans asked.

"I grew up here," Michael said. "I know the woods." He grabbed his jacket and put it on. "I need to go check on Joe first. Do you just want to hang out here? It won't take long. I know a good shortcut."

"Don't," the older man said. "I went there first."

Michael noticed that Evans's hands were shaking. There was dried blood on his fingers from when he got attacked by the guy with a crowbar. "Was it bad?" he finally asked.

Evans nodded.

Joe had three younger sisters. His parents were cool. Michael turned away from Evans, not wanting the man to see the tears burning in his eyes.

"What about your family?" Evans asked. "Any idea where they are? Should you leave a note? I mean, how old are you anyway?"

"My dad's in Denver," he said, trying to keep his voice from trembling. "At this point there isn't much I can do about him. I can't reach him on the phone and he's not due back for a few more days. I haven't seen my mom or sister in years. Mom's remarried. They're out east. And I'm seventeen."

"Good God, you're just a kid."

"Hey, you asked me for help."

Evans put his hands up. "I didn't mean it that way. You just seem a lot older. At seventeen, I'd probably have been hiding in the closet and sucking my thumb through something like this."

The comment made Michael feel oddly proud. He put his hand on Evans's shoulder. "We'll get through this. We'll find your wife and child."

MASON

Mason couldn't sleep. He moved across the house in the dead of night, the almost empty whiskey bottle firm in his fingers. He was drunk but it wasn't a good time. Happy hour was over.

There were pictures on the walls, chronicles of his life:

—Disneyland when he was seven. He cried because he wasn't tall enough to ride Space Mountain.

—A five-year-old Mason wearing his dress shirt and tie for his cousin's wedding. He'd been the ring bearer. Someone had spilled red wine on him just before he walked down the aisle. He'd cried.

—A baby with a bright red nose, laughing while playing in the bathtub. One of the rare times he hadn't cried.

—A picture of him and a bunch of his friends on the first day of high school. Tom had his arm around him. They'd dropped by the house after class and Mom had made the whole group sandwiches without complaining. A bunch of happy, hungry teenagers.

—Seventeen and standing in front of his new car. Okay, it wasn't new but he had been thrilled just the same. He'd saved up for it for a year by working part-time at the mall. Mom had come through at the last minute and chipped in a few grand so he'd buy something safe and not a relic from the eighties.

—Mason at four. Back when Dad was still alive. In the picture, his mother was holding him, they were both wearing sunglasses, and he had on Dad's baseball cap, which was several sizes too big. Mom looked so happy; her hair was loose and blowing in the breeze. Dad had taken the picture, and afterward they walked along the beach holding hands. The tide was out and Dad picked up some of the heavier rocks so that Mason could watch the baby crabs scuttle away. Afterward they had fried shrimp, and Mom laughed because Mason thought the marinara sauce was ketchup and poured it over his fries.

The picture slipped from his hands. He watched it drop in slow motion and hit the ground, the glass cracking across his mother's face. Dropping to his knees, he picked up the broken frame and shook away the glass, fingers trembling; he removed the picture from its casing and turned it over so he could read the inscription.

STANLEY PARK. SECOND BEACH. VANCOUVER, BC, MASON AND MOM— ENJOYING THE SUN.

He couldn't stand to look at it anymore. His eyes scanned the room, desperately seeking something else to grab his attention. Immediately he found his reflection in the darkened flat screen.

The television was no longer broadcasting.

Sometime around two the stations went off the air. There

was no warning. No emergency broadcast system. No lecture on how this was a test, only a test. Everything went dead, and black filled the screen.

The Internet was down too.

He didn't even bother to check his cell phone.

Before it went off the air the television was full of questions. News announcers told people to remain calm while glancing agitatedly offscreen. Stay inside. Lock your doors. If you feel you can't be alone or that you're in danger, call the local police for a listing of safe areas to relocate.

Remain calm.

Helicopter reporters circled the skies, their cameras shooting footage of riots in the bigger cities like New York and Chicago. People were behaving erratically all over the world, even in places where the earthquakes hadn't hit. Don't panic. Los Angeles was gone. All electronic communication was halted. No one knew the exact extent of the damage. A few reports came in from Seattle and Portland. The cities were in ruins. The death count was immeasurable.

Don't panic.

Something was happening to the citizens of the United States and the rest of the world. People were going crazy. Hurting each other. They were bombing schools and government centers. Strangers were setting things on fire. Reports of shooting sprees at restaurants and hospitals were popping up. Children were being hunted down in playgrounds and preschools. People were attacking randomly both loved ones and complete strangers. The melted bag of frozen peas on the couch was testament to the last one. No matter how much Mason drank, his shoulder still hurt. Several times during the evening he stood in front of the bathroom mirror and moved his arm as much as he dared. He flexed his fingers and worried about the swelling and bruising when he took off his shirt. He'd toyed with the idea of going back to the ER but didn't think he'd even get through the doors. He wondered if his mother was still in the intensive care ward, dead and forgotten. Was her body stiff by now? Rigor mortis lasted only so long, didn't it? Maybe her body was soft again, slowly decaying, cellular structures breaking apart, and there was no one there to put her in cold storage down in the morgue. She might never get a burial; instead the hospital bed would become her tomb. Would she mummify? Or would she simply rot away?

He should go back and get her. There was a shovel in the garage; he could bury her in the garden. It might not be as glamorous or sacred as a cemetery, but his options were slim. He couldn't bear to see her body again, though. What if it was already bloated? What if he'd been wrong and she'd still been alive? What if she was dying right now and calling out his name and he was selfishly pissing away her only bottle of whiskey? No, he couldn't go back. He just wanted to stop thinking. It was easier that way. The numbness hadn't left him; if anything it was spreading. When he looked at the pictures, there was no emotion, even though he knew there should be. He should be sad.

But he wasn't.

He felt nothing.

The drinking didn't help.

Somewhere in the darkest recess of his brain, a button was pushed. Everything he cared about simply vanished. He'd malfunctioned.

It was better this way, or at least that's what he told himself. Caring only led to heartbreak. He'd probably be curled up on the floor in his bedroom, crying like a baby, if it weren't for the numbness. This way he was able to still function, or he would tomorrow morning once he sobered up.

He was done mourning.

It was time to act. Whatever was happening was going to continue. He needed to find someplace safe if he was going to survive, a nice rustic cabin in the mountains where he could silently wait the whole thing out. Maybe he could find a beach, become a castaway where the sun could warm his body. He'd do it alone; he didn't want people around. They'd only hold him back. He didn't need anyone.

All he had to do was burn his bridges.

There was a gasoline can in the garage for the lawn mower. Drunkenly, he stumbled out to find it in the corner underneath some tarps. Back in the house he started with his bedroom. A clean start would make everything better. There was nothing he wanted. He sprinkled his bed with a healthy dose of the flammable liquid and then moved on. Next were the guest room and the bathroom. He passed his mother's bedroom—no need to go in there. He briefly considered taking her jewelry but then decided against it. It's not like he'd be able to sell it. The odds that the pawn shops might be open during this crisis were laughable. Downstairs he soaked the television and the couch. In the kitchen he baptized the microwave, table, and curtains. Methodically he moved from room to room until he finally ran out of gasoline. It was enough; he'd managed to do sufficient damage. When he lit the match the entire house would burn. Maybe he could roast marshmallows.

Back in the living room, he dropped the canister on the floor and looked around for the whiskey bottle. He found it, but somehow he'd tipped it over and the last remaining liquid had spilled out and stained the carpet. His brain became assaulted with white noise. Darkness clouded his vision. He couldn't even think straight enough to try and step back and figure out where the rage came from. Picking the bottle up off the floor, he blindly hurled it at the wall. It smashed against the television, cracking the screen and sending bits of glass across the floor.

It wasn't enough. Over at the wall he tore down the pictures. One by one, he slammed them to the floor, stomping on the frames and grinding the glass into dust beneath his heel. The bookshelves were next: Mom's paperback collection. He pulled them down, tearing the covers off and crushing the contents inside. The vase he'd given her was thrown at the fireplace, her plate collection used like Frisbees. In the kitchen he toppled the refrigerator, hurled the chairs out the window, uprooted the plants, and used the silverware for target practice.

He began to cry. Big whooping sobs that consumed him, blinded him, but still he carried on. He almost made it to the bedrooms but collapsed on the stairs when his legs refused to keep moving. Closing his eyes, he felt the rage disappear as quickly as it had come, and he was left there sobbing on the carpet, his back against the railing, completely unsure of what he'd just done.

When there was nothing left inside, he laid his head down on the carpet and stared at the wooden railing. He was even emptier than before. How was it possible that hollowness could dig so deep?

Breathing heavily, he wiped his nose with the back of his sleeve.

It was late and he was tired. He couldn't remember what he was going to do. The smell of gasoline was strong, but there was no memory of why.

Eyes closed, his body gained a few hundred pounds. It was too much effort to do anything except lie there awkwardly. All he needed was a few minutes, and then he'd get back up and do whatever he was supposed to do.

He slept. There were no dreams.

When he woke the next morning, his head was pulsating from the whiskey and the fumes. Picking himself up off the stairs, he couldn't remember how he got there. All he could remember was taking the whiskey bottle from its hiding spot and the first few swigs. His back was all messed up from sleeping crooked; he must have pinched a nerve. His shoulder throbbed; he could barely move his arm. Stumbling, wincing, grabbing his head with his good hand, he made his way into the bathroom to find some medicine.

In the mirror a worn-out person stared back at him. There were black circles under his eyes and his hair was tangled. Taking off his shirt, he winced when he saw the black-and-purple pattern across his shoulder. He splashed some water on his face, and the coolness quenched his skin. He chewed down two Tylenol without taking a drink.

The living room was a disaster. Everything was destroyed or lying on the ground. He was pretty sure he'd done it. But he couldn't remember exactly.

Did he pour the gasoline?

The Stanley Park picture was on the ground, and he picked it up, turning it over in his hands so he didn't have to see the smiling faces. Folding it carefully, he tucked it into his back pocket.

Mom and Mason in Stanley Park.

He'd felt safe there.

It would be nice to see Vancouver again.

The kitchen was worse. He wandered from room to room trying to retrace the steps he'd taken, but his mind was a blank slate. In his bedroom he tried turning on the television, but none of the channels were working. His cell phone said there was no signal.

The world was in chaos. He remembered that much. In the hospital his mother was rotting on a bed. Had anyone come to take her away?

He grabbed his jacket and car keys. If he was going to survive this, he needed to be where he could get news. The whole world couldn't be cut off. There had to be other normal people out there. He'd find them.

But he wouldn't care. Never again would he get close to someone. They'd only leave him, and he was going to do whatever it took to outlive this war. This sickness. Apocalypse? Who cared what it was. Out of sheer defiance he'd beat it.

He paused at the front steps before he left. The match lit on the first strike. The flame hurt his eyes, made his heartbeat throb at the back of his brain. He set the packet ablaze and dropped it in the closest gasoline puddle.

From the safety of the car he watched the flames eat away at the living room blinds. The street was completely empty; no one witnessed his crime. He didn't know if his neighbors were hiding away behind closed doors or if they'd fled like he was about to do. He didn't really care.

Something was happening to him. Mason didn't know what it was, but deep down inside his soul, he was changing. A tiny voice in the farthest corners of his mind was whispering things he wanted to hear, forcing him to behave in a way that was foreign to him. A new Mason.

"I'm going crazy," he said. The words echoed through the car.

He floored the gas pedal and, tires peeling, backed out into the street. As he drove off he didn't bother to take one last look at his house going up in flames.

ARIES

She stood in the hallway and wondered what to do next. Now that Daniel was gone, bravery leaked right out of her body and onto the cold tiled floor. The theater was only a few steps away, but her feet no longer wanted to move. They were stuck to the floor by all the panicky substances discharging from her pores.

He'd promised he wouldn't leave her.

What else did he lie about?

How long had she continued talking once he sneaked off? She'd been babbling away for a while, trying to avoid a horrendous panic attack. It took all the self-control she had to keep from screaming or bursting into tears. But it was better than the alternative. There was something terrifying about all the silence, and filling it with sound was her way of keeping sane. Now that she had no one to talk with, she could hear the stillness creeping in at her from all directions. Taking a deep breath, she continued on toward the theater. If there were people there, she'd become calmer. Daniel had lectured on the dangers of groups, but he'd forgotten about the comfort level of friends. It cut down on the silence. Someone would know what to do.

Right?

But somehow, deep down inside she knew Daniel was correct. Bad things were happening. They were going to get worse.

There were six people in the theater. They were huddled together in the first two rows. All eyes turned to Aries as she descended the steps. At least the emergency lighting was still working. The theater was dim and heavily coated with shadows, but she could make out the faces of her classmates.

"Aries?" Jack King stood up from his chair to get a better view, his sandy brown hair illuminated by the emergency lighting above him. He had the role of the White Rabbit.

"Thank God you're here." That was Becka Philips. She was the Mad Hatter. Colin had pitched a fit when she was given the part. It was the role he wanted, and he couldn't handle the idea that a girl was taking the other lead. He'd spent the whole week mumbling about sexism.

Speaking of Colin, he was sitting in the first row, being comforted by Amanda Steeves, the lighting technician. Aries's first reaction was to do something dramatic: walk up to him and slap him for leaving her to find Sara. But she managed to retain her calm. It wouldn't bring Sara back, and all she'd do was make a scene. She knew his character; it was exactly what she'd have expected of him. Sara may have overlooked his obvious flaws, but Aries wasn't fooled. Colin was not someone she could trust.

"Are you hurt?" That was Ms. Darcy, the drama teacher.

"I'm fine," she said.

"Were you in it?" Becka asked as she came over to give Aries a hug. "We were in here when it happened. The whole building shook. Ms. Darcy wouldn't let us go outside to check. Did you see the cars in the parking lot? They're all trashed. And no one's phones are working."

"I was on the bus. It's a mess out there. Lots of people are hurt. There's no power and the roads are wrecked. The ambulances can't get through."

"You were with Colin?" Becka looked back at Colin incredulously. "Why didn't you tell us you were with Aries? Where's Sara?"

Aries glared at Colin. He refused to look back at her. Instead he conveniently found something fascinating with the stage lights.

"Sara's dead," Aries said. "A lot of people died. I would have been here sooner, but I stayed behind to help. Well, sort of."

"Oh." Joy Woo, the Caterpillar, put her hands up to her mouth.

Colin stayed in his seat as he listened, an unreadable expression on his face.

No, there was pain in his eyes. He was trying to hide it, but she caught a glimpse. It was good to see he did care, even if he'd been all about saving his own skin at the time.

Ms. Darcy approached Aries, a pained expression on her face. Reaching out, she took Aries's hand and squeezed it gently. "Are you all right?" she asked quietly. "You're sure you're not hurt?"

"I'm fine. I was lucky."

Becka started to cry. She'd been as close to Sara as Aries was. They'd grown up next door to each other. Joy immediately put her arms around her. The others sat numbly, unable to respond. There was a long silence that followed, broken up by the occasional sniffle as Becka buried her face in her jacket.

"What do we do now?" Amanda muttered.

Colin stood up from his chair. "I'm going home."

"We should stay here," Aries said. "It's not safe outside."

"We're sitting ducks," Colin snapped. "What about after-shocks? This whole building could go down."

"I don't want to get crushed," Joy said.

"No one's going to get crushed," Aries said. "On the way over here I met this guy. He told me the safest place to be is the school, and I agree. Our parents know we're here. They'll come for us when this is over. We just need to be patient and stay put."

A lot of people are going to die, and it's only the beginning.

Daniel's words. She couldn't tell them he said that. It sounded crazy. But she'd seen it; the mob of darkened shadows tearing people apart on the street. She knew she should warn everyone, but Becka looked like she might fall apart. She didn't see the point in terrorizing her more. Besides, they were safe in the school. It was very unlikely that anyone would come searching for them as long as they kept hidden in the theater.

"I agree," Ms. Darcy said. "I think we should wait for your parents to come pick you up. It shouldn't take long once the roads are cleared."

"If they're okay," Becka said. "How do we know they're not dead?"

"I think right now we need to be more positive," Ms. Darcy said. "Until we're given a reason to believe otherwise."

The decision was made. No one dared question the teacher. She was the only adult and technically in charge. She was supposed to know what to do in these situations. But there was an anxious expression on her face and something odd with the way she tilted her head when she spoke. She was trying hard to hide it, and none of the other students noticed, but Aries saw through her fake demeanor. There was no mistaking it. Ms. Darcy didn't believe her own words. She knew.

"So where is this guy, then?" Colin said. "If he thought it was so safe here, then where is he?"

"There were others to save," Aries said. "It was more important to him than running like a coward with his tail between his legs."

Colin gave her a hard smile.

"Good for him," Ms. Darcy said. "Now maybe we should go down to the prop room. I saw an old boom box there a few weeks ago. If we can get it working we might be able to get the news on the radio."

"I have to leave."

Aries and Ms. Darcy were downstairs in the prop room. They found the boom box in the corner, half hidden under some stage wigs. It was monstrously huge, a forgotten relic from the eighties. Aries was doubtful it would work, but they wouldn't know until they managed to find some batteries.

"What do you mean?" Aries asked. "You agreed with me."

Ms. Darcy stared at her, her chin quivering. "I have two small children at home with a babysitter. I can't wait for a rescue party. I have to go and make sure they're safe."

"I understand."

"The others will, too. I'll make it simple. I'll slip out when no one's looking."

"But I don't know what to do."

Ms. Darcy grabbed her by the shoulders and pulled her close. "Just keep doing what you're doing. I wouldn't have put this on you if I didn't think you could handle it. You're one of my smartest students. The kids look up to you. They'll listen. Keep them at the school. Whatever you do, don't let them go outside."

"But what if they don't listen?"

"They will."

"Not Colin."

"Then let him go. You can't save them all."

"People are dying," Aries said. "I've seen it. Sara's dead. Maybe you can wait till morning. We can organize something. We can help you get back home."

"It might be too late by then."

"You know what's happening out there, don't you," Aries said.

"I do. That's why it's so important you keep them inside. Listen to me, Aries." Ms. Darcy pulled her closer and spoke directly in her ear, although there was no one else around. "Something bad is about to happen. It's already started. I know you're feeling it too." Ms. Darcy shuddered. "It's like an electric charge. I can't explain it. I've been sensing it for weeks. It's bigger than any earthquake, and in the end it'll be far worse than a few buildings collapsing."

"I feel it."

"The others don't."

"They're lucky."

"Be careful. But understand when I say I don't want you coming with me. Stay here while you can. Wait out the worst of it. If we're lucky it'll end soon and your parents will come and find you."

"It's not going to end." Once the words were out of her mouth, she realized they were true.

"I can't believe that."

Aries took a deep breath. "I hope your children are safe and that you make it home to them."

"Thank you." She took her keys out of her pocket and passed them over. "If no one comes by morning, try using the phone in the office. It might be working then."

"Okay."

The boom box didn't work even though they tried both sets of batteries. Leaving it behind, they went back upstairs to wait with the others for morning to come. Aries took a seat next to Jack and wrapped her jacket over her body to use as a blanket. It was done more out of need than comfort. There was no way she'd be sleeping anytime soon.

Ms. Darcy slipped out the door somewhere close to two in the morning when most of the students were dozing in their chairs. She made it look like she was going to the bathroom; she didn't even take her purse or jacket. Aries watched her go, swallowing the voice inside her begging silently for her to stay.

Ten minutes or so passed before Jack whispered in her ear. "She's not coming back, is she?"

"No."

Aries imagined her parents sitting in the living room, holding hands while watching the news. They were probably worried sick. Every ten minutes or so her father would get up and pace the room while her mother rushed off to make him coffee and check the phone lines. She tried to keep the image in her head, because the alternatives were worse. She didn't want to picture them dead just yet. She would continue to believe she'd see them again.

Not like Sara.

"If they don't come for us by morning, we'll figure something out," she said.

She woke to Joy gently shaking her. The last thing she remembered was checking her watch sometime after five a.m.

"What time is it?" Rubbing her eyes, she stretched in her

seat, her jacket sliding to the floor. The coolness of the theater bit against her skin, forcing her to shiver violently.

"Just after seven," Joy said. "Ms. Darcy's gone. Colin's pitching a fit in the lobby. You'd better come."

She was instantly wide-awake. The lobby had windows facing the street. He was right out in the open where anyone could see. The group of killers she'd seen last night might still be out there. If the wrong person happened to walk past, they'd all be dead.

Brace yourself. It's about to open.

Humanity has found a cure to a disease they never knew existed.

There was a connection between what the crazy man and Daniel had said. Something had been triggered with the earthquake. Something awful.

And more people were going to die.

They were all waiting in the lobby. The morning sunlight filtered through the glass, warming Aries instantly. She scanned the outside area, but it appeared empty. For now.

"Get away from the windows," she said. "We need to go back in the theater. We're too in the open here."

"Isn't that the point?" Becka said. "Don't we want people to find us?"

"Not if it's the wrong kind," Aries said.

"And what exactly do you mean by that?" Amanda's voice raised a few octaves.

She had to choose her words carefully. She knew how crazy it sounded. The others were still clueless about the dangers outside. For all they knew, last night was nothing but an earthquake. They hadn't seen those people being beaten to death.

"There are rioters out there," she finally said, completely aware of how lame the excuse was. "They might hurt us."

"You're joking, right?" Colin laughed loudly. "Rioters? That's your big fear? Who cares? You're such a girl, Aries. Go back inside and let the men talk."

"I did go back inside," she said. "I went back inside the bus and found Sara dead. What did you do? You ran like a coward. You left her."

"You take that back."

"No."

Jack stepped between them, putting his hands out as if he was afraid they might start tearing at each other's eyes. "Come on, guys," he said. "We're all tired here, and this isn't helping. Let's go sit down and talk about it. We'll figure it all out."

"I want to go home," Becka said.

"Yeah, well, we all want to go home," Colin said. His eyes never moved from Aries's face. "But the bitch here keeps going on about how we have to wait things out." He glared in her direction. "Why is that again? Really? Oh right, some stranger told you it's not safe and you believed him. And where is this mystery guy? He split—the exact opposite of what he told you to do."

"There's no need for that, man," Jack said.

"It's not just Aries," Joy said. "We took a vote and the rest of us agreed. We promised Ms. Darcy. We're safe here. It's something our parents would want."

"Don't you ever think for yourself?" Colin snapped back.

"Don't talk to her like that," Aries said. "You're really something, Colin. Left your girlfriend to die and now you're shouting at Joy?"

Colin pushed past Jack until he was inches away from Aries. "You'd better stop talking like that. I swear, I will hit you. I don't give a damn if you're a girl."

Jack grabbed his arms from behind, pulling Colin away.

Becka and a few of the other students got between them, making a wall of bodies. They all began yelling at one another, taking sides although none of them really knew what they were arguing about.

They were still in the lobby. Out in the open. Vulnerable. Loud. People would hear them through the glass.

She needed to get them back in the theater. Fortunately, Jack seemed to be thinking the same thing.

"Enough of this," he said. "Let's go back inside and sit down. We can discuss this like adults, right? Right?"

Jack's words worked. Colin stared him down for a few seconds before he finally nodded and turned and went into the theater without saying a word. The others followed.

The cold chill running through her subsided a bit once everyone was back inside. Jack waited in the lobby with her as she glanced out one last time to make sure the street was empty.

"He's being a real ass," Jack said. "I'm sorry."

"I'm not," she said. "I expected it."

They returned to the theater to find Colin putting on his shoes.

"Let's just wait a little longer," Aries said. "It's still early. There's no need to rush. People might be on their way as we speak. I'm sure it's just a matter of time."

"We don't want to do anything foolish," Jack agreed. "I saw some power lines on the street. They could still be active."

"And what are we going to do for food?" Colin snapped. "We could be stuck here waiting for days. I don't plan on going hungry."

"There's always the cafeteria," Joy said. "The main keys are in the office. I was a teacher's aid last semester. I know where they are. All we have to do is get them. I'm sure we can find plenty to eat there."

"Maybe we should do that now," Aries suggested. "I'll go. Anyone want to come with?"

"I'll come," Jack said.

"Me too," Colin said. He'd calmed down a bit. "I need to get out of here. I'm going crazy just sitting." He looked directly at Aries when he spoke, obviously implying that it was all her fault. Give him a few more hours and he'd probably find a way to pin the entire earthquake on her too.

It didn't help that he was trying to lead the group in a direction that Aries knew was dangerous.

"Try to find a radio or something," Becka said. "Maybe we can get some news. And check to see if the phones are working."

"I'd kill for some coffee," Joy said with a grin. "And maybe some pancakes? Bacon and eggs? Sausage? Do you think they'll have cake?"

"Stale crackers it is," Jack said with a grin.

Jack found a duffel bag behind the stage and emptied it of someone's gym clothes. Swinging it around his shoulders, he climbed the steps and headed back out into the lobby. They would all go except for Amanda and Becka, who stuck behind just in case someone happened to wander by and rescue them.

The cafeteria was on the other side of the school. It would take about five minutes to walk. The office was in the middle by the main doors. They would stop there first.

"I never realized how creepy the school is," Joy said. "It's so empty. I keep expecting something to jump out at us. Did it always echo like this?"

Everyone laughed except Aries.

"Would make a great horror movie idea," Jack said. "Student by day, killer by night, and the halls will run red with blood."

"Okay, enough already," Aries snapped.

"Sorry, just a joke," Jack said.

They walked the rest of the way in silence. The main office doors were locked, and Aries pulled the keys from her pocket.

"Where'd you get those?" Colin instantly wanted to know.

She ignored him and opened the door. They stepped inside. The office was dark, the blinds were closed, and Jack immediately went over to open them. Aries almost shouted out to him but stopped. What could she say? They needed the light to find the keys and she still wasn't ready to announce to the group about how unsafe the outside world really was. Plus, how could she explain when she didn't fully understand herself?

"I'll get the keys." Joy walked over to the administration desk and started rifling through the drawers. "It's really something. The master key opens every lock in the school. Maybe we should take a peek at our permanent records while we're at it. Do you think those really exist, or is it a myth?"

"I sure hope not," Jack said. "I peed my pants in the first grade. If that comes out I might never make it into university."

A black office phone sat on the desk next to a pile of papers. Aries picked up the receiver and pressed the line button. There was no dial tone. She checked the box to make sure it was plugged in and tried again. Still nothing.

"Oh, God." Jack's voice was stilted. His fingers gripped the last blind sash tightly, frozen in midtwist.

Aries made it to the window first. Her eyes followed Jack's gaze. Fifty feet away from the window, a body lay in the grass. The person was facing the ground, covered in blood, impossible to recognize.

Almost.

The bright green blouse gave her away.

"That's Ms. Darcy," Colin said.

Joy turned and promptly threw up all over the closest desk.

"Oh God, oh God, oh God," Colin chanted, putting his hands up against his ears as if he wanted to block out the sound of his own voice.

"What happened to her?" Jack said. "Why would someone do that? That's gotta be more than just rioters."

"It's evil," Aries said, and she finally understood fully what the crazy man on the bus meant when he said "game over."

There would be no bonus lives to help them get a higher score.

"Someone's out there," Jack said.

Just beyond the grass, closer to the main road, stood three people. They were staring at the school. No, change that. They were staring straight at them.

Aries pulled Jack away from the window.

"We need to get out of here now," she said.

No one seemed to listen to her. Time was moving too slowly. They weren't going to be fast enough. Her heart thumped loudly in her ears. Jack moved away from her in slow motion, his eyes focusing back on the outside world.

"We have to leave," she said again, louder, trying to block out her heartbeat. "We have to get Becka and Amanda."

Jack finally looked at her. "Okay."

But he still wasn't moving. None of them were.

"Come on," she screamed, pulling both him and Joy at the same time. "If we don't go now we're going to die."

"What's happening?" Joy said. "Who did that to Ms. Darcy?"

"They'll kill us next." That seemed to get everyone's attention. "Let's go." Thankfully Colin didn't argue.

They ran down the halls, almost making it to the theater before the screams started.

"That's Becka," Joy cried.

They all stopped and waited, frozen and unsure of what to do. The screams continued for what seemed like an eternity before abruptly stopping. Silence filled the halls, pressing down on Aries's skull. She couldn't speak; her tongue was glued against her teeth. She could feel Jack's body pushed up against her from behind, tense.

"What do we do?" he said.

"We have to leave now," Aries said.

"What about Becka and Amanda?" Joy whispered. She may have spoken the words, but she was already walking backward, away from the theater.

"We can't help them anymore," Aries said.

They heard the grinding noise of the theater doors opening. Footsteps echoed across the tiled flooring.

"Run," Jack said.

They did.

NOTHING

I can feel them. All of them. Their thoughts. Their voices whisper in my ears. I hear their prayers, and their pain passes through my body like a million electric volts.

I know their crimes.

They will make sure I witness every last one of them.

In New York City, a janitor blocks all the exits and dismantles the power supply before setting fire to the building. He spends his morning going from building to building, committing several acts of deadly arson before he finally traps himself in his own explosion and dies instantly.

In Houston, hundreds of inmates escape a local prison and go on a bloody rampage through the streets. The police force isn't capable of protecting the people, especially since many of the officers turn their weapons on the innocent crowds instead.

In Barcelona, a priest walks into a church with a gun and kills everyone during morning mass.

Riots in London stain the cobblestone redder than anything Jack the Ripper ever dreamed of.

A young preschool teacher in Toronto gives her students a

deadly mixture of arsenic and fruit punch. When she comes back long enough to realize what she's done, she downs the last remaining drops in two swallows.

Game over.

People are killing each other all over the world. Brothers attack sisters. Husbands and wives destroy their children. There is no explanation for the average person to understand. In the last remaining places where the media is able to reach the public, they have no answers.

But I know.

I can't block it out. They have dug their claws into my skull. There is no place in the world where I can hide, because they know where to find me. They don't even have to try. They've got the keys to my brain and they're emptying my thoughts and refilling it with theirs.

Not too long ago I think I was normal. I had a mother.

She'd need to light a lot of candles to save my soul now.

Somewhere through the darkness I catch a thought. A small memory. There is a lot of white sand; it stretches in all directions, farther than I can see. In front of me is a blue ocean. It's gigantic. But I'm very small. A child, perhaps, no older than three or four. I hold on to my bucket and shovel while my parents spread out a blanket over the white, pure sand. It's hot on my feet.

My father calls out to me.

My mother is smiling.

She looks so happy.

And then it's gone.

I want to grab these memories and hold tightly. I'm afraid that if they disappear, I'll never experience them again.

There must be a way to fight this. To block out the black thoughts and make the voices go away. But with each memory fading, their hold on me strengthens. Soon the person I was, still am, will be gone. I'll be hollow.

I am not the first and I will not be the last.

There are so many empty people walking around on this little planet. Lonely people. Angry people. Bitter. Forgotten.

They were easy to fill.

MICHAEL

"What do you think?"

The binoculars were cracked, and Michael saw the world in two halves, both of which were colorless and slightly out of focus. It hurt his eyes and he blinked several times to try and make the world look normal again.

What did he think? They had stumbled across the ranch house just before noon. They almost hadn't seen it; most of the building was hidden behind an overgrown acre of evergreens.

"Well?" Evans tapped his finger on the side of Michael's head. Hard. To get his attention.

"Empty." Michael scratched his head and raised the binoculars again. They'd been watching from the bushes for a few hours now. There had been no movement from inside, but that didn't mean anything. Nothing was ever empty or free. But they were farther away from the city; there was always the possibility that they weren't bothering to come this far out. They hadn't seen anything for several days. This could be a free zone. "Maybe," he finally said. "It's worth looking at."

"Maybe not."

"We can't take that chance." They were out of food, having

divvied up the remaining package of saltines for supper two days ago. They'd discussed hunting. There were plenty of wild animals, but lighting a fire to cook was too risky. They couldn't take the chance knowing that others would be drawn to the smoke. They were stuck. Who knew when the next meal might come? The last pizza had been delivered weeks ago. There would never be another. And they had a child with them. They'd found a mother with her four-year-old son a few days ago while searching through an abandoned lumberjack camp. It was a miracle they'd survived. But the kid was sickly, and Michael didn't think he'd last much longer without food, maybe some medical supplies, too, if they were lucky.

"There's no such thing as chance anymore."

Michael didn't answer him. They all had their ghosts. Three weeks ago they'd arrived at Evans's house to find his wife and baby daughter missing. His front door was kicked in and there was blood on the carpet. They never found out what happened.

"I think we should take a chance." Billy, one of the other group members, jumped in on them from behind. Landing on the soft dirt beside Michael, he grabbed the binoculars from him in one swift move and raised them to his eyes. "These things are useless, man. How on earth have you been staring through them for the past two hours? I would have shot myself." Tossing them back, he scratched his goatee. "Seriously, that kid don't look so good. We've got to do something and do it fast, or he ain't gonna make it till nightfall."

"I know," Michael said. "But we can't go in until we're absolutely sure it's safe."

"We've been here for hours," Billy said. "If they were in there, we'd have seen something by now. Them Baggers ain't gonna sit in there and wait for us to bore ourselves to death. They would have attacked by now if they's here."

Baggers. A hunter's term. As in "I'm gonna go out and 'bag' myself a deer." Only the Baggers were hunting something completely different. Billy introduced the word several days ago. He'd heard some poor guy mention it before one of the monsters tore him to pieces.

"Maybe."

"How far are we till the next town?" Billy scratched himself again. They were all itchy. Showers were a luxury that none of them could afford or find these days.

Evans pulled out the crinkled map for the tenth time that hour. "Hard to say. We still don't quite know where we are. Could be a few miles, could be a few hundred."

"No ways." Billy grabbed the map. "There ain't a single place here that's more than a few miles away. We ain't that far up north. This here's still civilization. You ain't able to spit without hitting a Taco Bell or Jack 'n' Box."

Michael glanced back at the mother, stretched out on the ground, her child's head resting on her thigh. The boy—Michael couldn't remember his name—hadn't opened his eyes in a long time. Shallow gasps escaped bluish lips, his chest barely rising against his shirt. His face was deathly white, eyes sunken deep into the recesses of his skull. The poor kid probably weighed as much as a small animal. Sure, they'd all lost weight, and most of them would probably run one another over for a hamburger, but this was different. This was a kid. They weren't supposed to go hungry.

Children weren't supposed to know that monsters existed either.

The mother didn't look so good. Blond, matted hair that probably hadn't been brushed since this whole ordeal started. She looked washed-out. Faded. There may still have been a sun in the sky, but its rays weren't warming her skin. She was singing softly to her son, a song that Michael hadn't heard since he was really young. He could barely make out the words.

She shouldn't really be singing. The noise might attract the wrong kind of attention. But Michael wasn't about to tell her to stop. It might be the last time the child ever heard her voice.

No one wants to go off into the darkness alone.

"Screw it." He turned his attention back to Evans and Billy. "Let's do it. Get the others."

There were twelve of them in the group. Michael and Evans joined them two weeks ago, back when they were five. Since then they'd picked up a few more as they traveled the road. The mother and son were the latest find. It was getting difficult now that the group was so big. There was no safety in numbers, just more and more people to try to keep an eye on. Bigger meant more food was needed. It also meant louder.

But Michael liked being in a group. It made him feel wanted. He liked being a part of something. It was the type of person he was. Right in the center of things he was confident and strong. Dad said he was a natural-born leader, and if he were around he'd be proud to know Michael was coping. Michael knew there was still the possibility Dad was holed up somewhere in Denver. He knew a lot about survival. He clung to the idea that they'd cross paths again one day, and he looked forward to telling his father about how well he'd done. He was, after all, leading this group and he was younger than almost all of them. Evans had to be at least forty. Billy was thirty, but he looked older because of his missing teeth.

At seventeen, Michael was the one they looked to when they wanted answers. He'd never planned it that way. It just happened.

He got up, wincing as his knees popped. He'd been sitting for too long. Wandering over to where the mother sat, he knelt down beside her. Why couldn't he remember the name of the child? He should ask her, but he didn't want to look stupid. It was embarrassing that the leader couldn't remember all the names of his flock.

"Hey." He spoke quietly.

She stopped singing and looked at him. Her eyes were unfocused, staring right past him. Blinking several times, she finally managed to look at his face. Her eyes were bright blue but clouded.

"We're going to go check out the house," he said. "Do you want to come? You can stay here, but I think it's better if we stick together. I can help you. Do you want help? I can carry him."

He reached out his arms, but she pulled away, clinging tightly to her child. "No," she muttered. "I've got him. Do you think there'll be a bed? It would be nice to lie down for a bit."

"We won't be able to stay long," he admitted. "We're just going in to see if there's food. It's not safe to stick around."

"Just for a bit," she repeated. "He needs to rest. He's not well."

Michael nodded. "We'll see what we can do."

She stood up by herself, still holding the child, and started walking toward Evans. Her legs were shaking but she managed to keep it together.

There was something oddly comforting about her strength. Michael wondered, if he ever had a child, would he have the same determination to keep him safe? No matter how weak she became, she'd never give up.

He planned on being that strong. Who knew how long this war would continue. The Baggers had the upper hand, but if enough people banded together, they might be strong enough to regain power. Even if they managed to take down one Bagger at a time, well, that would be considered a good start.

Michael wanted to believe that. He had to believe that. Even with the entire population on the brink of extinction, he preferred to remain an optimist. It was impossible to tell how many people had died, since there was no more communication. It would be nice to find a short-wave radio or something. There might be other survivors using such devices. But so far the group had found nothing in the houses they'd searched except cell phones, computers, televisions, and all the other sorts of now-useless communication gadgets he'd grown up with.

Once upon a time he'd thought his cell phone was the one thing he couldn't live without. Amazing how quickly the tides can turn.

The Baggers were definitely being smart. Rumors were, they were the ones who managed to shut down the networks so quickly. They were the ones who blocked the cell phone towers and destroyed the Internet. Without communication, the world was thrown into black panic. There was no one to tell them what was happening. No information on safe places to go or what sorts of steps to take to protect themselves. The only way to find out if your loved ones were alive was to get in a car and travel. That's how the Baggers managed to kill so quickly. People put themselves out in the open and became sitting ducks.

Or at least that's what the group speculated about late at night while waiting for sleep. They also talked about why some people had become Baggers and others hadn't. Why and how had the change happened? What would the Baggers do with the world they'd destroyed? And left unspoken was the fear. They weren't Baggers. Yet. Evans figured if they hadn't turned by now, they weren't going to. Michael agreed with him. But the fear always crept in. Was it just a matter of time? Would he wake up one night with one of his peers about to rip out his throat?

No, he wouldn't think like that. And whatever it was, it didn't appear to be catching. He had to believe that. They all did.

But for now there were plenty of other people out there. Still normal, hiding inside their houses, taking refuge in whatever safe places still existed. Michael planned on finding them.

"We ready?" Evans appeared, folding up the map carefully and putting it in his pocket.

"Yeah." Michael's stomach growled, reminding him of the important things. "Let's do it."

They both made fists with their hands and lightly punched each other. It had become their mantra, their good-luck charm.

Billy and he took the lead, with Evans following at the rear. They were the three strongest and the least affected by hunger. At least that's what they led the others to believe. In reality they were just better at pretending the grumbles in their guts didn't bother them.

It wasn't much of an army, but they'd managed to survive. They were tough enough. But they'd never gone this long without eating before. How much longer would their strength last?

They moved along the tree line, sticking closely to the woods in case they needed to run. Vigilance would get them only so far. Realistically, if they were spotted now, they wouldn't all get away. They knew this—survival came at a price. Over the past few weeks they'd all survived a Bagger attack. Or two. Or three. They knew the consequences. Not everyone got out alive. They'd seen loved ones die. Even worse, some had watched the people they cared about turn on them. But as long as they stuck together in a group, they were still human. As long as they were human they were still alive. Michael watched the house carefully for movement. A tiny flicker, parting of a curtain—anything he might have missed before. A bubble of icy liquid churned away in his stomach. He was getting so used to being afraid, he barely noticed anymore. Goose bumps on his skin were as common as breathing. It was smart to be scared; it was the one thing that was keeping them alive. "Caution" was the new secret word.

Wait.

Did something move in the window?

No. He was imagining things. The hunger was playing tricks on his mind.

But still . . . he couldn't afford to be wrong.

He paused to listen. Nothing seemed to be out of place. Squirrels chattered away in the trees above them, and in the distance he could see a thin V in the sky as a flock of Canadian geese chased the sun. The ranch house remained silent in front of them, a sentinel abandoned, just waiting to protect hungry strays. The back door was within their vision, closed and probably locked. They might find a key in the mailbox or hidden under a mat; if not they would break a window.

The yard was unkempt; the grass was growing wild and didn't look like it had recently been disturbed.

Everything appeared normal.

So why was his body temperature dropping at an alarming rate?

"I got a bad feeling about this," he said.

"You say that every time." Billy snorted and spat on a char-coaled evergreen.

"This is different."

"There's nothing here. You said so yourself. We've been watching the building for hours. I'm hungry, man. There's food inside that there house. I can smell it. Maybe they'll have canned ham. I could really go for some of that. Maybe some relish that hasn't gone bad and some potata chips to go with it."

Billy, deep into food fantasy, continued to discuss his dreams openly as he passed Michael and moved toward the ranch house.

"Hey!" Michael jogged a few steps to get back in the lead. Keeping his eye on the upstairs window, he led the group up to the backdoor. Nothing moved.

It was easy to exaggerate things when your body was fueled by adrenaline.

Michael and Billy climbed the porch steps while the others waited at the bottom. The mother held her boy in her arms, her fingers tangled in the child's white-blond hair. Her legs were obviously unstable, and even from a distance Michael could see them shaking under the extra weight. Evans stood close to her side, watching her carefully in case she might stumble.

The porch was empty except for a few folding chairs leaning against the side of the house. Brass window chimes hung from the corner, unmoving and silent. Piles of dead and burned leaves had collected in the corners. Off to the side were an old-fashioned push lawn mower and a slightly rusted barbecue grill. Nothing looked disturbed or out of place. The chimes were covered in cobwebs. No recent footprints in the dust either.

The door was shut, and when Michael tried the handle, it didn't budge. Locked. A good sign. There was always the chance that survivors might be inside, barricaded and waiting for help. Even better if they had weapons. Finding healthy people en masse would be proof enough that the Baggers hadn't reached this far north and they could let their guard down, even if only for a little while. It would be nice to sleep without keeping both eyes open.

No key in the mailbox. He ran his fingers along the top edge of the door. Then, bending down, Michael stepped off the welcome mat and turned it over. Nothing but a bit of dirt and a few pebbles.

Billy joined him, turning over the flower pots in the window. Dirt spilled onto the wooden floorboards.

"No key," Michael said.

"Let's break a window, then," Billy said. "No pain, no gain."

"No noise."

"Less is best."

Billy took off his jacket and wrapped it around his arm. Leaning against the door, he pressed hard and quickly, shattering the pane. The sound of glass breaking and hitting the floor caused them all to inhale deeply.

They waited.

The wind shook the dead evergreen branches, and the brass wind chimes crashed together. The icy-cold sensation was back again, and the hair on Michael's neck pulled away from his scalp.

Picking bits of glass from the frame, Billy cleared enough of a hole to reach his arm through and turn the lock. Metal scraped behind the wood, and the door creaked open a few inches.

"In," Billy said. "We'll be eating like royalty soon enough."

"Quickly," Michael said. "In and out. We're too open here."

"You're doing that paranoid thing again. You've got to chills out, bro. There ain't no Baggers here. We're safe."

They were never safe.

Michael knew this. But a lecture at this point wasn't going to work when Billy's mind was set solely on the purpose of fueling his belly.

The back door led into a small mudroom. Jackets for all seasons hung on wooden pegs, and shelves were filled with shoes and boots. One of the coats closest to the door was bright pink with a fake-fur hood. Mittens with strings hung on the peg beside it. On the floor was a school bag, unzipped, loose-leaf pages of children's handwriting poking through the opening.

Michael immediately glanced back at Evans to try and gauge his reaction. The older man stared at the pink jacket, a stony expression on his face. It would be hardest on Evans; he would never fully know what happened to his family. And there would always be reminders around to guarantee he never stopped thinking about it.

Evans reached out and touched the jacket gently. Michael stopped himself from asking if he was all right. No one else noticed the gesture, and it was too private to bring to everyone's attention. Michael found the light switch on the wall and flicked it a few times. Nothing happened, but he'd been expecting that. The last of the power went out weeks ago. He did it out of routine, and not because habits were hard to break but because it gave him hope. Maybe one day they'd have the luxury of pressing buttons again and getting everything they wanted. But right now there were more important issues at hand than dreaming—namely Billy, who'd pushed ahead of the group and entered the kitchen without double-checking for danger.

Michael chased after him and into one of the nicest kitchens he'd ever seen. It was enormous, bigger than the whole of the one-bedroom apartment he used to share with his father.

Billy was throwing open cupboards at an alarming speed. So far he'd found nothing but row upon row of dishes, coffee mugs, and Tupperware. The counters were filled with all sorts of fancy appliances. Toaster oven, espresso maker, blender, mixer—everything strategically placed, as if Martha Stewart did the decorating. A gigantic kitchen island had rows of copper pots hanging above it and a large silver fruit basket with moldy apples and pears. The rotten fruit was the only proof that someone had actually once used the kitchen.

"We should check out the rest of the house first," Evans said. He'd approached Michael and was standing beside him, watching Billy search. One of the other group members opened the stainless-steel fridge, and the smell of sour milk and rotten vegetables wafted through the room. Michael covered his nose. It was enough to make his stomach stop grumbling.

Evans moved across the room to help the mother, still clinging tightly to her son, sit down at the table. Michael went over to the fridge, suppressing the urge to gag from the smell, and sifted through the shelves until he found a small can of fruit cocktail. He pulled a spoon from the drawer and brought it over to the mother.

"Here," he said as he opened the top, sugar syrup dripping on his fingers. "See if he'll eat this."

"Thank you," she whispered.

"Jackpot!" Billy shouted from across the kitchen. Too loud. What the hell was he thinking? He knew better.

But Billy had found the pantry. All he could think about was the row upon row of groceries facing him. There was so much there. It really was a bonanza. Dozens of cans of food: soups, corn, peas, chili, tuna, salmon, pears and other assorted fruits. There were even some tiny cans of ham, just the thing Billy was dreaming about. Bags of chips and pretzels, boxes of cereal, granola bars, all sorts of things that didn't go bad—they would have enough food to last them a few weeks once they sorted through everything.

Billy tore open a package of granola bars and threw one at Michael. He fumbled the catch and picked it up from underneath a chair.

"I'm gonna go take a look around," he said to no one in particular. "Don't get too comfortable. We still don't know if we're alone."

The mother looked slightly alarmed at the thought. She perked up in her chair, spilling fruit cocktail all over her child's shirt.

"I'll come with you," Evans said. At least two of them still had their priorities straight. Michael understood that they were hungry and all that food clouded their judgments, but this was exactly the sort of thing the Baggers would expect. However, the group was spread out across the kitchen, many sitting on the floor, stuffing their mouths with anything they could grab. Going on about safety at this point would only make Michael appear whiny. That was one of the downfalls of being young.

Michael and Evans moved through the doors and into the living room. A leather couch, covered in a thin layer of dust, dominated the area. On the wall was a fifty-inch flat screen, complete with a bookcase filled with hundreds of movies, many of which were Disney cartoons. On the floor in front of the entertainment system was a doll, half undressed.

They found suitcases by the front door. Michael lifted one.

It was heavy. "Looks like someone left in a hurry," he said.

"Let's hope so," Evans said. They still hadn't checked out the upstairs.

Back in the kitchen they heard Billy whoop.

"That idiot's gonna get us killed," Evans said.

They walked up the stairs together and checked out all the rooms. There were five bedrooms and two bathrooms, all of which were empty, to Michael's relief.

"Water's still running here," Evans said as he came out from one of the bathrooms. "There's a barbecue out back with some working propane too. I can boil us up some heat. We're looking at showers tonight as long as we're quiet."

"Can't remember what clean feels like," Michael replied. When was the last time he showered? He reached up and scratched at his scalp. His long hair was greasy and the ends were beginning to dread.

"I'm looking forward to it. After living with you for three weeks, I can honestly say you need it."

"This coming from a guy who farts *and* snores."

"You've got to stop using that hair gel, kid. It's starting to rot your brain."

They grinned at each other.

Back in the kitchen, the group was looking slightly bloated from stuffing their faces. Only the mother didn't seem to have eaten, mostly because her son hadn't been able to swallow the fruit cocktail.

"Come on," Evans said to her. "There's a room upstairs. Let's get the boy rested for a little bit. I think it's safe for us to spend the night. But only one. We need to move on by sunrise. The rest of you better not get too comfortable. I'll be expecting us to work for our dinner. I want lookouts at both doors and even outside."

Michael nodded. He couldn't have said it better himself. He helped the mother to her feet. She refused his offer to take the boy but allowed him to lead her upstairs to one of the empty bedrooms.

They were safe. Miracles still did happen.

MASON

In the middle of downtown Calgary, his car finally gave out. There was a loud noise like a gunshot, and he instinctively ducked and hit the brakes at the same time. The steering wheel jerked in his hands as he ground to a halt. The engine sputtered, then stalled completely. The blacked-out traffic light swayed in the wind above his head. The only movement on an otherwise empty street.

Cursing, he pulled the keys from the ignition and flung them against the dashboard. What was left of the city seemed to be taking the destruction and death seriously and barricading themselves in their homes. How many people were still alive? How many of them weren't insane? Or infected? Or whatever the hell this was? Several weeks later and Mason (and probably everyone else in the world) had no clue what was happening. Communication was still down, anyway. If anyone out there did know what was going on, they couldn't share.

All he knew was that people were dead. Lots. If the televisions were still broadcasting they would call this an epic pandemic.

He was parked in the middle of the intersection. The traffic lights above his head stayed dark. The city was a graveyard of electric wires and appliances. He'd driven most of the night and hadn't seen a single light, because most of the rural communities were blacked out too, with the exception of the occasional farmhouse that was probably using a generator. Mason wasn't about to pop his head in the door to ask. The last thing he wanted or even deserved was company.

He would never feel anything again. Somehow he wasn't the same Mason he'd once been. His mother died so he could live. As far as Mason was concerned, she'd left him with a curse.

Several buildings off Deerfoot Trail were on fire. He could see the black smoke in his rearview mirror. Half an hour ago, he'd been right in the middle of it, holding his shirt over his nose with the windows rolled up tightly. It was slow moving, too many cars in the street, doors open and abandoned. There were dead bodies alongside the road. Burned. Mouths open in silent agony. The crazy monsters roaming the city must have chased them into the fire. Which was worse? Dying at the hands of insane people or burning alive? He wasn't sure.

When he'd driven past, he'd kept his eyes focused in front of him, pretending the bodies didn't exist, trying to convince himself that the smell in the air wasn't that of roasting flesh.

He decided he'd never drive through smoke again. The next time he found fire, he'd bypass the city entirely. It wasn't worth the memories. Or the smell. He'd have to ditch his clothing the first chance he got.

You forget the good and remember the bad. His mom used to say that. Bits of her still wormed their way into his memory when he least expected. The smell of her perfume. The way she smiled. He was trying so hard to forget. He'd traveled many miles over the past few weeks, but she continued to give chase. When he fell asleep she was there. When he stopped to take a break or let down his guard she was the only thing he thought of. Eyes closed, hooked up to machines, taking her last breath before giving up the fight. She never even got to say good-bye.

No. He wasn't going to remember this.

Leaving the keys in the ignition, he climbed out cautiously and wandered around to the front of the car to take a look.

Both front tires were blown.

Glancing back at the road behind him, he could see bits of glass reflecting the morning sun. How on earth had he missed that? Cursing again, he slammed his fist down on the hood.

Now he'd have to find another car. That shouldn't be too hard. There were probably a dozen dealerships within walking distance. He could have the pick of the lot. No Hummer or Porsche was beyond his reach. But he'd never cared about flashy cars in the past. He didn't know the difference between six cylinders and sixty, so now wasn't really any different. Besides, a fancy car would burn gas faster, and that meant stopping more. He didn't trust the gas stations. They were out in the open, and who knew what might be lurking around. No, the only car he wanted was one that worked—tires and all.

It wasn't safe being in the middle of the intersection.

How long till he was discovered?

"Need some help?"

Mason turned quickly, hands up in defense, but one look at the man behind him and he instantly relaxed. The guy had to be at least seventy. His white hair was neatly combed and slicked back. He was wearing one of those suits that hadn't been in style since the fifties, along with a tie and a red polka-dot handkerchief in the pocket. And he was missing a leg. Under his arms, his weight rested on a pair of crutches.

"Didn't mean to scare you," the old man said. "But I don't think there's any non-terrifying way to greet someone these days."

"Yeah, I guess," Mason said.

"I'm sure you can deduce I'm harmless," the man said, tapping his crutches on the ground to prove it. "I'm hoping the same of you. Never heard one of 'em making a fuss over such a little thing before. Not when there are thousands of available cars sitting about. So I think that makes you pretty human."

"I'm normal," Mason said. He wanted to do something too, so he turned around in a slow circle to show there was nothing behind his back or up his sleeves.

"Normal, huh?" The man laughed. "Is there such a thing as normal anymore?"

"Probably not."

The old man twisted around on his crutches and scanned the road. "I don't know about you, but I'm not overly fond of staying in the open for too long. I live just down the street. Why don't you come back to my place and I'll fix us up some tea and breakfast while we try and figure out how to get you on the road again. What do you say?"

Mason glanced back at the blown tires attached to the car he'd found just outside of Drumheller. His own car was abandoned at the side of the road outside of Rosetown. He'd had a terrible time leaving it behind. It seemed silly now, loving a car. It was just a piece of metal with some fancy bits that moved when he used a key. He couldn't remember why he'd been so attached to it. That seemed like a million dreams ago. Reaching through the window, he grabbed the bag he'd packed the morning he'd burned down his house. From the sun visor he grabbed the picture he'd carried in his pocket. *Mom and Mason—enjoying the sun.* Happy, cheerful Mason— when did he grow up?

"Let's go," he said.

"I'm Winston Twilling," the man said. "But everyone calls me Twiggy. At least, they used to call me Twiggy. No one calls me much of anything these days, I guess."

"I'm Mason Dowell."

"Pleased to meet you. Wish the circumstances were better. But we can't all be eating cake and crumpets these days. But I've got some good tea. Swiped it from the fancy market down the street. They have an entire aisle dedicated to the fine world of teas and coffee. Wouldn't shop there before—they used to just gouge people on their prices. But a free lunch is a free lunch. At least these days it is. Who's gonna complain?"

Twenty minutes later Mason sat in the only chair in Twiggy's bachelor apartment and waited while the man fiddled with the buttons on an old propane stove that now ran on gasoline. Mason stifled a yawn with the back of his hand. It was getting harder and harder to get a full night's sleep these days. Twiggy, however, looked like he'd had ten hours the night before. The old man's eyes were bright and energetic.

Twiggy's apartment was more like a museum than a home. There were shelves overflowing with everything imaginable. Thousands of books, notebooks, statues, loose articles, and knickknacks, piled and tossed until every corner was filled. On the walls were a collection of maps of the world. Maps of the solar system. Maps of subway routes and what looked like small towns. There were drawings and pictures, mostly of places—waterfalls, beaches, jungles, canyons, ruins of ancient civilizations, and even a few smiling people—stuck in place with thumbtacks and pushpins, several of which overlapped into one gigantic collage.

Binders and newspaper clippings were stacked in corners. Even the kitchen had boxes of books pushed up against the refrigerator and cupboard doors.

The place made Mason feel slightly claustrophobic, but it didn't seem to bother Twiggy in the slightest.

"It was a push-button generation," Twiggy said. "We never needed to work for anything. Anything you wanted was within your reach. If you were hungry you popped something in the microwave and pressed a button. If you wanted to drink you turned on the coffeemaker. We used buttons for elevators, cars, televisions, alarms—hell, if you could think it up, someone would invent a button for you to press in order to have it. Now, I'm not one of those old farts who goes around talking about how much better the world was when I was a boy. It wasn't. At least, it wasn't a few weeks ago. Can't really compare it to today, can I? Nothing is worse than this."

Mason nodded. He stared at a stack of books that looked dangerously ready to topple at the slightest breeze. Twiggy's apartment wasn't dirty, but it wasn't exactly clean, either. The dishes were done and neatly stacked in the cupboards, and the bedding looked freshly washed. But everything was worn— old and faded. Mason couldn't help but think it must be a depressing place to live.

Twiggy caught him looking around. "Yeah, it's not much, but its home. I've lived here a long time. I guess if I really wanted to, I could find myself a nice condo in the downtown core. I'm sure there's plenty of good real estate waiting around these days for someone to grab it. Might get a real steal of a deal."

Mason nodded, distracted by a smushed bug on the ceiling.

"But this is mine. It's not the building but what's inside that counts. Been here thirty-some years. Could have left it behind a long time ago, but never felt like I needed anything else. Aside from books and knowledge, I've always believed in a simple life. Never married, no kids, nothing but my job and that was enough. Even after I retired I still didn't feel like moving down to Florida or whatever it is old people do these days. Besides, can you imagine how much it would cost to move all this junk?"

"What did you do?"

The kettle began to whistle and Twiggy switched off the burner. He poured the water into mugs containing fancy-looking tea bags. For a one-legged man, movement was not a problem for him. Balancing on one crutch, he picked up a mug and brought it over to Mason without spilling a single drop.

"I was a sociology professor at the university," Twiggy said as he went back to the kitchen. He picked up a bag of cookies and tossed them at the bed before retrieving his own mug. "Don't look so surprised, us nutty professors always look like twenty miles of bad road. I think unmanageable hair and tweed suits are part of our chemical makeup."

"Cool."

"Extremely," Twiggy said. "I specialized in downfall, the destruction of societies. As you can imagine, this whole event has caused quite a stir in my attention span."

A scream sounded from outside the window, and Mason jerked his hands up, spilling hot tea across the front of his shirt. Swearing, he jumped to his feet, pulling at the cloth to try and prevent the scalding liquid from burning his chest.

Twiggy hopped over to the window and pulled aside the curtain to get a better look. "Can't tell if that was one of them or someone in trouble. Not that we'd be able to do much."

"Should we go take a look?" Shirt cooling, he joined Twiggy at the window, which faced an alley. There was no one in sight.

"Not a chance. I may be old, but I'm not looking to die just yet. I saw them tear apart a looter a few days ago. Dumb idiot was trying to carry one of those seventy-two-inch televisions. Don't know what he thought he was gonna watch it with? Maybe he thought it runs on pixie dust? Who knows? They did him in just the same. Never heard a man scream that way. You'd best keep low if you want mankind to survive."

Mason turned from the window. He knew Twiggy was right. It seemed irrelevant anyway—the screamer was gone. Or silenced.

Twiggy closed the window and pulled the curtain. Moving back toward the bed, he sat down. "You don't talk much, do you?"

"Not really."

"I doubt it's because you don't have much to say."

Mason shrugged.

"I'm not going to ask you who you lost," Twiggy said. "It's all over your face. But I'll tell you this. Going off into the wild and being a hero isn't going to bring them back. Now isn't the time to be getting survivor's guilt."

"It's not that," Mason said.

"You want answers? There aren't any."

"Why?"

"Good question." Twiggy scratched at his leg. "But I don't have that answer. Why does anything happen? I think the disease just got too deep."

"Disease?"

"Humanity."

Mason shrugged again, mostly because he didn't have a clue how to respond. Twiggy was staring at him intently, and he was getting uncomfortable. His algebra teacher used to do the same thing all the time, especially when he knew Mason didn't have the right answer. Maybe it was a teacher thing?

"Born into blood, raised by blood," Twiggy said. He hobbled over to the bookcase and took down a scrapbook, passing it to Mason. The first page had a black-and-white photograph of a wasted world. Broken buildings loomed in the background while hundreds of dead bodies littered the streets. "Humans are the most violent species on the planet. We have a brilliant history of all the ugly deeds we've done. We're rotted straight to the core. The disease finally won the battle. We've never had a cure, and the symptoms are out of control. We're finally doing something right by wiping ourselves off the face of this planet."

"So you're saying we're responsible? We created this?"

"Not directly," Twiggy said. He turned over a few pages for Mason until he found what he was looking for. Ancient ruins. A temple covered in vines and overgrown bushes. Mummified skeletons with their jaws forever open in agony. "It's the end of days, Mr. Dowell. Like all great societies before us, ours has begun to eat itself—cannibalize, if you will—from the inside. Think of all the great societies in the past. Mayans. Aztecs. Romans. All advanced for their time. All destroyed and gone today. They've left behind nothing but a few hints for people like me to come and dig up."

Twiggy pointed to a picture on the wall. Hundreds of dead bodies piled together. "Murambi Technical School in Rwanda," he said. "The genocide of an entire culture. Hundreds of thousands killed. Hacked into pieces with machetes. Slaughtered. Not pretty, is it?"

"That's messed up."

"It's our turn to eat ourselves from within. Something happened that roused the destruction on a universal scale. We are no longer a cluster of societies living off the land. We've globalized and grown too big. Now something's made us go strange in the head. Took away our free will. Humans are dogs, you realize. There is a pack leader that starts us off down the path to destruction. But someone or something always comes along to throw us a bone first. Philosophers like to argue that we have free will, but I think the majority of people can't stop themselves from following. Whatever is controlling this, it picked the perfect time to plan its attack. I think it was the earthquakes. Animals can sense them, did you know that? Fact. But something caused the ground to split, and it's angry. It's come for us, you see. And we've invited it in with open arms."

"I don't believe in that sort of crap."

"Doesn't matter what you believe in. Do you think things will stop or change because you've forgotten what the bogeyman looks like? Maybe that's what pissed it off, so to speak. It doesn't like being forgotten. So it decided to shake things up a little."

Twiggy took back the scrapbook and turned a few more pages until he came to a picture of total devastation. A woman held her dead child in her arms, her face taut as she tried to keep from falling apart. Dead bodies were lined in a row behind her. People stumbled around the debris, desperately searching out their loved ones. Another picture—the bodies of two young girls, side by side, rotting in the streets because there was no one around to bury them.

"There have been earthquakes before," Mason said.

"True. And maybe there were bad things lurking about during those disasters too," Twiggy said. "Maybe some were misdiagnosed. We'd have to go back and look to see if there's a connection. But that's a moot point right about now. I doubt I'd be able to get my hands on any research material these days. Just think, maybe millions of years from now they will find our cities buried under the dirt and try to understand what brought on our demise. Imagine what they'll think of our laptops and microwave ovens."

"I don't believe in evil."

"Once again, we're only tiny pawns in this game. Belief has nothing to do with it. For all we know, this evil could have killed off the dinosaurs. Or maybe it really was a meteor. Or maybe history was just created from God's hands to give us something to argue about over dinner parties."

From beyond the closed window, the muffled sound of glass breaking reached their ears. Mason's body stiffened, and it annoyed him that such things were still affecting him. Twiggy didn't even twitch. How long would it take before screams and breaking glass wouldn't even have Mason blinking his eyes? Would he ever become as calm as the old man in front of him? Maybe if he wasn't this highly strung he might be able to get some sleep at night.

"It'll be dark soon," Twiggy said. "I'd invite you to stay, but as you can see, I'm not exactly set up for company." He pointed at the single bed.

"I should get going anyway," Mason said, standing. "You wouldn't happen to know where a car dealership is, would you?"

"Hold on." Twiggy hobbled over to the dresser and opened it. Reaching inside, he pulled out some keys and tossed them at Mason. "Downstairs in the garage. Not much, I'm afraid. Just an old, beat-up Honda. I don't drive it a lot, but it'll do you well enough. There's a full tank of gas."

Mason squeezed the keys tightly in his fist. "Are you sure? Do you want to come with me? I'm not sure where I'm going yet, but you're welcome to—"

"Let me stop you right there," Twiggy said. "I'm not going anywhere, Mr. Dowell. It's not my world out there. I'm safe here. I have everything I need and the fancy grocery store down the street from which to steal. I'm not a man who deals well with change. I have no desire to join you in your adventure."

"Okay," Mason said. "I had to ask."

"Yes, of course you did." Twiggy laughed. "And now that you've asked, you can move on with a clean conscience. It's good for the soul. Now thank me kindly and start moving on."

"Thank you."

"You're welcome."

Twiggy saw him to the door. "Just follow the stairs to the basement. It'll be parked in the back corner. I doubt there'll be anyone down there. The door's automatic; you'll have to do it manually. Try not to let anyone in when you leave."

"Thanks for all your help." Mason turned to go.

"Oh, Mr. Dowell? One last thing."

Mason turned back to face Twiggy. "Yeah?"

The coffee mug sailed through the air, smashing into the side of Mason's face. White stars exploded in all directions, and the edges of his vision instantly distorted. He couldn't control his body—knees buckled, arms became dead weights, and his legs fell out from underneath him like some slow-motion dream. He cracked his head on the doorframe on the way down.

He couldn't move. Through blurry eyes he watched Twiggy hobbling toward him, his crutches stopping dangerously close to Mason's face. He wanted to do something, but his eyes weren't focusing. He couldn't breathe.

The last thing he saw before the darkness took him was Twiggy leaning over him, a crooked smile showing yellow teeth. His eyes were funny. Bloodshot. But the veins weren't red. They were black.

"Trust no one," Twiggy said.

Then nothing.

NOTHING

I don't feel like talking today. Go find someone else to bother.
  I mean it. Stay away.
  Don't make me hate you.

ARIES

She was cold. Freezing. Her fingers were white and stiff. Something was wrong. October never used to be this cold. And wet. The tiny Gastown apartment was waterlogged. Vancouver may be known for its precipitation, but this was overdoing it. It'd been raining for a week and there was still no sign of it giving up. The clouds were fat and gray, the land pregnant with swollen tears.

Funny how a gray sky made her want to curl up in a ball and start crying, especially after everything else that had happened in the past few weeks.

Depressing.

She pulled the blanket tighter around her shoulders. It was itchy and stained and smelled faintly of mold, but at least it kept her somewhat warm. There was no such thing as luxuries anymore. Besides, she hadn't showered in days; she probably didn't smell like roses either. When was the last time she saw her own reflection in a mirror?

Through the window she watched the solitary person walking in the rain, pushing a squeaky shopping cart. The person had no face, at least not one that was visible, and was covered in a makeshift raincoat; the eyes were blurry through the clear plastic.

"It's one of them."

She turned toward the voice. "How can you tell from this distance?"

"No one sane would be outside in this weather."

"Har-har. Very unfunny."

Jack shrugged. "I'm still not going to take any chances and invite him up here for a cup of tea."

Aries nodded. "Yeah, I hear you. Better safe than dead."

"The saying is 'better safe than sorry.'"

"I wouldn't be sorry. I'd be dead." Aries closed her eyes and leaned back from the window. She was tired. They all were. No one got much sleep these days. Who has time for napping when staying alive requires so much effort?

They'd done well so far. They were still alive. At least some of them were. That had to count for something. How many people were left? Ten percent of the city? Five? It was hard to tell when so many were in hiding. There weren't as many screams these days, and that was a blessing in disguise. But less meant less—not more. Should she include the monsters in her head count? Could you consider them human anymore?

"You should take a break and get some sleep." Jack leaned over and grabbed the water bottle from the window ledge.

"I'm fine," she said.

"You've been here for at least six hours. We're supposed to be doing this in shifts, remember? It's okay to give someone else a chance. They aren't going to come breaking down the doors if you close your eyes. I'm here. I'll watch over you."

"It's not that."

"You don't trust me?" He brought the bottle to his lips, but she could still see the smile concealed behind it.

"I trust you." She grabbed the bottle back before he got a sip. Water sloshed out, soaking his nose and forcing her to grin like an idiot.

It was nice having these moments when they could forget what was going on outside and share a silly laugh. The problem was, it didn't happen often enough. Aries placed the bottle back on the ledge and scanned the street below her. The shopping cart person was still moving steadily toward them. In a few minutes they'd be within earshot. That was enough to sober her up.

Whatever humanity had become, it still had good hearing.

They waited silently while the figure moved past the building. It moved slowly, pausing once to sniff the air and glance back down the road from which it came. It kicked an old soda can into the gutter and picked up something off the street: a bicycle helmet with a long crack down the side. It rustled around in the shopping cart for a few moments before pulling out a human head. Jack gripped Aries's shoulder. They both watched silently as the plastic-clad person placed the helmet on top of the severed head before stuffing it back under the tarp. Eventually the person started moving again, heading back down the street in a continuous shuffle. It wasn't until the monster turned the corner that Aries realized she'd been holding her breath.

"I think we're safe," she muttered. Her heart was thumping hard, and she was angry that she was still scared after three weeks. She wanted to be stronger. She had to be stronger if she was going to run this group. They all looked toward her, except Colin, but he still grudgingly went along with whatever she suggested. Well, most of the time.

Movement on the street caught her attention. A stray German shepherd stuck its head out from behind a parked car.

A smaller dog, maybe a shih tzu, crouched behind it. They'd obviously been waiting for the monster to leave too. The shepherd sniffed the air before cautiously moving out toward the middle of the road, where it stuck its nose into a pile of newspaper. When it raised its head, it was chewing something. Plenty of garbage for the animals these days.

"There are other survivors out there," she said suddenly. "There have to be. We can't be the only sane people left in the world. It would be nice to find them. We'd be stronger. We don't even have any weapons."

"We'll find others eventually."

She took a sip of water. Her throat was always dry these days. "We should be looking for them. Sending out search parties. It wouldn't be too hard to do."

"It would be suicidal. You said it yourself, we don't have weapons."

"Then we'll get some."

She yawned, and tried to cover it up by coughing.

"You're tired," Jack pressed.

"I just don't feel like sleeping right now."

"Who do you see when you close your eyes?"

Aries shot him a look. "That's personal."

"I see Ms. Darcy."

She nodded. "Me too."

And a million others.

It wasn't sleep that she feared. It was the time before sleep when she rested her head down on the pillow. She couldn't turn off her brain; it became an open invitation for all the events she'd witnessed over the past weeks. There were too many thoughts, and this was the prime time for them to creep their way into her head. Closing her eyes meant seeing and imagining the bodies of both strangers and the people she loved. Their screams echoed like a scratched record on an endless loop. She wanted sleep. She wished desperately for it to come to her. But she couldn't clear her head. She didn't know what tricks to use to make it all go away.

She blinked several times to try to ease the soreness from her eyes. Clutching the blanket, she pulled it back over her shoulders. "Where are the others?"

"Second floor. They're trying the laptop again, but I think the battery's about to die. Personally I would have given up on it a long time ago. It's broke, can't be fixed. Thing's useless anyway without the Internet. Colin's on the roof. He said something about needing fresh air, but I think he's just tired of the smell. Can't say I disagree with him. I wish we had drugs. If my head gets any stuffier it's gonna explode."

The building in which they were hiding had a foul odor of mold and fried eggs. It had been the brunt of bad jokes over several sleepless nights. What smells worse than ten-day-old maggot breath? This place. What smells worse than Colin's feet? This place.

They laughed silently in the darkness. You had to laugh if you wanted to live. But you did it quietly. Who knew what lurked in the shadows outside?

Six of them lived. Colin, Joy, Jack, and Aries were the only ones lucky enough to make it out of the school alive. They'd met up with Eve and Nathan a week later. They were a brother-and-sister team that managed to survive inside a 7-Eleven by hiding behind a bunch of boxes in the store room. Together they were six. Alone they were, well, alone. She remembered what Daniel said to her before he disappeared. Groups were a bad thing. People do stupid things when they're together. She disagreed. Being part of a group gave her strength. She'd never have made it out alive if it hadn't been for her friends.

Daniel. Was he out there somewhere, hiding in an abandoned grocery store or holed up in some earthquake-ravaged building like hers? She thought about him often, more than she'd ever admit. She wondered if he was still alive or one of the numerous corpses that littered the streets like the aftermath of some bizarre death parade.

When they'd escaped the school and ran blindly into the street, she'd been surprised that the group automatically headed toward the bus stop and the grocery store. Her heart exploded in her chest when she recognized the overturned bus, knowing that her best friend was still trapped inside with Daniel's jacket thrown over her. It would be her final resting place; no one was coming to give her a proper burial. Thankfully they ran straight past. No one thought of taking cover there.

Luck was on their side and they found shelter in someone's garage. They huddled in the darkness, listening to the screams, waiting for someone or something to open the door and find them. It was a miracle they made it through without detection.

"They're going from house to house," Jack informed her during the first night. It was three a.m. and everyone was dozing except the two of them. Jack was peering out through the window, cautiously.

"Who?" she asked. A waterfall of cold ice ran its way down her spine.

"Six or seven of them," he said. "They just dragged someone out into the street. She's in a bathrobe. Oh God, there's a child, too."

Aries joined him at the window. She couldn't help herself.

"Are you sure you want to see this?" he whispered.

She nodded and he pointed farther down the street where she could see the group of people circled around and tearing apart their victims. A soft cry involuntarily left her lips, and she covered her mouth with both hands.

Jack put his arm around her and pulled her close. She buried her face in his chest for a few moments before anger overcame her. No. She wasn't going to cower. She'd have to be stronger if she wanted to get out of this alive. Pushing away from him, she forced herself to watch the group finish up their job before moving on to the next house.

"They'll get here eventually," she finally said.

"There's a car cover in the back," Jack said. "We can hide under it."

"We need weapons," she said.

Luckily for them, the murderous mob never checked the garage. By the time they reached that house, dawn was breaking in the sky and the killers must have been exhausted. They broke down the door of the house across the street. Aries clung to Jack when one of the monsters threw a helpless woman through the living room window. After checking to make sure she was dead, the killer casually wandered back inside and closed the door. They must have decided to rest, because the house grew quiet.

Aries spent the entire day believing she'd be dead by nightfall. But when the mob resumed their killing spree that evening, they miraculously skipped their hideout.

The rest of the block wasn't so lucky.

Three days later Aries and her friends moved on. Mostly because they were hungry and if they stayed any longer they'd be too weak. They slipped out under the cover of night.

There were dead bodies everywhere. It was almost impossible to move without hitting a hand or stomach. Joy stepped on someone's fingers, accidentally breaking them beneath her boot. She threw up on a discarded book bag. Everyone

huddled around her, but not out of concern. They were terrified that the noise might draw attention. Although Joy was on
the verge of hysterics, she managed to keep it together. But
she was more cautious where she stepped from that point on.
They all were.

There was blood. It may have been dark outside, but Aries
could see the endless splashes of dried liquid on the cement.

It was the longest walk she'd ever endured. Every time
they heard a noise they jumped in the bushes or took cover
behind a car. When people screamed or called out for help
they turned and walked in the opposite direction. A body still
oozing fresh blood put them into a full-blown panic, but only
because it meant one of the psychotic humans was close.

Eventually they made it to the downtown core, where
they found Eve and Nathan. They spent the night under the
Granville Bridge, where they crawled up onto a cement pil-
lar. It was cold and miserable, and Aries spent the entire night
afraid to close her eyes. She couldn't get past the fear of falling asleep, rolling off the bridge, and hitting the dark waters
below.

The next evening they found the apartment block. Set
above a restaurant, it had no way inside on the first floor
except for two giant iron doors with heavy-duty locks. The
windows on the second and third levels were broken, and a
corner of the roof had caved in during the earthquake, but it
was secure. A dropped key by the steps gained them access.
No one else was inside.

It became their haven.

The building wasn't exactly livable. Many of the apart-
ments were empty; it seemed the place was undergoing reno-
vations when the earthquake happened. The few places that
had been inhabited were sparsely furnished. They found a

bit of food in the cupboards and the rest they managed to scrounge by sneaking out in the dead of night to the convenience store down the street. After a few weeks of living on chocolate bars and bags of chips, they were starting to get jittery. The sugar rushes were wearing down their bodies and tripping out their minds. Aries was tired all the time, and she was positive the others felt the same way. She knew there were other shops farther into the city, some maybe as close as a few blocks away. But getting to them would be risky. They were all running short on bravery these days. Maybe after a few days of starving, they'd change their minds. But it hadn't happened yet.

All they did was sit around and wait. The building was damp because of its age and all the rain. The lack of windows meant a constant draft they couldn't escape. Her body constantly felt soggy.

If they found other survivors, they'd be stronger. They could form a community. They'd be able to divide the responsibilities better and get more organized. It would be good to find a doctor. Even a police officer. They could learn more about self-defense. They could learn to protect themselves. The bigger the group, the tougher they'd be. Maybe eventually they could find a way to communicate with other cities.

If they could find a way to share their stories they might be able to find a way to defeat the monsters.

"Maybe I will take a break," she said. Forcing herself to stand, she ignored the strained ligaments and pulled the blanket off her body and draped it over Jack's shoulders.

"Good," he said. Sniffing at the scratchy wool, he made a face. "This is disgusting."

"Better than nothing," she said. "I'm gonna go make some coffee. Do you want?"

"Caramel macchiato with extra foam. Double shot of vanilla, too."

"Black it is, and if you're lucky I'll stir it with a Twix bar."

Jack laughed. "You're on."

She paused at the door, keeping her face hidden from his. "Sometimes when I close my eyes, I'm afraid of my mind going dark. Like I'll wake up changed into one of those things."

"If you were one of them, I think you'd know it by now."

"We don't know that. We don't know how any of this works. Why'd they change in the first place?" She turned to face him, and her eyes found his.

"You're right," he said. "We don't know. But I'm going to continue believing that no one else is going to change. Otherwise I'll just drive myself crazy wondering. I can't live that way."

She nodded. "You make sense. I don't remember you being this sensible back in school."

"I'm shockingly intelligent sometimes."

"I see that. One Twix bar coffee coming up for you." She left him by the window and headed down toward the kitchen they were using. No one was there, and she poured some bottled water into a pot. Placing it on the Coleman stove, she turned on the gas. They were running out of propane. Soon this luxury would be over too.

While she waited for the water to boil, she leaned against the counter and stared absently out onto the street. It was empty, but she couldn't help but think of all the people she hoped were still alive. She often thought about her parents. Were they safe? More than anything else in the world she wished she could stop by her house and see if her Mom and Dad were waiting. Their faces were strong in her memory.

She imagined the reunion several times a day, the surprised, relieved looks she'd get when she walked through the door. She'd give anything to curl up in her bed with her warm blankets. Her bed was the unreachable dream.

But her house was all the way on the other side of the city. Even if she managed to find a car, it would take hours just to try and navigate around all the stalls and accidents. All the bridges were jammed with abandoned cars. There wasn't a way in or out of the downtown core. Walking would be impossible. There were too many of those monsters just waiting to snatch up the last of humanity.

It was farther away than the moon.

CLEMENTINE

Dear Heath, I'm such an idiot and now I'm going to die. If there is a heaven, I hope you're waiting for me.

Lying on her back in the baseball dugout, Clementine held a shaking hand over her mouth. Less than two feet above her, strange voices held a discussion about what they'd like to do if they found a nice young girl.

"Getting harder and harder to find a chick," one of them grunted.

"That's cuz you keep killing 'em," said the other. "I dunno why you had to go and off that pretty brunette. I would have liked to spend some more time with her. Gotta appreciate it: soon good women gonna be a thing of the past. You know I only like the ones who scream, and they're gonna be extinct like the dinosaur."

"Better enjoy 'em while we can, then."

Thankfully it was dark, but if one of them had happened to glance down they might have seen the moonlight reflecting off her eyes.

It seemed like a good idea at the time. Hide in plain sight, where they'd never think to look—it was ingenious. She'd exhausted all other forms of safety. The first few nights she'd pulled off the highway and tried sleeping in the truck. But that never felt right. Every time she closed her eyes she'd visualize a hand smashing through the windshield, bits of glass pelting her body as thick arms reached out to grab her hair. Even if she drove down old service roads where the odds of anyone finding her were almost zero, she still heard imaginary noises every time she tried to relax. Saw shadows moving through the darkness. She started looking for abandoned buildings, farmhouses or gas stations where she might be able to lock herself in an upstairs room for a few hours' sleep.

She ended up bypassing Des Moines completely. It was obvious there'd be no police there to help. She'd seen the squad car half an hour before reaching the city limits. It was flipped over on its back, and the officers inside had been beaten to death, their weapons gone. They weren't the only victims on the side of the road. The highway leading away from the city was filled with cars, some abandoned, others filled with dead bodies. What happened in Glenmore was happening across the rest of America. On the other side of Des Moines, she ran into a couple of adults who told her that the crazy people were going from home to home, dragging out the hidden and killing them in the streets. After that, houses became a threat too. She couldn't even look at one without involuntarily shuddering.

No place was safe.

"They're barricading the main highways too," the older woman told her before they parted. "Disguising themselves as military. Pulling people out of their cars and shooting them. Up north they were everywhere. Dead zones. Miles of cars filled with bodies. Be careful. Avoid the main roads."

She continued on, refusing the offer from the couple to

join them. They were heading south and she wasn't about to abandon her goal of reaching Seattle. Her parents were gone, their bodies abandoned with the only town she'd ever lived in. She owed it to them, especially her mother with her eerie premonitions, to try to let her brother know what happened.

But it was slow moving. Getting gasoline could end up being an entire day's ordeal. Luckily for her, she'd spent the past two summers working at the Gas N Go and knew how to get gasoline out of the underground reservoir. It wasn't an easy job and often took her hours of surveillance before she even attempted to go near the station.

Avoiding the vulnerable highways was the other major distraction. Many of the service roads weren't mapped, and often she'd reach dead ends after driving for hours.

She was on her third vehicle since she'd left her parents' house three weeks ago. Her original truck she abandoned after she swerved into a ditch while trying to avoid hitting a couple of cows that had wandered into the middle of the road. She took the second car off a lot but lost it in the first major barricade outside of Sioux City. She spent several days hiding in the back of someone's van, trying to gather enough courage to move on. Eventually hunger and the smell of her unwashed body was enough for her to sneak along the road until she reached what remained of civilization. Luckily for her, most of the area was already abandoned or dead, so she picked up some supplies and a new ride from a grocery store parking lot.

She kept telling herself it wasn't theft, that the cars and trucks she took weren't being used and it's not like the real world existed anymore.

I'm coming, Heath.

She refused to believe he was dead. Naive or not, the hope kept her strong.

Sleeping in the baseball dugout was a good idea. Who on earth was going to come searching for her there? It wasn't like anyone was going to try to get a team together for a friendly competition. The field was beside a burned-down high school, so she didn't have to worry about people being attracted to the building. There was no one left alive to hide in it, anyway.

She had a sleeping bag. It was unzipped in case she had to make a hasty retreat. But she'd fallen asleep at the wrong time and been awakened by the sound of the two men walking across the dirt. The chance to escape had been twenty minutes ago.

Now her brilliant idea lay thrown in the mud, and the hope of surviving the night diminished with every second.

They must have heard her heartbeat. How could they not? It was hammering against her rib cage, threatening to tear its way right out of her chest.

"Town's dead," one of the voices said above her. Clearing his throat, he spat in the dust, inches from Clementine's face. Spit bubbles popped in the moonlight.

"Was fun, wasn't it?"

A throaty chuckle drifted downward.

Remaining calm was impossible. Every vein in her body ached to run. Dendrites exploded, sending false information to her brain. A million insects crawled around on her skin; spiders scratched their legs through her hair. Knees ached, longing to expose her through involuntary kicks. A tickle in the back of her nose threatened a full-blown sneeze. Even her eyes begged to be blinked.

"We should call it a night, then."

"Sounds good."

Footsteps crunched and she almost cried out in relief. But then one of them paused.

"Hold up, gotta take a leak."

The sound of the zipper almost brought her to tears. Even though she knew it was coming, she still jerked when the stream of urine hit her opened sleeping bag, sending a stream of liquid across the waterproof fabric and straight onto her shirt. Why hadn't she thought to cover herself properly? She bit down hard on her lip to try to prevent the fumes from reaching her lungs.

It went on forever, the liquid soaking through her clothes, touching her skin, staining her body.

"That's better." The zipper went back up, and the man moved away from the dugout.

She continued to lie there, soaked and frozen, long after the footsteps faded away. Part of her kept thinking they were waiting for her. She hadn't fooled them one little bit. The second she stood up they'd be on her, tearing her apart, doing deeds a million times worse than anything her mother ever warned her about.

It was the smell that finally jerked her into action. She couldn't take it anymore. Carefully she rolled the sleeping bag aside, trying to avoid any more urine reaching her clothing. Waiting on her knees, she listened to the night, ignored the chirping crickets and swaying prairie grasses, until she was satisfied she was truly alone. She'd have to take the chance. Otherwise she might fall apart and start crying.

Standing up quickly, she scanned the surrounding field, and it was empty. The urge to cry again struck her, but she kept busy by examining her shirt. Her first instinct was to rip it off, but she didn't have anything else to wear. Removing it would leave her even more exposed, and she didn't think she was strong enough for that.

No, she'd have to find something else. The main area of town was just two blocks away. Surely she'd find a clothing store or gas station that sold souvenir shirts. Urine-covered girls like herself couldn't be choosy. Glancing down at her sleeping bag, she decided to leave it behind. It would only stink up the truck, and there was no way she'd ever sleep in it again now.

The truck was parked out past the burned high school, down a side street where other parked cars added camouflage. She'd leave it where it was for now. The two men (and lord knows who else) were still close enough that they'd hear if she tried to drive. But if she hurried, she could find a store, grab some clothes, and be ready to head out within the hour. There would be no more sleeping tonight. Hopefully tomorrow she'd have better luck.

She moved slowly across the baseball field and back toward town. The silence was good but also unnerving. There were no alleys here to sneak down, so she kept to the sidewalks, shadowing the houses, prepared to run and hide at the slightest breaking branch.

The main street was actually Fourth Avenue. There were no working street lamps, and she was happy about that. A quick glance showed row upon row of empty parking spaces. Not even a single abandoned truck. The street was lined with glass-windowed shops, a hardware store, a pharmacy, three bars, a grocery store, and an insurance and travel place combined. Two motels offered satellite television and air-conditioning. At the end of the block she found what she was looking for. A small thrift store with a rack of secondhand shoes still left out on the sidewalk. The door was shut, but when she tugged at the handle, it opened.

Bells immediately chimed above her head.

It took every ounce of willpower to keep from turning and running off into the night.

Nothing happened. The bells stopped rattling, and the sounds of empty street filled her ears. She couldn't even hear the crickets anymore.

Why hadn't she thought to check the door for bells? She was getting careless. She'd never have done that a few days ago. She'd have waited about half an hour to make sure the store was empty, gone around and checked the back for exits, made sure she really was alone—and then she would have cautiously checked the door for bells and whistles before she opened it.

But she was tired. People make mistakes when they're tired. *Fools and their lives are soon parted.*

Glancing down the street, she shrugged and entered the shop. Might as well go ahead now that the whole town knew she was there, but she'd check for an exit before she allowed herself to go on a shopping spree.

She found it in the back, a locked door with a darkened exit sign. Unlatching the lock, she pushed the door open and found herself practically in someone's backyard. It would provide a good escape if she needed one. Satisfied, she closed the door, latched it up again, and proceeded to the front, already dreaming of how good it would feel to remove her shirt and put on something fresh. There was a small bathroom and half a bar of green soap and an orange towel. She returned to the front, where she found a bottle of water behind the counter— that would help rinse off some of the grossness.

Picking through the rack, she discarded the first few items because they were either too large or too bright. Darker colors were safer. Pushing aside a worn pink cardigan, she found a blue-and-green plaid shirt that looked to be about her size. She glanced back at the front door to ensure she was alone before yanking off her top and dumping the stinking garment on the floor.

She soaked the towel with water and ran it along her body, trying to remove all traces of urine. Using the soap, she cleaned quickly, her eyes constantly keeping watch on the door. She moved quietly, a tiny mouse removing all traces of scent so that the snakes wouldn't find her.

She almost cried out in relief when she pulled the shirt over her body and did up the buttons. It fit perfectly, and there was such a wonderful feeling to be free from that rank odor. Turning to leave, she paused, thinking that it might be a good idea to grab an extra change of clothing in case something like this happened again. Who knew when she might come across another clothing store? She should grab a coat, too.

She found a jean jacket a size too big and slipped it on. It would do. Back at the rack, she pulled out a black sweater and a shirt that said Michigan State. She found a bag behind the counter and shoved her new items inside.

Dear Heath, that's quite possibly the quickest shopping spree I've ever been on. You'd be proud. You always said I had too many shoes. Now I'm down to one pair. They're made for walking, and I'll be heading out soon enough to find you.

She came from behind the counter but froze when she looked out the window and saw the men from the ball park on the sidewalk. Quickly she dropped to the ground, her heart thumping against her chest and pounding in her ears. Icy saliva filled her mouth; she couldn't swallow it.

The bells chimed as the door opened.

"Come on, sweetie," the first guy said. "We know you're here. We saw you from the window."

Her eyes darted across the counter shelves. She needed a weapon. Anything. Behind the assorted bags she saw a letter opener. Fingers closed around the metal. It would have to do.

"We ain't got all day, girlie."

She raised her head and stood her ground. She didn't want them coming around the counter to grab her. At least this way there would be space between them. Maybe she still had time to run. But could she get to the back room and unlatch the door before they caught her? She couldn't tell.

Dear Heath, give me strength.

"Well, ain't you a pretty one."

They knew what they were doing. As the first one talked, the second started leisurely moving his way toward her, trying to get around the counter so they'd have her cornered.

"Stay back." She raised the letter opener in defense.

"And what are you going to do with that, sweet pea? Stab me?"

Number Two was almost on top of her. She had to act. Hurling the shopping bag with all her might, she turned and darted toward the back room.

She made it to the door, but a hand clamped down on her shoulder before she could unlatch the lock.

"Bitch, I'm gonna—"

She didn't think. The letter opener moved through the air of its own accord; she was positive it wasn't her using it. Silver metal sliced the stomach flesh of its victim. How could something travel through tissue and muscle so easily?

The man grunted. She couldn't tell which one—it was too dark to see much of anything. He slouched against her, pressing her body up against the door, his breath heavy on her face. She could smell beer and potato chips. Onions. Shoving him with all her strength, she managed to twist around until she could reach and turn the lock. The door swung outward, sending both her and the man sprawling into the street.

She didn't pause. Kicking at the dropped man, she squeezed her body from underneath him, crawling away until she managed to get her legs up, and tore into a run. From behind she could hear the other man screaming at her, but if he gave chase, he wasn't fast enough to catch her.

Six blocks later, she unlocked her truck and started the engine before she even got the door closed. Slamming her foot on the gas, she tore off into the night, leaving behind the town and everything in it.

It wasn't until she got several miles away that she pulled over, letting the engine idle, and finally scrubbed at the tears that threatened her vision.

There was fresh blood all over her shirt. Her body was sticky again.

And after all that trouble, too.

MICHAEL

"Hey!"

A voice reached through the darkness.

"Hey! Idiot. Wake up. We've got to get out of here now."

Michael forced his mind away from the haziness that wasn't his dreams. When did he fall asleep? Wasn't he supposed to be on watch?

"Whatisit?" His mouth tasted like raunchy cotton balls. His neck was against the window frame, bent at an unusual angle. Already he could feel the knot worked into his muscles. There would be pain once he stretched out.

"There are bodies in the basement."

He was off the floor in an instant. "What? What do you mean, bodies? Who?"

"People. I dunno. Maybe the ones who own this house. Who the hell cares. We've got to get outta here. It's a bloody trap is what it is."

Evans's face was pale, his eyes wide and looking in every direction except at Michael. He rushed over to the window and stared out into the night. Michael joined him, but there wasn't anything to see. It wasn't a clear night, even the stars were invisible. When did it get dark? The sun was still in the sky last he looked. How could he do this—falling asleep while on duty? These people depended on him. He'd told Evans and Billy he would search the upstairs for useful things: weapons, clothing, that sort of stuff. He hadn't even made it past the first bedroom. What kind of leader was he if he couldn't do a simple thing like stay awake?

If this was a trap, then the Baggers would be coming. They might already be here; it was too dark to tell. The surrounding acres of forest made the ranch house the perfect hideout, but it was also a great location for an ambush.

Why hadn't he thought about that earlier?

"Who else knows about this?"

"No one." Evans pulled away from the glass. "I was checking the basement for the hot-water heater. Wanted to try and get some heat. I found them way in the back by the utility room. Stacked in the corner like wild meat. Something put them there. They didn't just die like that."

"That's screwed. Where are the others?"

"Billy and the rest are sleeping in the living room. Idiots ate too much and they all crashed. I think the mother's still in the bedroom with her sick kid."

"Get her up first," Michael said. "She'll take longer than the others. Make sure all the doors and windows are locked. Then tell Billy to try and gather up as much food as possible. But not too heavy. It'll just slow us down if we have to run."

"What are you gonna do?"

"Find some weapons."

Evans rushed off, leaving Michael alone in the master bedroom. He set to work, going through the closets, pulling boxes off the shelves and emptying the contents over the hardwood floors. What kind of people lived this far out in the middle of nowhere and didn't keep weapons? There had to be something. He tried to remember if he'd seen a shed in the garden, but he couldn't think hard enough. His mind was still hazy from being asleep for so long.

Maybe they were overreacting. Just because the bodies were hidden in the basement didn't mean the Baggers were watching the house. These killers were all sorts; it was possible that these ones just happened to be the neat-and-tidy kind after a kill. Maybe they spent the night and didn't want to deal with the smell? Or maybe they found the family hiding in the basement and finished them there. If they'd killed them elsewhere in the house, wouldn't there be some sign of a struggle? Pooled blood on the floors or streaks on the walls—there'd be evidence somewhere, right?

The bed.

Michael turned around and looked at the duvet. It was burgundy with a black-and-silver design. On top were half a dozen pillows arranged against the post. The bedroom was neat and orderly; even the clothing in the closet was arranged according to color and style. He'd gone through the contents of the bathroom earlier, and all the toiletries were neatly stacked and freshly dusted.

So why were the pillows crooked?

Michael reached out and picked up the closest, pulling them off two at a time until pillows littered the floor. Grabbed the side of the duvet and yanked the entire thing back in one dramatic heave.

The sheets were stained with blood. No, that wasn't the right word. They were swimming in the stuff.

"Oh, God."

He had to get Evans. Crossing the room, he put his hand on the doorknob, twisted, and started to open the door.

From downstairs came the sound of breaking glass. Wood splintered as the back door was kicked in. Billy shouted something, but the words were lost in the distance. Someone screamed.

Too late.

Slamming the door, he instinctively turned the lock. As he moved toward the bed, his heart jolted its way into his throat. Screams echoed up the stairs, voices he recognized. Something or someone thumped against the wall. More glass shattered.

He should move. Do something. But he couldn't. His legs were stuck to the floor. Blood rushed to his head, pounding in his ears, blurring out the screams and crashes. They were being slaughtered down there and he couldn't do a thing to stop it.

"Michael."

A fist slamming against the door broke his paralysis. Jumping, he stepped backward, tripping over the side of the bed, where he fell and cracked his back against a wooden hope chest. He sat down hard, chomping down on his tongue. He tasted blood; it filled his mouth, forcing him to gag. Stomach clenched, he crawled toward the bathroom and shoved his head in the toilet.

"Michael, open the damn door. We need help."

He could hear Evans screaming at him, but he was too far away. The voice was distant and blurry, like something out of a bad dream. He banged a few more times, his fist rattling the frame.

Then nothing.

Michael stood up on shaky knees and turned on the faucet, splashing water on his face. His sense of reality had gone out the window. He needed to think, get his brain working.

If he didn't act soon, they'd finish up downstairs and come for him next. But something turned off inside of him. All he could do was stand in front of the mirror and stare at his wet face. Brown eyes stared back at him. He brought his fingers up and pulled at a few of the long strands of greasy hair.

Is this what a coward looked like?

"What the hell are you doing?"

He started to scream, and Evans covered his mouth with lightning speed. How could he not have noticed there was an adjoining door to the bathroom?

"I. I can't. Don't touch me. I'm okay, man, I'm okay." The words regurgitated from his lips, no rhyme or rhythm. Babbling.

Evans slapped him hard. "Snap out of it."

It worked. The pain burned across his cheek, kicking his body back into action.

"You didn't have to do that," he lied.

Evans didn't respond. He turned and headed back to the other bedroom, where the mother sat on the edge of the bed, rocking her half-dead child and whispering to him that everything was going to be all right.

"We've got to get out of here," Evans said. He moved past the mother and looked out the window. "We'll have to climb out on the ledge."

"I can't do that," the mother said. "We can't. We're not strong enough."

"I'll carry him," Evans responded.

Michael looked at him with resentment. Evans was taking charge. Just like that. He didn't throw up or lose all control of his body. He kept cool.

"We could try hiding," he said. "They may not know we're up here."

"Don't be daft," Evans snapped.

Michael's eyes hardened.

Something slammed against the door. The mother let out a yelp, pulling her child closer, nearly to the point of suffocation. There was a low, guttural hiss from the landing outside the room, and someone tested the lock.

A second bang.

A third.

The door cracked and groaned under the weight. They were coming.

Evans couldn't get the window open. He pulled at it with all his strength. "Help me," he snapped at Michael.

The wood of the door splintered.

He didn't want to die. Not here. Not like this.

The door gave way. The Baggers filled the room. Four of them in total: three males and one female. Two of them were holding hands as if they were on some sort of psychotic honeymoon. Clothing soaked and stained, they dripped blood all over the floor, grinning like wild hyenas closing in on the kill.

I now pronounce you husband and wife. You may kill the congregation.

The ridiculousness of the thought almost reduced him to hysteria.

The choice was easy. It wasn't actually an option, just picking life over death. Michael stepped back into the bathroom, slamming the door and locking it.

The last thing he saw was the look on Evans's face. They locked eyes, Evans's narrowed until almost completely closed. Hands curled into tight fists. Disgust. Pity. Not because of the Baggers.

Because of him.

Betrayer.

No time to change his mind. Already one of the Baggers was working on the bathroom door, slamming his body against it. Michael had only seconds to act. Turning, he fled over to the bedroom window. It wouldn't open either; there must have been some sort of locking mechanism he wasn't seeing. Figuring it out would take too much time. On the bedside table was an alarm clock. Michael picked it up and threw it straight through the glass. He grabbed one of the pillows off the floor and used it to clear the frame of the remaining shards.

Evans shouted. The child was crying. Loud wails abruptly cut off. Evans screamed again, but he couldn't hear the words. Something slammed against the wall, shaking the foundation. A painting over the bed fell, raining glass over the bloody mattress.

He stepped out onto the roof. Scrambled to the edge and jumped without looking. He hit the ground and rolled; his ankles and knees screaming in protest. White-hot heat shot through his side, knocking the wind out of his lungs. His face took a dive in the dirt; twigs and pebbles grinded against his tongue. Lying on the ground, he gasped, unable to move, unable to breathe.

For half a minute he lay helpless, tears leaking out of the corners of his eyes and soaking the ground where his cheek rested. His body slowly came back to life as the air started to reach his lungs. Pressing his hands into the ground, he got onto his knees, puffing as if he'd just run a marathon. Dirt-colored drool escaped his lips.

He needed to move. They would be on top of him in seconds.

Finally his legs had enough strength and he managed to

start running, wobbly at first, swaying back and forth with drunken steps. He headed straight for the trees without looking back. He knew if he saw them coming after him, he'd freeze again, useless, and they'd be all over him, too.

MASON

Pop.

Pop.

Bang!

The world returned in an instant. His brain struggled to place mental imagery to the sounds. Not a car backfiring. Not gunshots. He knew that sound. He'd heard it enough times in the past. Someone was shooting off firecrackers just outside the window.

He couldn't have been unconscious for long. A few minutes, maybe—not enough time for Twiggy to do anything. Mason was still lying on the floor, head throbbing, hair soaked in tea. At least he hoped it was tea. The broken mug lay inches from his nose.

Twiggy was over at the window, head sticking out, leg bopping up and down as he screamed at the intruders.

"Heathens. Leave. You're not welcome here. Don't make me come down there and get you."

Mason sat up too quickly. Stars exploded across his vision, forcing the room into a spin faster than any amusement-park ride he'd ever encountered. He raised a hand to the side of his head; the fingertips came back bloody. Struggling onto his knees, he managed to stand by leaning against the wall for support. The door was still open; Twiggy hadn't bothered to close it after the attack.

"You." Twiggy turned his attention away from the window. He'd left his crutches by the bed. Bouncing up and down on his leg, he seemed to be deciding if he could cross the room before his prey got out the door.

Mason was closer. Reaching out, he picked up the crutches and threw them into the hall. His legs continued to sway, but the stars were gradually beginning to fade. Vision growing stronger, he found his bag on the floor and picked it up.

"You woke up sooner than I expected," Twiggy said. "What a shame." His face showed visible disappointment.

"Why?" Mason asked. "You could have killed me back on the street. Why all the acting?"

"Had you fooled, didn't I?" Twiggy said. "I always liked a show. Better than simply putting a bullet in your brain. I needed to see if I could convince you first."

"What the hell did I ever do to you? What did any of us do?"

Twiggy's face erupted in various shades of red. "Are you that stupid? Wait, don't say a word. You kids today think you know all the answers. You're nothing but a bunch of lazy bums. You're the reason society is faltering. It's because of you that the world needs to be cleansed. Because of you the voices come to us, turning some of us into mindless pack dogs. The rest of us receive clarity. I see everything that needs to be seen."

"That's an excuse."

"No excuse," Twiggy snapped. Spittle flew from his mouth. "We've been around for a long time, Mr. Dowell.

Longer than you or any of your stupid little friends could ever conceive. Sleeping in the shadows and waiting for the right moment. A disease you might call us. A plague. Evil. From beneath the ground, it rises as it has done many times in the past. It's given us our mission. We're cleansing. Removing the world of the filth it created. Rewriting, erasing the slate. How lucky we are to be a part of it. It chose me for a reason, and I am happy to serve. I'm one of the special ones, still able to keep my intelligence. My orders will be more complex and fulfilling than those of the insane heathens outside."

"So you're nothing but a dog, then," Mason sneered.

Twiggy laughed. "Do you know why some of you are allowed to stay alive? It's the fear. The pain. The enjoyment we get as we tear your skin to shreds. We feed on it."

"Maybe I'm just smarter than you," Mason replied. "Isn't that what you said? Free will? Maybe I'm able to fight it. But you're just weak. A sucker."

"You won't be singing that song when I tear the tongue from your throat."

Mason's legs were stronger. He calmly turned and stepped through the door. "Good luck with that, hoppy."

"You're all alone now," Twiggy screamed behind him. "We'll find you. You'll never hide long enough. We'll find you and kill each and every last one of you. All alone. Run, Mr. Dowell. You won't get far. Don't sleep! Don't sleep!"

He was fine with the hallway. The stairs required a bit more navigation. His balance was off, but he managed to get down by holding on to the banister and taking the steps one at a time. Twiggy continued to scream, and every time Mason glanced back, he half expected to see the old man hobbling toward him at full speed. But the staircase stayed empty.

Whatever world savior Twiggy thought he was, he knew his limitations. Next time he'd just have to hit his victim harder and make sure he stayed down.

Outside, the light burned straight into his brain, making him cringe. He paused at the door, unsure of what to do next.

First things first—he needed to get as far away from the building as possible. Then maybe he could find someplace to crawl into for a while until his brain stopped punishing him. What was the deal with concussions again? No sleeping. He'd have to stay awake. Maybe he could find a hotel with a swimming pool. Cold water would be a blessing and it would keep him clearheaded. It was a good idea. Up ahead he could see some signs for a Travelodge. Only a few blocks away; he could manage that. Close enough to walk to without dying, and far enough that Twiggy wouldn't follow.

It was hard moving. The sun pounded down on his back, making him sweat through his shirt. Squinting made his head want to explode, but the bright light made it throb worse. He kept his eyes on the ground, concentrating on moving each foot forward without tripping. His backpack weighed heavily on his shoulders, digging into his back, pushing him down.

He saw the couple cautiously coming toward him when he finally looked up. They were both wearing hiking clothes, with backpacks and sleeping bags. He froze, trying hard not to sway back and forth.

Keep cool, Dowell. Stand your ground.

"Hey," the guy said. "Need help?"

Mason didn't say anything. His knees shuddered. He was 100 percent positive he couldn't move another step. Something happened when Twiggy hit him: damage to his central nervous system or something.

"Hey," the girl said. They were closer now, almost on top of him. "You're really hurt."

"Stay away," he muttered.

"You're bleeding." She reached out to touch him, and he jerked back, almost toppling in the process.

"Watch out, Chee," the guy said. "He's scared."

"Screw you," Mason said.

"It's okay, man, we're cool."

"How do I know you're not one of them?"

The girl snorted, her hair flipping up behind her. "How do we know *you're* not one of them?"

"If I was, you'd be dead by now."

The girl stepped backward. "Well, if you're going to be a jerk about it . . . Come on, Paul. We don't need this."

But the guy didn't move. "We can't leave him. He'll be hunted down."

"He is pretty messed up."

Mason didn't know what to do. They seemed normal, but so had Twiggy. Who was he supposed to trust in this new world? More than that, who could trust him? Maybe that's why he was still alive and Twiggy hadn't killed him.

There was too much darkness inside his brain.

Until he knew for sure, he was better off alone. He knew this.

The guy sensed his wariness. "Look," he said. "We're cool. We're not gonna hurt you or try and rob you. We're in the same boat, man."

Mason decided to take the chance. "I'm sorry," he said. "Some crazy guy with one leg just invited me up to his place for tea and then tried to bash my head in with a mug. I'm a little short on trust right now."

"One leg?" The girl snorted again. "And he still managed to do that?"

"He seemed pretty normal at the start," Mason snapped, but a grin started to appear on his face. "I mean, how much trouble can a one-legged person be?"

"Is that some sort of bad joke, or are you really asking?" The girl grinned back.

"Little bit of both."

There was a short, awkward minute, while the girl visibly grew impatient. She glanced back and forth between them, shuffled her feet, and finally decided she'd had enough of the silence.

"I'm Barbara Flying Eagle, but everyone calls me Chickadee or Chee 'cause I'm so tiny. I hate Barbara, so don't ever call me that. Yuck. And this here is Paul Still Waters. We just call him Paul. But he's so tall, he won't hear you unless you shout."

Mason grinned again. The girl was definitely small. She had to be a little less than five feet tall. Her hair was long, almost down past her bum, making her appear even tinier, if it were possible. The guy beside her, Paul, was the complete opposite. He towered over her, gawky and serious; Mason instantly knew they were one of those couples that people always joked about in a friendly way. Night and day. Fire and ice.

"I'm Mason Dowell," he said.

"It's good to meet you," she said. "Now that we've got all that out of the way, I suggest we get the hell outta here. Didn't you hear the shots earlier?"

"I thought they were fireworks."

"Sure, the kind that come flying out the barrel of a gun."

They started walking, moving slower for Mason's sake. His legs were working again, but his head still felt fuzzy. Pain clawed at the insides of his skull. Chickadee and Paul stayed in the lead, walking about five feet ahead. They may have exchanged names, but neither side was taking any chances.

They were still strangers.

"Where are you headed, Mason?" Chickadee asked, keeping her voice low. She nodded toward his backpack.

"West," he said. Absently he reached his fingers into the back pocket of his jeans to make sure the Stanley Park picture was still there. "Vancouver."

"Cool," she said. "We're going north. Paul's got an uncle in the Yukon and we figure we'll head up there. Not a lot of people. Can't imagine it's been affected like it is here. His closest neighbor's about an hour away."

"Sounds like a good idea."

"It will be if we can last that long," Chickadee said. "It's pretty scary. We had some trouble this morning coming through the city. Did you see the fire? Couple of the crazies chased us, but we lost them in the smoke. They're bloody everywhere."

"I drove through some of it," Mason said. "But my car broke down a few blocks away. That's how I met Twiggy."

"We drove for a bit. Got stuck in one of those roadblocks a few weeks ago. They came at us with shotguns. I've never been so scared in my life. Luckily it was nighttime and we managed to hide in a wheat field. But we lost Trevor. He was my sister's boyfriend. My sister, she died a few weeks ago when this all started. I still dream about her every night. Paul lost his entire family because his older sister went crazy. Attacked everyone in the middle of the afternoon. I still don't know where my mom is. I'm hoping she's all right, but I doubt it. She didn't deal well, if you know what I mean."

Mason nodded. Chickadee waited a few minutes to see if he'd talk, but Mason wasn't ready to share. They'd just have to wonder. When he didn't speak, she continued to prattle on in a half whisper, filling the dead air with endless banter as they walked. He only listened halfheartedly, though. It was hard concentrating when his head throbbed the way it did.

"I need to stop," he said after a while. They were at the hotel he'd spotted earlier. "My head hurts," he added when they both looked at him. "But you can go on. I'm fine by myself."

Chickadee and Paul glanced at each other before she spoke. "No, it's cool. This place is as good as any, and I'm pretty tired myself. We can get separate rooms and lock each other out if you're still scared."

"I'm not scared of you," he said.

"Okay, just wary, then." She giggled. "But it's a good idea. It'll be dark soon. I don't like being out at night. Too hard to spot them coming."

The hotel had an indoor pool, but it would be a long time before people were able to enjoy the chlorine water again. They took adjoining rooms on the twelfth floor, figuring they'd be safest at the top. It was a long hike up, and by the time they got to their rooms Mason was ready to collapse. Normally he was in excellent shape. If Tom and his friends were watching him from heaven they were probably laughing their asses off.

They came to Mason's room first. Chickadee opened the lock and passed over the key. "Remember," she said. "We're right next door if you need anything."

"I'll be fine," he assured her. "Just need to lie down for a bit."

"You sure you don't have a concussion?" She eyed him cautiously.

"No," he said. "I don't think so. Just a headache. Wish I had some Tylenol, but I'll make do."

"I'll go get you some," she said. "Just let me drop my stuff. I saw a gift shop downstairs. I'll probably find a bottle there."

He didn't want her going back down all those stairs just for him. "I'll be fine," he said. "Honest."

"Okay."

"See ya," Paul added. It was the most he'd said in the past half hour. From what Mason could tell, Chickadee did all the talking for both of them.

He closed the door and tossed his backpack on the floor. The room was dark—no electricity of course—so he moved to the window and opened the curtains a little bit. He didn't think anyone would notice him that far up, but it was better to be safe than sorry. Glancing down onto the street below, he could see some people trashing a car with what might have been a baseball bat or a crowbar. A few blocks over to the right, a group of people had cornered someone. They were closing in on the kill. Even farther away, a group of people were stacking bodies into what looked like a gigantic bonfire.

Mason didn't watch after that. He lay down and tried not to think about it. Next door he could hear Chickadee jumping on the bed. Her muffled voice was cheery.

He wanted to be alone. Yes, he knew that. But at the same time, he was thankful he'd run into them. Chickadee's cheerfulness was contagious, and Paul looked like the kind of guy he'd want on his side if he was backed into a corner.

Closing his eyes, he fell asleep.

He awoke to a small tapping on his door. It took him a moment to remember where he was. The darkness was disorientating, and he couldn't understand why he was sleeping in a strange bed. Twiggy must have hit him harder than he first thought.

"Mason?" Chickadee's voice was soft through the wooden frame.

"Yeah, hold on a sec." Rolling over, he pulled himself up into a sitting position and immediately checked his head. There was a lot of dried blood, and it hurt when he pressed his fingers at the spot, but his headache was gone, along with the dizzy sensation.

His knees didn't buckle when he stood, and he took that as a good sign. Stumbling over his shoes, he maneuverd through the darkened room and tried to find the door. Chickadee waited with a candle in one hand, a gift shop bag in the other. Paul stood behind her munching on a bag of tortilla chips.

"I brought you some stuff," she said. "Don't bother to pay me back. I'm loaded these days. Money to burn."

Mason grinned. "Hold on," he said. "I've got the curtains slightly open. Let me close them before you come in with that light."

They waited at the door while he checked the window. The streets looked so tiny below him; he couldn't see much of anything. If the monsters were out there, they were camouflaged by the night.

"I brought you some Advil," she said. She pulled a tiny bottle out of the bag and tossed it at him. "Couldn't find any Tylenol."

"Thanks." He turned the bottle over in his hand but didn't open it. "My head feels better. I'm not sure I need this."

"That's good." Reaching back into the bag, she pulled out a six-pack of root beer. "I didn't get any booze," she said. "I had a feeling you probably wouldn't want any and Paul doesn't drink."

"That's fine," he said. "Yeah, I think I've had enough head pain to last me a while. I'll stick to sugar." He cracked the can and took a long drink. The root beer was warm, but he didn't mind.

"Most of the food's gone bad in the kitchen," she said. "But I managed to find some peanut butter and crackers." She turned the bag over and dumped it on the bed. It was mostly junk—potato chips and chocolate bars—but there were also a few wrinkled apples, along with the aforementioned peanut butter and box of saltines.

"Wow," he said.

He didn't touch the food. His stomach was too jumpy, so he stuck with the root beer and ended up swallowing a few of the Advil just to play it safe.

Paul and Chickadee divvied up the crackers, sticking their fingers in the peanut butter since she'd forgotten to grab a knife. They ate in silence for a while, the candle flickering softly on the bedside table.

"We'd like to come with you," Paul said eventually.

"Huh?" He'd been absorbed in his own thoughts.

"We want to go west," Paul said.

Mason stared at him blankly.

"We're not really heading north," Chickadee said. "I mean, we want to, but we don't really know where Paul's uncle lives. We don't even have an address. I guess it's just kinda a pipe dream?"

"Oh." Mason shrugged. "I guess that doesn't help."

"But if we go with you, at least we'd be together," Chickadee said. "We like you. Paul and I. We'd be safer as a group."

Mason shrugged.

"We don't take up much space," Chickadee said, sensing his reluctance. "Really, Paul may be a giant, but he's quite quiet. You won't even notice he's here. I'm a different story. I have this habit of talking endlessly, but most people find it charming. Why else would I be named after the cutest bird in history?"

"It's not that," he said. "I'm just not sure it's a good idea." How could he tell them the truth? That he didn't want them to come because of his darkness. He didn't deserve company. He wanted to be left alone so he didn't have to watch out for others and take care of anyone else too. He could be tougher by himself.

"Three pairs of eyes are better than one."

Mason swallowed.

Chickadee leaned in close. She continued to stare at him, refusing to blink. He couldn't help it; he broke into a smile.

"See," she said, leaning back and grinning, too. "You can't resist me."

He glanced over at Paul, but the taller guy didn't seem to be paying him any attention. Looking out the window, Mason figured he was obviously happy enough letting her do the negotiating. Paul knew what Mason was just learning for himself. Chickadee was good at getting her own way.

"So you want to go west, then?" he asked.

"West is warmer than north," Paul said. "Hell, it's warmer than here, even with the Chinooks. It's gonna be cold soon. Polar bear cold. I think we should head for the coast. Vancouver's really the best place to be. It doesn't get cold there. Mostly just a lot of rain. It'll get us through the winter alive."

Chickadee nodded. Her mouth was full of peanut butter. She chewed several times and swallowed. "I love Vancouver. I haven't been there in about two years. I'd love a chance to swim in the ocean again."

"Okay," Mason said. "Let's do it."

He'd worry about everything else later. It's not like he couldn't leave them if things went downhill.

"I'm so excited," Chickadee said. "This is the first time in a long while I've felt happy about something."

"Me too," Mason said, and he was surprised because it was true.

The next morning they gathered in the lobby, where Mason grabbed a map book from the gift shop. There were only a few roads between Calgary and the coast. They'd have to be careful.

NOTHING

I'm back.

I think I missed me.

There's blood under my fingernails. Dried on my clothing; matted in my hair; stained on my shoes. It's seeped through my skin, mixed with my own DNA, and I've absorbed all of its power.

I'm pretty sure it's not mine.

Life is a blur. I go in and out of time. The gray light takes over my body, eats my mind, and leaves me with the voices. I hear them. They curl up inside my frontal cortex and force all the warmth from my blood. Existence. Am I existing?

Why am I conscious when so many others are not? Are they doing this on purpose, and if so, why? Or is my brain wired differently from the average person's? What makes me stronger? Sometimes I wake up, and even if just for a moment, I'm aware of the things I've done. I'm pretty sure there aren't a lot who go back and forth the way I do. If all of them are having the same moments of clarity, I think there would be less killing. Less destruction. I can barely live with myself.

I wish I could stop remembering. I don't want to remember.

If they're going to steal my mind and control my body, why do they insist on giving me occasional freedom? If I must kill, then why do they torture me with blow-by-blow replays?

The girl. I remember her. So young. So pretty. I wanted to help her, but I can't be trusted. She was confused and I understand that. She wanted to be a part of something good. But I could see her darkness. The potential to kill was already inside her soul. She was no different from the others, only she didn't see it yet.

Eventually they will come to all of us. The chaos they've created will transform to a new world order.

Death will be a dream.

ARIES

"I'm not doing it."

"You agreed. Just like the rest of us."

"I changed my mind."

They sat in a half circle in a tiny one-bedroom apartment on the second floor. Jack was in the middle, holding a cardboard box with all their names thrown in. The rules were simple, and everyone agreed to it. Three names would be drawn, whoever got picked would take the trip. They were running out of food. This needed to be done.

Joy's name was the first drawn. She didn't say a word.

Aries's name came next. She'd planned it that way with Jack when she first approached him about the idea.

"Make sure you put my name somewhere you can easily pull it," she said. "I'm not sending them off without me. Consider me a silent volunteer."

"Let me come too, then." Jack brushed a strand of sandy brown hair from his eyes. "You're not going without me."

"No," she said. "You need to stay here in case I don't come back. So make sure you don't pick yourself."

Anyway, that was the plan. They all agreed. With Joy and

Aries on the list, they needed only one more. But Colin wasn't so eager when his name was chosen last.

"I'm not doing it," he said.

"Christ, I'll go," Nathan said. He took the box from Jack and started searching for his name. "I don't mind. I want to go."

"No," Aries said. "We all agreed. He can't go back on his word."

"I've got a cold," Colin said. "I'm not leaving this building unless I'm in perfect health. It's too risky."

"It's one excuse after the other with you," Eve said. She lowered her voice to try to match Colin's tone. "I'm too tired. I can't cook. I don't wanna!"

"Eve, stop it," Nathan said.

"I'm just tired of it," Eve said. "He's not very useful. And now he's going to screw everyone else because he's a coward."

Colin jumped to his feet. "You take that back."

"Make me."

"Children!" Jack jumped in between them. "Play nice. I'll go. I'll take Colin's place."

"No," Aries said.

"Okay, this needs to end," Nathan said calmly. "It's not worth the argument. I'm going and that's final."

Aries nodded at him. Nathan was right. Lately Colin picked a fight over every suggestion. He never wanted to do anything or be helpful. He wouldn't take a guard shift at night; instead he made excuses about how tired he was. He wouldn't help search the rooms for useful items; it was Joy who found the bicycles in the storage room. The world may have changed, but Colin hadn't. He was arrogant as always; being difficult was just another day for him. Of course, he wasn't the only one. They were all at each other's throats these days. Blame it on the lack of food, lack of space, lack of comfort, the inability to remain calm and collected. But Colin seemed to go out of his way to work the others into a pissing frenzy.

Nathan was right. It wasn't worth the argument.

"Fine," she said. "Nathan, Joy, and I will make the trip."

Jack slammed the box down on the table and left the room.

Aries started to chase after him and then stopped herself. She couldn't make everyone happy and she was tired of having the peace-keeping job. Jack would cool off on his own. There were more important matters to deal with.

"Let's plan this, then," she said.

"I'm going to go make some tea," Eve said. "Anyone want?"

Eve left with her orders. Aries stared at Colin, who sat back down on the floor and started leafing through an old magazine. He acted as if the argument never happened, as if he hadn't just forced Nathan to make a trip that he'd agreed to when he put his name in the box. It was *Alice in Wonderland* all over again, with Colin making a scene because everything wasn't going according to *his* plan.

Finally she turned her back on Colin and sat down with Joy and Nathan. She would be the bigger person. She'd get over it. Being this annoyed was terrible. It was a side of herself she didn't like seeing. Plus it was too exhausting, and she needed to save her strength.

"I'm thinking we should take the bikes," she said. "They're in good shape, Jack looked them over. We'll be faster that way—but more in the open."

"What happens if we find other normal people?" Nathan said. "I think you're right. There's got to be lots out there."

"That's why I want to pick up some handheld receivers. If we're going to start searching the city, we need to keep in touch."

"Agreed," Joy said. "Let's make a list of the important things besides food. Less stinky blankets for one. I need a coat, too. And let's not forget weapons. We need to arm ourselves."

"We all need coats," Nathan said. "This could get heavy. Are you sure we can manage with bikes? We could steal a car. Anyone know how to hot-wire?"

Colin snickered.

Aries ignored him. "Cars are loud. Might as well slap a Here I Am sticker on our foreheads. They'll follow the sound. If we can make it in without them knowing, we'll have more time to shop. I don't want us getting trapped inside."

"And we don't want to drag them back here either," Joy agreed. "So far they haven't found us. I'd like to keep it that way."

"Me too," Aries said.

"Okay," Nathan said. "Bikes it is. Maybe we can get some of those large camping backpacks. That way we can take more stuff."

Colin snickered again.

"Do you have something you'd like to say?" Aries asked.

"Nope," Colin said, never taking his eyes off the magazine. "You're doing just fine. Keep on planning. If you find any hot female survivors, send them my way. I could use a change of scenery."

"Why are you even here?" Joy asked. "You've made it clear you don't want to be a part of this. So why don't you just take off? Go read somewhere else. I don't want to look at you."

Colin threw the magazine aside and jumped to his feet. "Wish granted," he said before disappearing into the hallway.

"He's horrible," Joy whispered after he stormed off. "He complains about everything and everyone. Yesterday he screamed at me because the coffee's gone. I don't even drink coffee."

"He's having trouble adjusting," Aries said. "I think he . . . misses Sara too."

"If he's so miserable he should just leave."

"Where would he go?"

"Right now I don't care."

Aries didn't either, but she kept her comments to herself.

Part of her wished that she'd never gone to the school. She should have ignored Daniel's warnings and tried finding her parents. She might have reached them or ended up someplace completely different, with people she'd never met before. People who didn't constantly remind her of everything she'd lost. She still couldn't look at Colin and not see Sara. No, that wasn't fair. Both Joy and Jack were good people; together they'd helped one another. She couldn't have come this far without them.

She had to take the good with the bad. She'd put up with Colin because no one else would. She'd continue to defend him because they were a group and they had to stay a group in order to survive. If things got to the point where they started turning their backs on each other and kicking people onto the street, well, then they weren't any better than the monsters.

"Let's go take a look at the bikes," Nathan said, trying his best to change the subject.

"Okay," Joy said. "I get the blue one."

Night came quickly.

Aries had a list. It was tucked away in her jeans pocket. Nathan and Joy each had one too. They discussed it for hours, trying to reduce the necessary items to the bare essentials. No point in carrying what they didn't absolutely need. If they pulled this off successfully, then they'd try again. Her job was to find clothing and sleeping bags. Nathan and Joy were on food duty.

The store was roughly eighteen blocks away. One of those big all-in-one, shop-till-you-drop, everything-under-one-gigantic-roof places. They weren't even sure they'd be able to get inside. They didn't know who might be there waiting or if it was still standing. The earthquake destroyed so much, and lately there'd been lots of fires. The city was covered in a smoky haze. So many what-ifs. But they had to try.

They waited behind the locked door while Jack and Eve checked to make sure the streets were empty. Aries absently squeezed the brakes on her handlebars. It was like psyching themselves up for war, bicycle messengers heading out to acquire foodstuffs to save their troops.

"I feel like I'm getting ready for a journey into hell," Joy said. "I used to love shopping."

"Me too," Aries said. "But I don't remember it being such a violent sport. Except maybe on Black Friday."

Nathan gave them a forced grin through the murky room.

"All clear!" Eve poked her head out from the top of the stairs. "Don't go right. A group of them just headed off in that direction. Straight ahead is clear, but there's a lot of smoke two blocks over by the Irish Pub. Low Road's clear. I'd head that way."

Nathan waited while Eve raced down the stairs. It would be their first time apart since this whole ordeal began. Although she was trying hard to be strong, Aries could see the worry in her eyes. She threw her arms around him and held on tightly.

"I'll be back," Nathan told her when it became apparent she was having trouble releasing him.

"You'd better," she whispered, reluctantly letting go. "I still need you."

Nathan nodded and turned back to the group. "Let's do it." Reaching out, he unlocked the deadbolt and gave the iron doors a hard shove. Fresh night air swept over Aries's face. For the first time in weeks she found herself wishing it was raining. The pelting drops would have helped cover the noise they were about to make.

"Remember," Aries said, "if we get in trouble, split up. We'll meet again at the back of the store. The loading docks. It'll be darker than the parking lot. And if there's trouble, go inside and get what you can."

"Sounds good," Nathan said.

Joy nodded.

Pushing her bike out into the street, Aries placed her foot on the pedal and lifted her leg over the saddle. The bike was small and Jack had raised the seat so that her knees wouldn't be hitting the handlebars. He'd found a small bottle of oil in the maintenance room and spent most of the day oiling the chains to guarantee less friction.

They pushed off silently into the night. Tires crunched against the cement, but the noise was minimal. Unless they directly crossed paths with one of the killers, they'd be able to make it to the shop without being discovered. Although her heart jumped around in her chest, the muscles in her arms relaxed a little. The air cooled her face, and she inhaled deeply, such a wonderful change from the moldy apartment.

It was hard.

The earthquake destroyed a lot of the city. Most of the buildings were still somewhat attached, but glass littered the streets, and pieces of concrete and brick made everything more challenging. There were holes in the roads too, some of which sank deep into the earth.

Abandoned cars filled the streets, making it impossible to

bike in a straight line. The roads became a maze in which they were forced to crawl along, weaving in and out between the silent machines. Many of the car doors were left open, adding to the obstacle course. Aries turned left to bypass a van and swerved to avoid riding straight into a mailbox.

There were bodies on the roads, on the sidewalks, in cars, on benches, everywhere. Some of them were seriously starting to decompose. The fresh air that felt so wonderful on her face began to change. The smell of rotting flesh reached her lungs and was absorbed into her clothing.

She began to breathe heavier. The ride got even harder; she was out of shape after hiding out in the apartment for the past three weeks. Her calves ached and sweat poured down her forehead and into her eyes. She kept rubbing her face, and soon her hands were slippery with perspiration. Her handlebars grew sticky. She glanced over at Nathan, who barely looked winded at all. Joy, however, lagged behind them, and Aries felt better knowing she wasn't the only one having trouble.

When they got through this, she would start exercising on a daily basis. Running up and down the stairs or doing push-ups—whatever she could do to keep healthy.

She almost didn't notice when Nathan hit the brakes. Pulling on the hand gears, she stopped hard, almost flipping herself right over the front tire.

"What's going on?" Joy whispered.

"Over there," Nathan said.

They all looked at once.

A block ahead, a group of people moved down the street. The darkness made it impossible to see any faces, but there were too many of them to take a chance on finding out.

"This way," Nathan said. Turning his bike to the left, he

jumped the sidewalk and headed straight into a courtyard. Aries and Joy followed.

"Do you think they saw us?" Joy asked. They were moving slower now. The cobblestone was slippery and the tires wobbled side to side on the uneven surface.

"Not sure," Nathan said.

They passed through the courtyard and into the next street over. They continued in the direction of the store, but Aries knew something was wrong. It was too quiet.

They were waiting for them at the intersection. Two dozen people or so emerged from the shadows. They came from all directions at once, running, closing the gap.

"Split up!" Nathan screamed.

Aries turned her bike left, toward the closest group. She took the direct approach, straight through the crowd. Someone grabbed hold of her shirt, almost yanking her backward. She managed to stay on her bike by delivering a blind kick. She heard a loud grunt as her foot struck home, and the hand on her shirt loosened.

She didn't look back to see how the others were doing. There wasn't enough time. Hitting her brakes, she swerved to avoid a greasy-haired attacker, turned sharp toward the right again, and pushed all her weight onto the pedals, picking up speed but going in the wrong direction.

The street ahead was clear. Behind her, shoes slapped the pavement, and people screamed and swore, but the sounds began to decrease as she gained speed. She kept up the pace for a few blocks and then turned again. There was a path she knew would take her back in the right direction. There were no more sounds behind her, but she was too spooked to turn around and look. Up ahead she could see the road she needed to take. Increasing her speed, she pumped her legs with everything she had.

She hit the corner too sharp and felt the tires slide out from underneath her. Her jaw clamped down as she hit the pavement, cutting off the scream that should have come from her lips. Her jeans tore as she sailed across the ground; gravel and dirt bit through her skin, blazing a trail of white-hot fire against her leg.

When she opened her eyes, she expected to see a group of people staring down at her. But the streets were empty. She listened, but there were no more footfalls. No screams. Nothing. All she could see was the night sky glaring down at her. Pulling herself up, her entire body resisted, screaming at her. Everything hurt—even her eyelids complained.

But she couldn't afford to listen.

Legs shaky, she picked up her bicycle from where it lay spread out beside an abandoned car. The forks were a little bent and the handlebars were scuffed, but the chain was still on and the tires looked like they'd turn. Limping, she pushed the bike a few feet to make sure it wasn't broken. Climbing back on, she ignored the pain and started pedaling. When she got to the store, she'd take the time to check out her damage. Until then she'd grit her teeth and fight the throbbing mess that used to be her body.

It took her a few blocks before she got back on track. She wasn't overly familiar with the area, and it was even harder at night with the shadows mixing up her sense of direction. But eventually she found the path that led along the inlet and farther into the city. She moved silently, aching, her heart beating rapidly against her chest.

She almost cried out in relief when she saw the store. It stood out against the night, the bright white building with miles of empty parking spots. It didn't appear damaged. Even the windows were intact as she pedaled up to the front. She tried the doors, but they were locked. Cupping her hands against the glass, she peered inside but couldn't see much. The store was dark, the aisles empty. Nothing seemed out of order.

It was a miracle that it had lasted this long without being looted. But they chose it because it was farther out in the industrial area and hopefully there'd be fewer people. Maybe this had saved it. The Costco was much closer, but it was in the middle of downtown, and they'd all agreed it was more of a risk.

She decided to head around to the back and see if the others were there. A small voice in her head spoke to her, asking her what she'd do if Nathan and Joy didn't show up. She tried to ignore it, but it was strong.

She'd have to be stronger.

Behind the building, she climbed off her bicycle and pushed it as she walked the length of the store. The loading docks were at the other end. The big double doors were pulled down and locked tightly. She stepped up to the side entrance and tried the handle. If it was locked she'd have to try and find another way in. She didn't know the first thing about breaking into buildings.

It opened.

Stale air hit her face. It was pitch-black inside. She stood at the door for a few minutes, listening to the emptiness of the building. If someone was inside they might not have heard her open the door. But if someone was inside hiding, wouldn't they have locked the door to begin with? It would have been the first thing she'd do. She pulled out the flashlight Jack found back at the apartment block and turned it on, shining it inside the massive room. There wasn't much there, lots of boxes, a receiving desk, and two hallways that led off in different directions.

There was no indication that anything had been disturbed recently. None of the boxes were opened, and the receiving desk had a thin layer of dust on it. She tried shining the flashlight on the floor, looking for fresh footprints in the dust. She couldn't see anything.

Pushing her way through the back doors, she moved onto the sales floor, carefully scanning the area to make sure it was clear.

She stopped in electronics first to grab some batteries. They were a much-needed asset for the flashlights. At the Duracell section something caught her attention and she moved farther down the aisle. In front of her were dozens of handheld receivers. Walkie-talkies, her father used to call them. He had given her a pair when she was younger. They used to take them camping and talk to each other, pretending they were survivors in the wilderness. She pulled down two of the most expensive packages she could find.

She was about to move on when someone coughed.

She ignored the pain in her leg and spun around. The aisle was empty. Cold shivers ran along her spine. She'd definitely heard something. But from where? And who? It couldn't be Nathan and Joy. They would have said something.

Cautiously she moved along the row, stepping quietly, preparing herself for the moment when something jumped out at her. But nothing happened. She turned the corner, holding the flashlight ahead of her body, ready to use it as a weapon if need be. But the main aisle was empty too.

Maybe she was hearing things. But then something caught her eye over by the bedding displays, a pink futon with purple pillows.

A shadow moved. She heard the click of another flashlight as the bright light shone straight into her eyes, blinding her. She squinted, trying to see.

The light fell away from her face as the person in front of her dropped to their knees. A man wearing a black hoodie and torn jeans rocked back and forth several times before toppling over on his side, the flashlight falling from his fingers. He didn't make a sound as he landed on his stomach, his face away from her. Black hair spread out across his cheeks. She moved toward him, wondering if she should say something. She wished she had a proper weapon. She should have gone into the sporting-goods section and grabbed a baseball bat. Why didn't she think of that before?

Aries moved closer until she could see the man's face.

The breath caught in her throat.

It was Daniel.

CLEMENTINE

Her sneakers had a hole in them. She couldn't remember ever wearing a hole through a pair of shoes before. Not like this. Not from walking.

She was tired. Her legs ached in a way they'd never hurt before. Her feet were on constant fire. There was a permanent knot in her lower back, and her shoulders hurt from carrying the backpack. She knew she should be taking breaks but was afraid she'd be unable to get up again once she sat down. For two days she'd continued down the road. Two days without seeing a single person. The latter she wasn't complaining about, although in this new world she missed having people to talk to.

Dear Heath, I talk to you a lot these days. It's kinda nice, although I wish you could actually talk back. I miss you. I don't think I ever thought about it before. You were always there, even if it was just a phone call. But did we ever have full conversations? You're my brother. Shouldn't we have said more?

I really hope you're alive and waiting for me. It'll justify all this talking in my head. I'll know that I really am reaching you and not a ghost.

She thought about the last sentence and repeated it a few times over in her mind. She didn't want to believe but secretly accepted that there was a good possibility her brother no longer existed in this world. She tried not to think about it. She wanted to continue being the optimist. She needed that destination; if Heath was dead, then her journey was pointless. Where else would she go?

If you are dead and in heaven or whatever sort of afterlife you've discovered, tell Mom and Dad I'm doing fine and that they don't need to worry about me. They raised one tough cheerleader daughter. Go team!

She stopped, reached back, and grabbed her water bottle, which had been filled at the last stream she'd passed. Taking a long drink, she barely even noticed the cool liquid slide across her tongue. Nothing tasted right anymore. Even her taste buds were exhausted. When was the last time she ate? She couldn't remember. Food no longer held any interest.

Night came, but she barely noticed. Her feet continued to slap the pavement, one step at a time. Right, left, right, and again left. One and two and three and four, one and two and three and four, two-four-six-eight who do we appreciate? Yay, Glenmore Goblins! Football seasons and forgotten cheers haunted her mind. A repetition of rhymes echoed with each step. A few times she almost walked right off the road, only noticing when her shoes stumbled over grassy hills instead of pavement.

When she finally fell, it didn't register in her brain until she was tumbling through the air. Surprised, she didn't even have time to put out her arms to brace herself. She hit the grass sideways and rolled down the embankment and into the ditch. Landing on her back, she blinked several times before realizing she was staring up at the night sky.

It was glorious. Millions of stars glittered down at her, the moon full and bright, a perfect circle. She could see the craters etched on its surface. She reached out her hand and tried to touch it, but it was just beyond her reach.

"The Big Dipper," she spoke out loud. "Cassiopeia. Orion's Belt."

These stars would always be here. Hundreds of millions of years in the future, when mankind was gone from this earth, they'd still exist.

How long till she was gone?

I'm going crazy, Heath. I've heard of that happening before. Lack of sleep can do strange things to people. I just need to rest, but I can't sleep. I'm so afraid. I don't know what to do. Help me.

There were no answers. Heath wasn't taking her calls.

It was peaceful lying there in the ditch. She knew she should get up and continue on. But she couldn't. Her legs finally decided they'd had enough.

I'm paralyzed.

The fear left her. Nothing she could do. Nothing except close her eyes. It would be so wonderful to do that.

So she did.

She woke with a start. Confused, she sat up abruptly, immediately scanning the area for clues. Her clothing was damp and covered in evening dew. She couldn't remember why she was there.

As she pulled herself up, her knees popped, and her legs were stiff. Stretching, she walked back up to the road and looked around. She was in the middle of nowhere, on a road she couldn't remember. Bits and pieces came back to her: tripping and falling into the ditch, staring up at the stars.

The sun was in the west. She looked down at her watch

and saw it was a little past four. That meant she'd been asleep for over sixteen hours. She didn't remember a single thing. There were no dreams, just blissful, obviously well-needed, deep sleep.

So that was the big secret, huh, Heath. All I had to do was walk myself to the brink of death before I finally managed to get some shut-eye. I guess in a way it was a good thing. I didn't die. They didn't find me. Maybe now my brain won't start to freak out every time I try to sleep.

She took a long drink of water and started walking.

She found the main highway around six. She followed the sun and turned right. The road was completely empty, not even a single parked car that she could borrow. By seven the sun was beginning to set, turning the sky a brilliant reddish pink.

She didn't exactly know where she was anymore. Maybe Montana. The countryside was changing. No mountains yet, but they were coming. She could see them just beyond the horizon, small, bumpy breasts on the landscape. Soon she'd be right in the middle of the Rockies. Hopefully she'd have a car again by then.

Dusk was completely upon her when she turned the corner of the road and saw the beginning of a town. Stretched out in between the trees was a gas station with a large parking lot filled with empty cars. She could see a sign up ahead but couldn't read it from where she stood.

"Finally," she muttered.

She would tread carefully. She stepped off the road and into the woods, determined to walk around to the back of the building first to make sure it was empty. But it was easier said than done. She was a prairie girl, used to wheat fields and flat open skies; going through the underbrush was alien territory. Branches snagged at her hair. Her arms collected scratches, and twice her feet got stuck in the millions of roots that seemed to have no purpose except to trip her up.

Ahead she could see a clearing in the fading twilight. Excited, she pushed herself along, climbing over some rocks and navigating a monstrous tree stump. The terrain spread out before her, a strange puzzle that required full concentration. Her focus was so intense, she almost walked face-first into the legs. A small yelp poured from her throat when she looked up and saw the body attached to them.

Scrambling sideways, she hit another one. The body jolted, spinning around lazily from her touch.

They were everywhere. Dozens of bodies hung from the trees. Some of them had their hands tied behind their backs. They swayed in the breeze. The ropes around their necks continued up into the high branches above. She moved forward into the clearing until she was surrounded. The smell hit her, assaulting her stomach, forcing the water she'd drunk earlier to rise into her throat. Pulling her shirt up over her nose and mouth, she held her breath.

She studied the clearing until she found a path that led her from the death site without her having to touch any more of the bodies. Running along the trail, she couldn't get away fast enough. She didn't stop until she came out at the side of the gas station.

She would go in and get what she needed. Find the keys to one of the parked cars and get the hell out. She didn't want to linger. Not while all those bodies were so close.

The front doors of the gas station were busted. Glass covered the ground, and she carefully stepped over it, trying to make as little noise as possible. Inside, the place was trashed. The aisles were littered with chocolate bars, chips, and all other sorts of roadside goodies. Motor oil bottles had been opened and thrown against the walls, leaving a slippery pattern on the floor. Footprints led behind the counter, where the cash register lay opened and emptied. Cigarette packages were strewed across the surface.

The glass doors to the cooler were shattered. Most of the items were gone, but she managed to grab a few bottles of water and a can of Pepsi that had a big dent in it.

Just beyond the counter were doors that led into the truck-stop restaurant. She decided to try her luck over there. More than anything else in the world she wanted to find food that didn't come from a can. Stepping past a toppled gum machine, she carefully avoided the colorful marble-sized balls. The last thing in the world she needed was a broken ankle.

The restaurant was gloomy. The sun was almost completely set, nothing left but a bit of reddish glow. The blinds had been pulled down, the coffeepots smashed; the remains of month-old key lime pie stuck to the walls.

She wouldn't have even seen the guy in the corner except he moved. Instantly she froze, debating how many steps to the door and whether or not she could get there before he grabbed her.

"You can relax," he said. "I'm cool."

He sat in the back booth, his hand cupping a mug, spinning it around casually as if he was simply waiting for the waitress to bring him a refill. He was young, around her age, his long brown hair combed back from his face and tucked behind his ears. She couldn't make out his eyes in the fading light, but the look on his face was gentle. Sad. But everyone looked sad these days.

"Are you?" she asked. "Why are you sitting there in the dark?"

"No place else to go."

She nodded. She completely understood that.

"But you can get what you want. I won't move." The guy held up his hands and placed them on the table. "I'd leave, but I just don't think I have the energy."

She moved closer to him. The voices inside her head didn't scream to run. There was so much sorrow in his voice. If he was tricking her, then he was the best actor she'd ever met.

"You're not going to run?" He sounded surprised.

She shrugged. "Should I?"

The guy chuckled. "I said I was safe, didn't I? Maybe I need to be more cautious of you. But you strike me as normal. Though, what is normal these days? I don't think I know anymore."

His fingers were long and graceful. She'd always been attracted to hands, something about them, the way they moved. His looked like a musician's; they tapped against the table to a silent tune.

"Do you live here?" she asked. "I mean this town. Not this diner."

He shook his head. "Just passing through. You came from around the back. I watched you walk past. You saw the bodies, didn't you."

"Yeah."

"I think they rounded up the entire town. There are more in the streets. They've hung them from the lampposts. I think they gathered them up and hung them like some old-fashioned vigilante thing. Only I don't think the Baggers are extracting justice."

"Baggers?" She sat down across from him at the table. "Why do you call them Baggers?"

"I dunno. Got it from Billy. Said he overheard it from this

guy down South. It's 'cause when they catch you, they bag the hell outta you. Like when someone says 'I'm gonna go bag me a deer.' But they're killing more than deer, aren't they."

"Makes sense." She wanted to ask him who Billy was, but the look in his eyes when he mentioned the name was enough to make her not do it. Instead she offered up her hand to shake. "I'm Clementine."

"Michael." He took her hand and gave it a quick pump before going back to twisting his cup. There was a bit of liquid at the bottom, and she could smell the alcohol on his breath. Not like it mattered out here—no one was going to card him.

She pulled out her dented Pepsi and opened it. Took a long drink. The carbonated sugar water felt wonderful on her tongue. She put the can down and waited for him to speak. It was awkward; she didn't really know what to say. It had been too long since she'd talked to someone.

The last of the sun was gone and they were sitting in the shadows now. Soon it would be too dark and they'd have to use a candle. She had some in her backpack but didn't bring them out. They'd have to go into the back room. From where they sat, a little light might attract someone.

"Where are you headed?" he finally asked.

Relief washed over her. She could answer this one. "Seattle. My brother, Heath, is there. At least I hope he's there, I don't really know for sure. We couldn't get ahold of him after the earthquake, and my mom and I were going to head out together. But that didn't work out so well. My . . . my parents were shot down along with the rest of my town. I think, well, I'm pretty sure I was the only one who got out."

"Does that make you lucky?"

She shrugged. "I guess you could say that. What about you?"

Anger flashed in his eyes. His fingers froze on the mug, gripping it until his knuckles turned white. "My family is dead," he finally said through gritted teeth. "At least I think so. I haven't seen them since this started. And so is the group I was traveling with. The Baggers found us, and if it's all right with you, I'd rather not talk about it."

"I'm sorry."

"It's not your fault." Reaching down onto the seat, he pulled out the bottle of whiskey and poured himself another. "Want some?"

She shook her head. She wasn't much of a drinker; she tended to get physically sick once the room started to spin. It made even less sense to drink these days, but she wasn't about to tell him that. It wasn't her business.

"I'm done anyway after this," he said. "I can tell you're not impressed. But I'm not drinking to get drunk. Just needed one. It's been one of those days."

"It's okay," she said. "I understand that."

"Besides, it's not safe to get too whacked out. Never know if they're watching."

She nodded again. "Do you think they're still around?"

"The ones who did all the hanging? No, they're long gone. I spent the afternoon searching the town. If they were here, they would have found me by now. I've been sitting in this spot for a few hours. Made it real easy for them to come get me."

She didn't know what to say. It almost sounded like he had a death wish, waiting in the dark for the monsters to come.

"Why don't we make some dinner," he said, as if reading her mind and wanting to change the subject. "Are you hungry? I found a little Coleman stove and some propane back at the hardware store. There's not much to work with, but I'll bet I can throw something together. I'm pretty decent. Used to do all the cooking for my dad."

"Sure."

They moved into the kitchen, where she was able to bring out her candles and get them some light. The only windows into the room were on the door, and she covered them up with newspaper and taped it in place. Anyone passing by wouldn't see a thing.

She found some potatoes that looked pretty decent and started boiling water on the stove while Michael went through the cans looking for something decent to work with. To their surprise the big walk-in freezer was still cool, and they found some semi-defrosted hamburger meat and decided to take a chance. They ended up with chili burgers, mashed potatoes, and some half-melted ice cream for dessert.

"Enjoy," he said. "This is probably the last time you'll ever get ice cream and hamburgers. It'll be a long time before anyone makes anything that doesn't come out of a can. It's not like we can start planting gardens anytime soon. And I don't know about you, but I'm not really the type to go out and kill a cow."

"As long as I'm not forced to eat Spam and canned turnips, I'll survive," she said. "I don't get Spam. What exactly is it? Ham? Lunch meat? It's creepy."

"Maybe a bit of both?" He bit into his second burger, leaving chili sauce at the corner of his mouth. "I agree, it's nasty."

"I guess I can't complain," she said. "I've been living off Oreos and Goldfish crackers since this whole thing started. I think I've drank enough Red Bull to last a lifetime. And I don't even like Red Bull. It tastes like cow pee."

Michael laughed. "You're a connoisseur of fine tastes. However will you survive this apocalypse?"

"I don't know. Maybe I can find a sushi place that still delivers."

It was nice. The food tasted amazing and the conversation was fun. It reminded her of happier days. For the first time in weeks she was enjoying herself. She let down her guard and forgot about all the dangers outside. She hadn't realized how much she needed it. Michael seemed to be doing better, too. The pained expression on his face softened, and when he laughed, she saw some sparkle in his eyes.

"I never asked you where you're going?" she said after they'd finished their meals. She sipped on a bottle of orange juice while he drank one of her water bottles.

"Haven't really been going anywhere," he replied. "I was with a group of people and we were pretty much just going around looking for food. Never had any destination in mind, just wanted to be somewhere safe. That didn't work out so well."

"You're welcome to come with me."

He looked away from her and studied the kitchen for the longest time. She became embarrassed. Had she done something wrong? Asked too soon? Was there some sort of grace period in this new world? Maybe he thought she was coming on to him. He probably thought she looked terrible or maybe she smelled. She hadn't had a chance to clean herself up in days. She must look awful.

"Yeah, maybe," he finally said.

Her cheeks flushed.

"I don't mean to sound like a jerk," he said, reading her mind once again. "It's not you. It's me. I'm terrible at this stuff. The last group of people I was with are dead. Maybe I'm unlucky. Are you sure you want me tagging along?"

"I'm willing to take my chances."

"Okay, then."

She looked down at her dishes, the remains of the ice cream sticking to the bowl. "I guess we don't have to clean up. It's not like anyone's going to complain."

"One of the benefits," he said. "Look, there's a motel just down the road and I'll bet we can spend the night there. Or if you want we can head out. I'm not really tired anymore. Might be better to set off in the daylight, though. It gets pretty dark around here, and we can't exactly use flashlights. We'd be spotted a mile away."

"Yeah," she said. For the first time in weeks she wasn't tired in the slightest, but it probably wasn't logical to go back on the road now. He was right. They'd be better off waiting till morning. "We can check out the motel. Would be nice to clean up a bit."

"There's a clothing shop in town too," he said.

She looked down at the plaid shirt she was wearing. She'd forgotten it was covered in dried blood. It seemed like ages ago that she'd stabbed that guy, that Bagger, who tried to hurt her.

"Yeah, that's a good idea also."

"Then let's go find your brother," he said.

She smiled. Having him around was going to be nice. Safe. He made her feel safe for the time being.

MASON

"I don't think it's such a good idea." Paul stroked his chin, which was now covered with several days' worth of stubble.

"You said the same thing about Canmore. We need supplies. We've got no more food. And I for one am starving. You've got a hungry bird here, and my tail feathers are starting to get heated up. I need sugar."

Mason snorted. "What exactly does that mean?"

Chickadee laughed. "It means I'm getting bitchy."

They were crouched in the woods at the turnoff to the town of Banff, once a major tourist resort. Now the roads were lined with forgotten cars and camper vans. And bodies. It wasn't pretty, and Mason spent a lot of time averting his gaze toward the gravel. A few weeks ago he'd told himself that he no longer cared. The numbing effect still hadn't worn off; the anger inside him lay dormant, wrapped around the darkest corners of his brain. But as time went on, little bits pushed their way forward. Certain memories refused to be forgotten. He thought about his mother a lot, wondering if she was still in the hospital and what her body might look like. He thought about Tom and wondered if his friends experienced terror as their bodies crushed and snapped. Or had it been over quickly and painlessly? Did they even have a chance to run as the school tumbled down around them?

Too many thoughts whispered inside his head.

Despite this, he found it was hard not to be cheerful at times when Chickadee was around.

"You must have been a Buddhist monk or something in a past life," she had proclaimed a few days after she met him. "I swear, people who have taken vows of silence say more than you."

Mason had shrugged and turned his head, but he knew full well she'd seen the smile on his face. At first he resented it, hated the fact that he was enjoying the company of his new friends. A good part of him still didn't believe he deserved it. But as the days went by, a little bit of company went a long way. He was lonely. He hadn't realized it. Having some new friends made the nights a little easier.

"I think it's too big," Paul said again. He was by far the most cautious of the group. Mason figured he was the reason Chickadee was still alive. She was spontaneous, always ready to jump in without checking things out. It was almost as if she didn't realize the danger actually applied to her. Or she didn't care. Paul was the opposite; he took time to assess the situation, carefully thinking through his actions, constantly aware of the consequences.

"It's not really a big town at all," Chickadee said. "I've been here. Nothing but hotels and bars. I think we'll be safe."

"We should go on."

"The next town is days away," she said. "I can't wait that long. There's a Safeway there. I need a pharmacy." She gave Paul a long look, and Mason saw the way he turned and avoided her gaze.

"Why do you need a pharmacy?" Mason asked, alarm bells going off inside his head. "Are you okay?"

"I think I'm coming down with a cold," she said a little too quickly. "Nothing serious."

She didn't look sick, but she did look tired. There were bags under her eyes, but all three of them looked like they were dying for a good night of uninterrupted sleep.

"You sure?" Mason put his hand up to her forehead, and she quickly knocked it away.

"Just a cold, nothing else." She bit her lip and frowned, a look he knew meant she wasn't planning on saying anything else.

"Then we go in," he said.

"Two against one," Chickadee said.

"Fine." Paul stood up and headed off. When he was in the middle of the road, he paused without looking back. "Well, are you coming?"

Mason and Chickadee shrugged at each other and started to follow.

They headed down the center of the road. There weren't as many abandoned cars there, but lots of garbage lined the concrete. Opened suitcases—stripped and rummaged through—candy wrappers, even a smashed laptop.

"Looks like there was one hell of a party," Chickadee said as she stepped around a broken gin bottle. "Can we stop for a second? I've got to pee."

"Sure," Mason said.

Paul didn't say anything, but he turned around and knelt down on the road to study something. Chickadee pulled some tissue from her pocket and dashed into the woods. Mason watched her go, making a mental note of where she was before turning his attention to an abandoned iPod.

Picking it up, he tried to make it work, but the battery was dead.

"She's not my girlfriend," Paul said.

"Huh?"

"We're not dating. I kinda get the impression you think we're a couple. But we're not. Chee and I have known each other since we were babies. I think of her like a sister. She's tough as nails. Had a really rough life. Both parents were drunks. They beat her too. She'd come over to my place in the middle of the night with bruises all over her body. I used to wish I could help her, stop her pain, make it go away. But I was too little then, and now it's too late. You need to know this."

"Why?"

"I won't stand by and watch her suffer."

Mason shrugged. "I won't either. That's why it's cool that there are two of us. We can protect her."

"We can't save her from everything."

"What are you saying?"

Paul didn't answer. Chickadee emerged from the woods, her braids bouncing against her chest.

"Much better," she said. "Now let's go rock this place!"

At the edge of town was a plaque that gave a brief history of Banff. Someone had spray painted the words "Baggers Rule" in bright red letters over it. But Chickadee strode by as if it wasn't even there.

Five dead bodies lay at the entrance to the Safeway. Stacked on top of one another like some sort of bizarre card house. Blood still drained from the cuts on two of them. It was enough to make Mason want to turn around and head back to the highway. But Chickadee calmly walked past them, too, and headed into the store. Mason and Paul had no choice but to follow.

He liked her bravery. In fact, the more time Mason spent with her, the more he grew to adore Chickadee. Now that he knew Paul and her weren't a couple, he began to look at her in a different light. She wasn't what someone might consider beautiful; her nose was crooked and she was too short. She was also about twenty pounds overweight, but none of that really bothered him. Her personality trumped everything. The more she talked, the more beautiful she grew. She probably never had trouble getting dates.

But this wasn't the time or place for falling for a girl, Mason reminded himself as they walked past the doors and into the grocery store. It wouldn't do any good to start complicating things. It could be dangerous to have a crush. Better to concentrate on other stuff.

They walked through the aisles, checking to make sure the place was empty first. Aside from a few dead bodies, the store was clear.

"I'm so sick of canned food," Chickadee said. "If we were back at home I could have cooked you up a great meal. I'm a totally fantastic chef. You'd fall in love with me instantly. I'm that good."

"Really?"

"Yup." She picked up a box of Kraft dinner and frowned at it. "My grandmother taught me how. She used to tell me stories too about how enchanted Indian maidens would cook special foods in order to snag fancy warrior braves. I think she was hinting at something, but at that age I mostly found boys icky."

"And now?"

Chee laughed. "It made me a great cook. But I still scare the boys away. I think it's my dynamic personality. Mom always said my name should have been Barbara Talks Too Much."

Mason snickered.

"And if you ever call me that, I'll torture you for all exist-ence. Even after I'm dead . . ." She paused as Paul reached out and took her hand. They stared at each other for several seconds before Chickadee pulled away.

"Not so loud," Paul said. "We don't know who is listening."

Chickadee lowered her voice to a whisper. "I'm gonna go get some cough syrup. Why don't the two of you finish grab-bing the food?"

"Are you sure that's a good idea?" Paul asked. "Maybe I should go with you. I don't like you being alone."

"I'll be fine," she said. "Only fifty feet away. You'll hear me if I start screaming." She turned and scooted off down the aisle before either Mason or Paul could respond.

"I don't like this," Paul said. "We'll just grab whatever and get the hell outta here."

"Sounds good," Mason said. He immediately opened up his backpack and started shoving canned food inside, barely even taking the time to read the labels. They split up, him heading off toward the granola bars and trail mix, while Paul headed toward the produce to see if he could find anything worth scavenging.

The store was thoroughly looted, almost empty, but Mason still managed to find some granola bars lying on the shelves. He opened the packages and tossed the individually wrapped bars into his backpack. The secret was to get rid of as much packaging as possible. That way he'd have more room for extras. Reaching down on the floor, he scooped up a few bags of fruit snacks and shoved them in too.

It didn't take long to fill his bag, and he wandered over to the produce section, where the smell of rotting fruits and vegetables assaulted his nose. Everything was covered in green mold. Covering his mouth and nose with his shirt, he looked around but couldn't find Paul. Heading over to the pharmacy, he decided to see how Chickadee was doing. He didn't see her at first, but then he heard the sounds of jars being pulled off the shelves behind the pharmacy counter.

He rounded the corner and saw Paul and her tossing bottles on the floor.

"There's nothing here," she said. "They've looted everything."

"That's it, then," Paul said.

"That's not it," Chickadee said. "We'll find something. There's got to be something here. Check the fridge again."

"It's empty. Everything's on the floor."

"What about this one?"

"Expired. It's useless."

She tossed a few bottles aside, breaking one. The sound of glass cracking filled the store.

"What are you guys doing?" Mason asked.

Chickadee jumped. "Don't do that. You scared the crap outta me."

"If you're into hard-core stuff, that's just not cool. I'm not into that." Mason stood his ground and glared at Paul, who simply stood up and walked away from the mess.

"We're not looking for drugs," Chickadee said. "And I'm really insulted that you'd think that, Mason. Haven't you listened to anything I've said? I don't swing that way. I don't even drink. I was just looking for some penicillin. I'm worried that this cold could turn to strep throat. It happens to me a lot. That's all. Honest."

"And there's nothing here," Paul said. He calmly walked over to where Mason stood and grabbed a red-and-white bottle of cough syrup off the shelf. "You'll just have to make do, Chee. If you get worse, we'll deal."

Mason didn't know what to do. He wanted to believe them, he really did. But it was awfully suspicious. Neither of them seemed to be the types to do drugs, and he hadn't caught them behaving oddly or spaced-out since he'd met them. But something was definitely up. He just couldn't figure out what.

"Don't be mad, okay?" Chickadee said. She came around the counter, and Mason could see she wasn't holding anything. She opened her bag and showed him the contents. Nothing but protein bars. "I'm not into drugs. In fact, I'm hurt that you'd think otherwise. Please believe me."

Mason nodded. "Yeah, okay. I believe you."

From outside a gunshot sounded. Footsteps pounded on the cement, and one of the store windows shattered.

"Time to go," Paul said.

They headed around back to the storage area and exited through the loading bay. Outside, the sky glowed red and pink.

"Let's find a place to spend the night," Paul said. "There are enough hotels here that we should be able to grab one without being found."

"Let's do it," Chickadee said. She gave Mason a big grin.

They ended up in one of the cabins on the outskirts of town. Mason went into the lobby and found some keys while Paul walked around the perimeter to make sure no one was lurking in the bushes.

The room was small with bunk beds and a couch that folded out.

"I get top bunk," Chickadee said. She ran over and climbed the ladder to settle in. She bounced up and down on the mattress, her head nearly hitting the ceiling.

Mason sat down on one of the chairs and watched while Paul checked the windows. Pulling the curtains closed, he double-checked the lock on the door before heading into the bathroom to make sure they had an exit strategy.

"I'm exhausted," Chickadee said. She yawned three times in rapid succession. "It's been forever since we've had a bed. How long has it been since we left Calgary?"

"Four days," Mason said.

"That's crazy. I used to make the drive all the time and it only took about an hour and a half. We could make it to Vancouver in two days if we drove fast. Never dawned on me that walking would take so long. No wonder my poor feet hurt. I need a pedicure. I'll have crusty granny feet if this keeps up."

"If it weren't for all the roadblocks we'd be able to drive," Mason said. "It might get better outside of Banff, but it'll probably be worse once we hit the Fraser Valley."

"You know a lot about the area, then?"

Mason shrugged. "A bit. We did go camping there almost every summer. It was Mom's favorite place."

"I'm sorry."

"Why? You didn't kill her."

"I'm just sorry. Sorry that there won't be any more camping trips for kids or rock bands or even new books to read. No more movies or fresh bags of popcorn. It really sucks when you think about it. Of course, there is the possibility that we might be able to win this war, but not for a very long time. Probably longer than you and I will ever exist in this world."

"I try not to think about it."

"Sometimes it's all I ever think about."

"Why? It'll only bring up bad memories."

Chickadee jumped off the bed and walked over to where

Mason stood. She paused less than a foot away from him. "There are different types of people in this world. There are people who accept what's in front of them unquestioningly. They live in the dark. In defeat. Ignoring what the future might bring or how they might help to make things happen. Then there are people like me. Optimists. They too live in the dark, in times like these, but dream of the light. I trust in the possibilities of betterness. I believe there is more to life than this. I have to. There's no other choice for me."

She leaned toward him and he could smell her hair. Coconut. One of her braids brushed against his arm and she looked up into his eyes. He realized he wanted her to look up at him like that forever. Her beautiful face, bright and shiny and full of life—there was no one else as truly amazing as her left on the planet. Mom would have loved her.

"Bathroom's clear," Paul said as he came back into the room. "There's a window there, big enough for us to squeeze through if we have to make a quick exit."

"Excellent." Chickadee bent down to retrieve her backpack. "So what's for dinner, then?"

They tossed their findings on the floor and ate a meal of canned beans and granola bars, and split between them two apples that somehow managed to avoid growing moldy. They washed it down with cans of warm root beer and orange Crush. Afterward they sat and listened to the silence while the room steadily grew darker. They were too close to the main road to risk having candles.

"Tell us a story, Paul," Chickadee said after a while. She turned to Mason. "Paul's great-grandpa used to be a real storyteller back in the old days. Paul knows all the old legends. They're really good."

"Cool."

"You've heard all my stories," Paul said.

"Yeah, but Mason hasn't. You've got to tell one to him. Tell him about the coyote stealing fire."

Although the room was dark, there was no mistaking the look Paul gave Chickadee. Mason didn't know what to make of it. Maybe they had a fight earlier and he missed it. But Paul didn't really seem angry. He looked hurt, not physically, but mentally. His eyebrows were tight together, and there was a deep longing behind his eyes. Maybe he was in love with Chickadee—that might explain it—but he'd said himself that he thought of her as a sister.

Whatever it was, Mason's chest tightened when he saw the way Paul looked at her. There was such deep sadness in his eyes.

"I'm going to tell a different story," Paul began. "Once, thousands of years ago, there was a tribe that lived along the banks of the Pacific Ocean where Vancouver stands today. They were hunters and gatherers. The men would travel the forests and the wives would collect the oysters and clams from the shore. This was before the arrival of the white man, and the people lived somewhat peacefully with their neighboring tribes.

Most of the people in the village were happy, but there was one warrior brave who always wanted more. He wanted to travel and visit the world beyond his borders and fight in wars he knew he'd win, but he came home disillusioned. There was no place impressive enough to claim his heart. He wanted love, but no woman was beautiful enough for him; he wanted to eat great foods, but the oysters tasted like sand and the deer were never tender enough to his tongue. Because of this he became cold and bitter, and he'd spend his days away from his family and tribe, refusing to help or contribute anything at all to the community.

One day he decided to go for a walk. While down by the ocean shore, he came across a canoe with a strange man. Unbeknownst to him, this stranger was Khaals, the great transformer, a spirit of legend and fear. Khaals had the ability to change people into animals or even trees and rocks. He often punished people for their wrongdoings and was known for not being sympathetic. If a warrior boasted about his kills, Khaals might show up and turn him into a deer so that he'd know what it's like to flee in fear. If a man chased women other than his wife, Khaals would turn him into a tree so he'd never be able to run again.

"Why do you walk along the sand?" Khaals asked. "I hear your people celebrating in the distance. Why are you not with them?"

"There is nothing worth embracing," the brave said. "What is the point of living when I know I will just die? What is the point of loving when all the women are shallow and ugly? I have seen all there is to see, and there are no wonders for me to behold. I've done everything worth doing. Life is no longer a challenge. I'm bored."

Now, Khaals was not the type of spirit to anger, and the brave's words displeased him. He looked down on the warrior and read deeply into his mind.

"You think life is boring? I'll show you what it's really about," Khaals said, and he turned the brave into a wide, polished rock.

"I'll be back when you find something worth living for," Khaals said.

The brave lay trapped in his rock prison for thousands of years. The world grew up around him. He watched his people fall to the white man, watched the city grow and surround him, and saw the horrors that mankind was capable of doing. His mind never softened and his desire never grew.

Then one day a woman appeared. She was an ordinary woman—nothing special about her. But she carried herself on the wind, and the scent of wildflowers blossomed in her hair. She sat down on the rock and brought out a book to read. The softness of her touch moved the warrior, and he found himself missing her when she left a few hours later.

To his delight she returned the next day with book in hand, and the next day after that. Soon he found himself waiting only for her arrival and devastated with each passing. He longed to talk to this ordinary woman, touch her hair, and tell her how important she was to him.

One morning, after several months, the warrior was surprised to see the shape of Khaals's boat on the water. The transformer had returned for him as promised.

"Do you know why I've come back?"

"I've found something worth living for," the brave replied.

"But she is not a great beauty," Khaals said. "She will not bring the world to you. She will not make the food taste any better. She is nothing but ordinary."

"Her hair holds the wind and her eyes will see my soul," the brave said. "The oysters will taste of the ocean instead of sand because she will help me see their true flavor. She is beautiful enough for me."

With that, Khaals transformed the rock back into his true self. When the woman returned she found the warrior in its place. They instantly fell in love.

For many moons they shared all their time together. And the food did taste better and the rain that fell from the clouds was soft and warm on their skin. The warrior reached up into the skies and plucked the stars from their cushions and placed them in her hands.

But the woman was sick. She was dying.

When the warrior found out, he was beyond angry at Khaals. What was the point of bringing this beautiful woman to him if he would only lose her? Khaals had given him a taste of life, and now he would take that away.

The woman grew weaker. His fury grew, and realizing he couldn't stand to watch her wither, he did the only thing possible. He told her he no longer loved her. He looked deep into the pain in her eyes, but he couldn't take back the words.

He left.

He walked back to the ocean shore and called for Khaals.

"Why did you do this?" he asked when the transformer appeared. "You gave me life and then took it away. I was better off as a rock. At least then I didn't have to feel. You tricked me, and for that I left her."

"You left her because you couldn't face the pain," Khaals said. "You had true love, but you were selfish and turned your back. You are not strong. And because of that I shall leave you as you are. An empty husk to walk for all eternity."

And the warrior became a rock again, only this time he could move and speak. But he never tasted the ocean or smelled the wildflowers on the wind. He never felt the rain on his face or knew the joy of living.

He was never strong again.

Chickadee was crying. She tried not to let anyone hear, but a few sniffles filled the room. When Mason looked back at her, the tears on her face were as big as crystals.

"I'm such a girl," she said.

"That's okay," he said.

"It was just a really sad story," she said. "I can't imagine what it would be like going through life without feeling. Or feeling so much that you couldn't stand to watch someone you love die."

"Maybe he couldn't bear to bury her," Mason said, thinking of his own mother. "So that's why he left."

"Either way it's just a story." Paul yawned and went over to the couch and picked up a blanket. "I'm tired," he said. "It's time for bed."

Mason wanted to ask him why he told that particular story, but Paul rolled over on his side, facing the wall, making it clear he had nothing more to say. Chickadee reached out and touched Mason's arm, getting his attention.

"I'm tired too," she said. "Can I still have top bunk?"

Mason gave her half a smile. "Sure. I'll take first watch."

"I'll take second," Paul said. "Wake me in a few."

Mason went and used the bathroom and tried washing off some of the dirt and sweat on his face with a water bottle and one of the towels on the rack. It helped a bit. He rubbed his tongue along his teeth, deciding they'd have to remember to grab some toothbrushes soon. The face in the mirror was unfamiliar; it felt like years had passed since he last saw his own reflection.

Yawning, he returned to the room and sat down in the chair by the window. The air around him was quiet, but he knew no one was sleeping yet. When he roused Paul several hours later, he had the feeling Paul still hadn't slept at all. They silently traded places and Mason crawled into the bottom bunk, pulling the covers up to his chin.

He lay in the dark, staring at the wood above him until his eyes grew heavy enough to close.

At the moment before he fell asleep, he heard Paul's voice reach out through the blackness.

"I'm not strong enough."

But he was too tired to respond.

When he woke the next morning, Chickadee was sitting in the chair by the window. Her body was stiff and she held her head in her hands as if she couldn't keep her neck upright without the help. Her entire body trembled. How long had she been sitting there? Why didn't she wake him up?

"What's wrong?" he asked.

"He's gone."

"Huh? Who, Paul? Where'd he go?"

"Just gone. He left me. Us."

Mason pulled at the blankets wrapped around his legs. They clung to his body, refusing to let go. Eventually he freed himself and moved over to the window where Chickadee waited, tears streaming down her face.

"He can't be gone," he said. "Maybe he just went for food."

"We have food."

"Did you look outside?"

"He's not there."

"Why would he do such a thing? I don't know Paul as well as you, but I can't imagine he'd wander off like that. He cares about you."

"That's the problem." Chickadee finally looked away from the window. She reached over and took Mason's hand. "He cared too much to watch me die. Just like the story."

Her fingers were soft and slightly damp from the tears. Mason didn't know what she wanted him to do. She was seeking comfort, but there were no words he could use to make things better. There was something visible just behind her eyes, an answer to a question he didn't want to ask.

"Are you dying?" The words hung in the air like a bad smell.

"We're all going to die."

"But are you sick? Is there something you're not telling me?"

"I'm not sick."

"Okay."

A can of lukewarm Pepsi rested on the table. Chickadee reached for it and took a long drink. "I'm so thirsty," she said. "I think I've cried all the liquid out of my body over the past few days. How much more before I shrivel up into a husk?" She squeezed his hand and pulled him closer to her, so their noses were almost touching. "Please don't leave me, Mason. I don't think I could stand it if you go."

"I'm not going anywhere."

"Promise me."

"I promise."

Her lips brushed his, a small kiss. It happened so quickly he couldn't fully decide if it was actually real or his imagination. Opening his arms, he pulled her into him, wrapping himself around her and trying to keep her safe.

They stayed that way as the minutes passed and his arms cramped, but he didn't let go. The front of his shirt grew wet and uncomfortable, but he barely noticed. Finally she pulled back, and he released her reluctantly.

"Do you want me to go look for him?"

She sniffled and shook her head.

"What do we do now?"

"We move on."

Mason nodded. It sounded like the right thing to do.

ARIES

"Daniel?"

The figure on the floor rocked back and forth, but his eyes remained closed. Aries moved around to the side, trying to get a better look at his face. Daniel's eyelashes were fluttering, but he didn't wake up.

From behind her she heard the sounds of people. Nathan hissed her name. She could see their flashlights from across the store.

"I'm over here," she half whispered, half shouted.

Aries turned her attention back to Daniel, still sprawled out across the ground beside her. She couldn't believe it was him. She'd spent countless hours remembering their brief conversations, playing his words over and over in her head like a broken record. She never thought she'd see him again.

But here he was.

Serendipity?

There was a deep cut on his forehead. He was no longer bleeding, but his hair was matted from where the blood had drained out while he slept. A small red stain spread out like an inkblot on the yellow tiling. His face was pale with the exception of a bruise on his cheekbone.

She picked up the flashlight he'd been holding. It was small and blue. The same one she'd given him. He'd kept it. Not just kept it; he'd been holding it. Did that mean he thought about her, too? This was an entire store filled with better flashlights—why did he still have this one?

She smiled, even though she knew it probably wasn't anything worth getting excited over. But still, it might be a sign. A good one.

The black jacket covering his body didn't look very warm. The corner of the sleeve was torn. Something shiny stuck halfway out of the pocket. Without thinking, she reached over to touch it. The object was metal and cold to the touch. She pulled it out, a small switchblade with blood on the blade. Shuddering, she dropped the knife on the floor.

He moaned and his eyes fluttered again. She was worried that he might be sick, so she placed her palm against his forehead. His skin was boiling.

"Aries?"

She jerked back in surprise. Daniel's eyes stared up at her, dark brown and piercing but still rather dazed. He looked past her as if she wasn't really there.

"You remember me," she said. Her stomach gave a little leap, as if she'd just gotten on the roller coaster at Playland.

"Aries, but you're a Gemini."

She nodded.

"I'm happy you're alive. I thought you might be dead." He tried to hoist himself up on his elbows but winced instead, his head resting back on the cold ground. All his strength seemed to drain out over the tiles.

Yes, she was alive. Anger flared through her, if for only a

moment. He'd left her after making a promise. For the past several weeks she'd thought about all the things she'd say to him if they crossed paths. Why did he help her and then disappear? How come he knew so much? He'd told her this would happen—he knew people were attacking and that the world was ending. How did he know? How come she knew? She remembered her conversation with Ms. Darcy before she left.

Something bad is about to happen. It's already started. I know you're feeling it too. It's like an electric charge. I can't explain it. I've been sensing it for weeks.

She *had* been feeling it. At the time she didn't know what it was. It started small, a strange sensation in the back of her brain that swept across her nervous system, like receiving dozens of small static shocks. She'd thought she was coming down with something. When the earthquake happened, she'd been too distracted with Sara to fully understand it. But afterward, trapped in the abandoned apartment, she'd had plenty of time to work through the details. Her thoughts always returned to Daniel. He was the key. He knew something that she didn't.

But now, with him lying on the floor, looking so wilted, she couldn't bring herself to verbally attack him. Her concerns and fears changed to whether or not he was dangerously ill.

"Looks like I'm doing better than you," she said, reaching out to touch his forehead again. "You've got a fever. How long have you been sick?"

He shrugged. "It's nothing. Comes and goes."

"Do you think you can be alone for a few minutes? I'm going to get you some Tylenol from the pharmacy section. I should get you up on one of the bed displays. It'll be warmer."

He smirked and started coughing violently. She waited for him to finish.

"I've been alone for a long time. I can handle a few more minutes."

"That's right. You don't care much for company."

"Aries?" Joy appeared with Nathan by her side, staring down at the unconscious boy in surprise.

"This is Daniel," Aries said. "Remember? I told you about him."

"The guy who helped you after the bus crash," Joy said. Her eyes lit up immediately. "I'm Joy. This is Nathan."

Daniel blinked a few times, trying to hold back the pain. "I'd shake your hand but I'm not sure I have the strength."

"Are you okay?" Nathan asked.

"He's got a fever. Maybe you can help me get him onto one of the beds."

Ignoring Daniel's protests, the three of them managed to get him over to one of the displays, where Aries helped him lie back on a bright pink bedspread. She grabbed a blanket off the shelf and covered him.

"We should check the pharmacy," Aries said. "Maybe we can find something that'll help."

Joy nodded. Nathan looked a little uncertain. Aries grabbed his sleeve, pulling him along whether he liked it or not. "We'll be right back."

Daniel didn't say anything. Closing his eyes, he relaxed into the pillow. It wasn't like he'd be going anywhere soon.

"Sorry we're late," Nathan said once they were out of earshot. "Had a little bit of trouble. Took us a while to shake them. Man, those psychos can run."

"I lost my bike," Joy said. She was bleeding from a cut on her arm, but aside from that they seemed fine. "Nathan had to double with me. Not fun."

"Good thing you're light as a feather," Nathan said. "Otherwise we might not have gotten out."

"They brought me down," Joy said. "Pulled me right off my bike. One of them tried to bite me. Can you believe it? Just like a bloody zombie movie. I would have been toast if it hadn't been for Nathan. He's my new hero."

"We were lucky," he said. "I managed to knock one of them out. It felt amazing. I haven't been in a fight since I was a little kid. What happened to you?" He'd noticed Aries's torn jeans leg.

"Took a spill," she said. "Cornered too fast. My own fault. Luckily I'd already lost them."

"We'd better find something for you, too," Joy said. "That might get infected. Does it hurt?"

"Yeah, it stings but I'll live."

"We'd still better be careful," Nathan said. "Do you think you can trust that guy? I mean, how well do you really know him?"

"I can't believe you found him," Joy said. "What are the odds?"

"It's weird," Nathan said. "Why is this guy here of all places? And he's just sleeping in the store when the back door was unlocked? Does he have a death wish?"

"He's sick. Maybe he just got desperate. And he doesn't like groups," Aries said. "He's got this idea that people are safer being alone."

"Not me," Joy said. "I don't think I ever could have gotten this far by myself. But aren't you mad at him? He left you, right?"

"It's not important," she said. "He's here now, and he needs help."

In the pharmacy department, they found the fever medications, but there were a lot to pick from and she was momentarily overwhelmed.

"This one's good." Nathan handed her a bottle filled with burgundy liquid.

"How do you know?"

"My mother was a nurse. She always kept this stuff on hand. It tastes disgusting. But it works."

"Okay." She opened the box and slipped the small bottle into her pocket. "Anything else? I mean, what if he needs more?"

"Give him some Tylenol."

Joy grabbed the closest red-and-white bottle from the shelf. "Got it."

"And you're going to need this," Nathan said, pressing a bottle of saline solution and some gauze bandages into her hand. "For your leg. You're bleeding."

She'd forgotten about her own problems. They seemed so unimportant compared to everything else. But Nathan was right. She'd have to clean herself up or she might find herself with a nasty infection. Such things could be fatal in this new world. A clean pair of jeans would help too.

"Look." Aries glanced back toward the housewares section, but of course she couldn't see anything from where they were. "We've got to change our plans. I can't leave him, and I doubt he's strong enough to travel. I think you guys should get the stuff we need and head back without me for now."

Nathan looked at her in disbelief. "I don't think that's a good idea."

"I'm not leaving him. He saved my life."

"It's not safe."

"It's as safe as anywhere else," Aries said.

"But we need you," Joy said. "Who's going to carry your stuff? We promised the others."

"Look," Aries said, taking both Joy and Nathan by the arms

and leading them away from the pharmacy. "You can take my bicycle. There's a whole bunch of them in the sporting-goods section. I can always grab another. We can get one of those baby carriages that attaches to the back of the bike. You guys can carry more stuff that way without being slowed down. And I got some handheld receivers from electronics. We can keep in touch now. You'll be able to reach me whenever you want. I'll be back as soon as he's well enough to travel. One day, two tops."

"I don't like it," Nathan said. "And I don't think the others will either."

"I owe him my life," she said. "I have to return the favor."

An hour later they were ready to go. Both Joy and Nathan were loaded up with the goods, but not enough to slow them down if they got in trouble. Aries made sure of that. It was still dark outside, but in the east, the sky was beginning to lighten. If they were going to leave, it had to be now.

"We'll call you when we get back," Joy said. The handheld receiver was strapped to her backpack, making her look like an overburdened bicycle courier.

"Be careful," she said.

"You too."

Joy turned and unlocked the door. She pushed her bicycle through the opening, a tough job considering she now had a baby trailer attached to the back. Aries helped her navigate the stairs. Outside the air was cool and fresh. She could smell the salty scent of the ocean, along with faint traces of smoke. Because of the earthquake, then the looting and killing, a lot of buildings were still on fire. She couldn't remember the last time the sky didn't look like a giant smoke screen. Everyone's clothes constantly smelled acrid.

"Lock the door behind us," Nathan said. "If they break the window, go into the office. You'll be safe there."

While searching the store, they'd found a small office with no windows and a nice lock on the inside. If something were to happen, she'd be able to get Daniel in there without much effort. They'd be trapped, but at least they would be out of harm's way.

"Will do," she said.

Joy gave her a quick hug before climbing on her bike. Aries watched them ride off, wondering if she was doing the right thing.

Sighing, she turned and headed back into the building to wait for Daniel's fever to break.

He hadn't moved since she'd last seen him. She sat at the edge of the bed for a bit and watched his chest as he breathed. People always looked beautiful when they slept, vulnerable and innocent. She wanted to gather him in her arms and hold him tightly until he woke up. Reaching out carefully, she brushed a bit of hair away from his eyes. He didn't move. Running her finger along his face, she was amazed at how soft his skin was. Her heart began to beat faster; she could feel it pounding in her chest. His mouth was parted slightly, straight white teeth barely showing. She touched his lips and then drew her hand away quickly.

In his sleep, he mumbled something she couldn't understand. His lips curved into a slight smile. But at least he didn't wake up. She wasn't sure how she could have explained her sudden desire to touch him.

Embarrassed, she got up off the bed and pulled the covers over his chest, tucking him in gently to make sure he stayed comfortable.

Sitting down on the floor next to the bed, she removed her jeans and rubbed the saline solution over her wounds. It stung but not unbearably so. Gravel was stuck to her skin, and she picked out the pieces she couldn't wash away. The process was painful, and it didn't help that her muscles ached and trembled every time she jerked back in agony. Eventually she managed to clean herself enough to be satisfied, and she wrapped the gauze around her leg.

She threw her ruined pants aside and picked up the pair of sweatpants she'd found in the clothing aisle and put them on. At least they'd be more comfortable and less clingy than the jeans.

Yawning, she grabbed some pillows and a blanket from the shelf and made herself a little bed on the floor beside Daniel.

What would happen if the medication didn't work and he got worse? It's not like she could take him to the hospital. It was such a strange thought. There would be no help in this new world. Even simple things like fevers could kill.

"You're not going to die," she whispered in the dark. "I won't let you."

Covering herself up, she lay on her back, eyes opened, and waited for morning to come. It took a long time before her brain stopping working overtime with all the what-ifs and her eyelids grew heavy.

She didn't mean to fall asleep.

She woke, disorientated, not understanding the sharp discomfort in her lower back and why she was lying on the hard floor. Sitting up quickly, heart pounding in her chest, she looked around wildly.

"Good morning."

"Daniel?"

"Were you expecting someone else?"

Pushing her hair back from her face, she winced. Sleeping on a frozen floor was never a good choice.

"Bad dreams?"

She shook her head. "Nope, just forgot where I was for a second."

"That happens to me sometimes too."

"You sound a lot better." She pulled the blanket aside and climbed to her feet. Stretched. Felt her joints pop in her legs and back.

"I am, thanks to you. I think the fever's gone."

"Really? Excellent."

He did look better. Although his face was still pale, it didn't look as pasty or sweaty. Last night she'd taken some baby wipes to his forehead and gotten rid of most of the blood. She'd covered the cut with white gauze and used nonstick tape to keep it in place. He looked like a wounded soldier straight off the battlefield. At least his eyes were no longer glassy and he focused on her without difficulty. Such an intense stare, as if he was drilling straight into her brain.

"You still have my flashlight," she said.

He reached into his pocket and pulled it out. "Of course. I knew if I kept it, you'd find a way to come back to me."

"Um . . . I . . . ah." Brilliant conversation at its best.

"But now that you know I'm healthy, you need to leave."

"What?" She glared at him in disbelief. "No. It doesn't work that way."

"Yes, it does. I haven't changed, Aries. I still don't want to be in a crowd. You're a nice girl and I like you a lot, but it's not safe for you to be around me."

"You said that before. I don't believe you."

"You're still alive, aren't you? Because of me. Because I took you to the school, even if I did leave you there."

236

She couldn't argue that. It was true. She decided to take a different approach. "Why are you against people? It's worked for me. We need to stick together if we're ever going to stand up for ourselves. You're acting as if you're one of those monsters."

"Maybe I am."

"You're not. I'd know if you were."

"Would you?"

"They're crazy."

"Not all of them."

"They kill for no reason. That makes them crazy."

A water bottle sat on its side where Aries left it last night. Daniel picked it up and took a long drink. "Some of them are crazy. I watched one of them break its own neck the other day. Got its head between two metal railings of all things. It tugged and yanked until the bones cracked. Took a long time to die. So yeah, some of them really are stupid. But not all. That same day, a group of them got together and burned a library to the ground because they knew people were hiding inside. They waited at the exits and pegged their victims off one by one as they tried to run. It was a calculated plan."

"That doesn't mean they're not crazy."

"Some of them could fool you," he continued. "Some of them can talk normally. They can trick you into believing they're innocent. That's why you can't trust anyone. Do you really know these friends of yours? Would you trust them fully with your life?"

"Yes." She didn't even have to think about the answer. Colin's face, however, did flash into her thoughts, but only for a moment. He was too much of a coward to be a killer.

"You're stupid, then."

"And you're nothing but an ass."

"Because I'm trying to help keep you alive?"

"I don't need your help."

Daniel chuckled. "You know, I believe you're right on that one. You've managed to do quite well. Very few people have made it this far. I'd ask you where you're holing up, but I don't want to know."

"I want you to come back with me." There. She said it. She had a million questions to ask him, especially how come he knew so much? But they'd have to wait until she got him somewhere safe.

"No."

She wanted to grab him by the shirt and slap some sense into him. He infuriated her. What made him this stubborn? "Fine. Have it your way. But don't expect me to come running the next time you can't get off the bed."

"Then you'll leave?"

"Not until nightfall. It's not safe to go anywhere during the daytime."

She was surprised to see him nod. "You're right. I guess we'll just have to put up with each other until then." Getting off the bed, he peeled the dirty shirt off his body and dropped it to the floor.

She blushed and looked away. But not before she caught a glimpse of toned muscles and yellowish bruises on his abdomen.

"I'm going to find a new shirt," he said, and she could hear the amusement in his voice. "Then I'm going to get something to eat." He began to walk away, his bare feet slapping on the tiled flooring. "You're welcome to join me. I promise I'll wear something a little less revealing."

A dozen retorts came to her mind, but every single one was too lame to repeat. After he turned the corner, she picked up her pillow and threw it in his direction. Not exactly the world's greatest comeback, but it made her feel a little better.

She took the handheld receiver from her bag and turned it on. She put her mouth up to the speaker and then paused. What was she supposed to say? She'd talked to Joy briefly last night once they made it home safe and she'd promised she'd call again in the morning to give an update. Sure, Daniel was feeling better and that was something to report, but she didn't know where to go from there. It was her responsibility to bring him back, but he seemed intent on staying behind. It was odd.

"Anyone there?" she said into the tiny receiver. She felt stupid. Wasn't there something else she was supposed to say, like "over" or "ten-four" when talking into these things?

There was a pause and then a click. "Aries?"

"Hey, Jack."

"Wow, the reception is amazing. No background noise or anything. Are you still at the store?"

"Yep. I'm pretty much here till nightfall. How's everyone doing? Nothing bad happen?"

"No, things are great here. Everyone changed their clothes and ate some food. They're all in good spirits. Even Colin. How's the guy? Better?"

"Yeah. His fever's gone."

"Brilliant. I'm looking forward to meeting him. We'll see you later tonight, right?"

"Yep." She didn't exactly know why she lied, mostly because the truth was too complicated to discuss through a little plastic box. They'd just have to get the whole story once she got back.

And who knew? Maybe Daniel would change his mind. It was a long ways till the sun went down.

She went looking for him and found him in the toy department. He'd put on a fresh shirt, a black top that fit snugly. He'd also changed his jeans. His feet were still bare. The makeshift bandage on his head was gone and his hair was wet. He'd taken the time to clean himself up.

"You look good," she said, immediately regretting the words when he gave her a sideways glance, one eyebrow raised, and a crooked grin. "I mean, even less sick. Better than last night."

He laughed.

That's it. She'd had enough. She was done talking. If she kept her mouth shut, she'd stop putting her foot in it.

"You're looking a little stiff yourself," he said. "What did you do to your leg? You're moving as if you've forgotten how to use your knees."

"Just a scrape," she said. "Nothing I can't handle."

Actually her leg hurt even more than it had last night. When she took the tumble she'd somehow managed to pull all the muscles in her inner thigh, and the long wound was making it difficult to walk. Every time her skin stretched she wanted to scream, but there was no way she'd ever admit it. Especially to him.

"You don't strike me as the princess type."

"What's that supposed to mean?"

Daniel smiled. "It means that I'd still go out of my way to rescue you, but you'd probably smack me across the head and try to slay the dragon yourself."

"Let's not forget who rescued who last night."

"If you want to call it that, sure. So as a reward, I've got a gift for you," Daniel said. She realized he was holding something behind his back.

"What?"

"Something that'll make our day a little more bearable," he said, bringing the item out for her inspection. Monopoly. World Edition.

She laughed. "I'm gonna kick your ass."

"You're on. But I get to be the car."

Unwrapping the plastic, they spread the game out over one of the display tables back in the housewares department. They played three games, two of which she won. They raided the junk-food aisle and brought back bags of potato chips, cheese-flavored popcorn, and cans of iced tea.

Several times she tried questioning him about whether he knew more about what was happening. He seemed to know so much, but he refused to answer or he quickly changed the topic. Eventually she stopped asking.

"I think I've officially had enough Monopoly to last a lifetime," she said after the last game. She checked her watch. Six thirty. She stood up and walked to the edge of the main aisle. From across the store she could see the large entrance doors. Outside the sky was beginning to darken.

"Days are getting shorter," Daniel said.

"It's gonna be a cold winter," she agreed. "Especially with no heat or power. We should have gone south."

She was joking, but as usual he didn't get it.

"You never would have made it."

"Aren't you ever optimistic about anything?" She crossed her arms over her chest. Funny how just talking about the weather could make one cooler.

"Nope."

Earlier she'd taken a cardigan off the rack that she liked, dark forest green with brown wooden buttons and a hood. Daniel picked it up off her chair and handed it to her. She pulled it around her back, but her arm got tangled up in the sleeve. Reaching over, he touched her arm as he helped. Continued to hold her as he looked down into her eyes.

"You've got to go soon," he said.

"Come with me."

"No."

She yanked her arm away from him. "What is wrong with you?"

But he wasn't paying any attention. Instead, he stared over her head, his eyes focused on the main entrance, a taut look on his face.

"Did you hear that?"

She instantly stiffened. "What?"

Ignoring her, he brushed past her and into the main aisle. She followed just behind him, moving closer to the front of the store. Daniel knelt down behind a laundry-detergent display and she joined him.

Outside, the parking lot looked empty. But it was dark and there were a lot of shadows. She couldn't really see anything.

"They're out there," he whispered.

"What? Where? I can't see them."

"I feel them."

Glass shattered. Something bounced across the floor, coming to a full stop twenty feet away from them. A rock.

Daniel turned and grabbed her arm. He began walking quickly toward the back of the store and the loading docks. Earlier she'd packed up her backpack and left it in the bay along with her new bicycle.

"Aries," he said as he dragged her along. "Listen to me. You've got to listen. I need you to leave. Get out while you can."

"I can't leave you. Come with me."

He shook his head. "You don't understand. They're here for me. Not you. Just me."

"You're right. I don't understand." She tried to yank her arm away from him, but he was too strong. "Stop it. You're hurting me."

He ignored her protests all the way to the loading docks. Pushing a flashlight into her hands, he checked through the peephole in the door before unlocking it. She waited stupidly while he pushed her bike out into the back lane. She tried to listen for sounds coming from the store, signs that the insane people had made their way in, but she couldn't hear anything.

Once Daniel finished checking outside, he came back for her. Grabbing her arm again, he literally dragged her out into the lane.

"I'm not leaving you here," she said. Tears formed in her eyes. She couldn't do it. There was nothing he could say that would make her go away. She wouldn't leave him to die. Enough people had died already. She wouldn't allow another.

"It's okay," he said. Pulling her toward him, he drew his arms around her, hugging her tightly. Whispered in her ear. "I'll be fine. You're going to have to trust me on this."

"No." She tried to untangle herself from his grasp. He was just too strong.

"Aries." When she didn't respond, he grabbed hold of her chin and forced her to look at him. "I'm going to tell you something important and I don't want you to forget, okay?"

She nodded, choking back a sob.

"They're not all bad. Remember this. Some of them still feel the light. I'll be fine. I promise. And I'm not going to break that promise either. When this is over I'll find you."

"We're on Alexander Street. It's the only building with the roof caved in. You can't miss it."

He sighed. "I told you not to tell me."

"I'm sorry."

"I have to leave now. Let me go."

She did.

He didn't say another word. Instead he ran up the stairs toward the store and disappeared into the darkness of the receiving bay. The door closed behind him and she was alone.

When her paralysis broke, she took the stairs two at a time and grabbed the handle. But the door was locked.

She didn't know what to do. Everything had happened too quickly. Sitting down on the steps, she tried to weigh her options. She couldn't get in from the back. It would be suicidal to go around to the front.

He'd won. He'd gotten his way. Now she had no choice but to leave. She'd have to believe him.

Red-hot anger pulsated through her body. Jumping to her feet, she grabbed her backpack and pulled it over her shoulders. Fine. If that's the way he wanted it, then let him go. She was through playing his game. If he'd rather get himself killed than be with her, well, she wasn't going to fight him.

By the time she reached the apartment, the butterflies were still rioting inside her stomach. The fear of the unknown. Daniel. The monsters disguised as people.

How could she prepare for a war she knew she couldn't win?

NOTHING

We forget how truly fragile we are.

Skin. We do so much to it. Burn it. Tattoo it. Rub chemicals into its surface. Sometimes we scrape it, pierce it, poke holes through its softness.

Skin holds us together. It keeps the blood inside. Without it, we die.

When the knife slashed through her skin, she gave a look to suggest she couldn't believe I'd hurt her. Such surprise. Shock. She would die. The blood rushed past her skin, no longer trapped inside her flesh, and pooled onto the floor beneath her toes.

She thought she'd live forever.

"You need to have thicker skin," I told her. Famous last words. Spoken to me in my former life by someone I once loved.

Thicker skin.

But in reality I needed a stronger brain.

I have three scars aligning my body. They are a diary of sorts, chronicling my life according to the things I've done. The things that have been done to me.

1. A round scar the size of a quarter on the middle of my right palm. At the age of five my father punished me by pouring boiling water onto my skin. Forced me to hold out my hand and poured the water straight from the kettle once it boiled. It was for my own good. I'd been bad.

2. A large scar on my knee from falling off my bicycle. I was seven. I had stolen something trivial and the grocer came after me. Of course I got caught. I had my finger broken as punishment, and he refused to take me to the hospital. My skin still wasn't thick enough.

3. A thin line along my wrist from where I tried to let the blood come out.

I'm not proud of the things I've done. Or of the things I know I will do in the future. We became evil because we deserved it, not because we lived our lives as saints. The darkness cannot go where the light holds warmth. Sometimes it is easier to embrace the pain than fight against the fire. Free will isn't always about choice; often weakness plays the game.

If you heard all about my childhood, you'd refuse to lay the blame on my side. You'd say I was a victim. Not guilty. But the voices know better. They still saw fit to judge me. To claim my soul.

I want to stop. I want someone to help me.

Help me, before I kill her.

MICHAEL

"It's cold," Clementine said.

They'd stopped for a lunch of canned spaghetti and dried fruit, stuff they found in an outlet store a few days earlier. A rest stop next to a lake, one of the many dozen tourist attractions spread across the Rocky Mountains.

"It's going to snow," he said.

"How do you know?"

"It smells like snow."

Clementine sniffed the air and gave him a confused look.

He'd forgotten that she'd never traveled through the mountains before. She was from the prairies, a place where everything was wide-open. So different from his upbringing in the valley, where lakes and trees were just another part of the boring scenery and the winters were cold and uncomfortable.

"I guess it's one of those things you get good at noticing," he said. "I can't explain it, but you can always tell the way snow smells out here. I dunno."

"We're not dressed for snow," she said, and he realized she was right.

They wore jean jackets and hoodies. No winter coats or

gloves or scarves or even boots. Why didn't he think about it
when they passed their last outlet store?

Because other things were on his mind. The thought that
haunted him the most was of the mother and her small son.
Had it hurt? He hoped the Baggers had shown mercy and
killed the child quickly. Why hadn't he done something to try
to save them?

Besides, September had been hotter than hot. Yeah, sure, it
was October now, but it was still warm. Or it had been. Yet
he should have thought about how unpredictable mountain
weather could be.

"Let's get going," he said. Jumping down off the table, he
picked up his backpack and slung it over his shoulder. "If we
keep at it, we should be able to find a cabin or something to
spend the night. There's lots of places around here. We just
have to find them."

"Okay."

"Having a bit of snow might be a good thing, too. If we're
lucky it'll send the Baggers south. It's gonna be a cold one
without electricity."

"Seattle will be warmer," she said. "Heath said it just rains
there."

The first flakes hit them as they stepped out onto the road.
Just a few tumbling lazily down from the darkened clouds
above.

"See," he said. "Can I call them or what?"

"It's beautiful," she said, her head tilted upward. "I love the
first snowfall of the season. I always liked to take a walk in the
fields and just stare up at the clouds. It's almost as if the entire
sky is dancing just for me."

Michael hated snow, but he didn't tell her that. It meant
shoveling and frozen faces, hibernating in the basement and

playing video games until he grew bored to death. Winter always made him want to curl up and sleep. Mom used to joke that he was part bear. He'd been planning on going to university in California or Arizona, someplace he knew would be hot all year long.

The snow melted at first when it hit the pavement, but after thirty minutes or so, a fine film of white began to cover the surface. Large flakes dominated the sky, falling faster and harder with each new footstep. Michael grew worried but tried not to show it. He didn't want to frighten her, but the world around them appeared to be getting ready for an all-out blizzard. A strong wind blew up behind them, pressing against their clothes, trying to rip the hair right off their heads. The sun was fully gone. Not even three in the afternoon, but the woods were dark. The snow blocked everything else out.

They needed to find shelter.

"How is this even possible?" she yelled over the howling wind. He could hear her teeth chattering in between words. "It was sunny and warm this morning."

"I've seen worse," he shouted back.

"Really? You could actually see it? I can't even see the road in front of us."

It was true. Visibility had completely gone down the toilet.

"Just keep your eyes peeled for turnoffs," he said. "There's gotta be something around here. I grew up in this area. There are hundreds of cabins nearby."

All right, it was a bit of a lie. He'd lived farther south where dozens of ski hills dominated the terrain. Right now he didn't have the foggiest idea where they really were. For all he knew they could have gone too far north and crossed the border into Canada. He'd been going around in circles a lot lately, not paying attention to where the road led. With the group, their main priority had been to find food. But alone, well, no matter how much he traveled, he couldn't seem to get far enough away.

But he didn't mention a word of this to her. The last thing in the world he wanted to do was scare her more than she already was.

He hadn't wanted to scare the others, either. Look where that got them.

The blizzard continued, and it wasn't long before they were up to their ankles in the white powder. The sun disappeared completely and nightfall took over. The wind howled at their backs. Michael's face started to hurt and his toes grew alarmingly numb. Clementine didn't complain, but he could tell she was suffering as much as him. She pulled her jacket tightly around her neck with both hands, trying to keep the snow from falling down her shirt. Her cheeks and forehead were bright red and her blond hair whipped uncontrollably around her head.

They trudged along.

If they didn't find shelter soon they would freeze to death. It struck Michael as ironic. This seemed like the wrong way to die considering the circumstances.

But he wasn't ready to die. Not when he still wanted to live.

"What's that?" Clementine shouted over the wind.

Michael looked and didn't see much at first. But then he spotted a shadow through the storm. Thin and long, stretched out along the road. It took him several minutes before he finally realized what it was.

"Mailboxes," he said. "Those are mailboxes."

A big rectangular row of metal boxes, stacked on top of one another, the kind in rural communities. Three rows of four. Often people lived too far out for the post office to travel to, so they grouped them together in one area.

"There must be houses close by," he said. "We're saved."

But Clementine wasn't rejoicing the way he thought she would. Instead she peered back the way they'd come, staring into the white nothingness.

"What do you see?"

"Something's moving back there."

Michael turned his attention back toward the road behind them. At first he couldn't see anything except snow, but then it was there for a quick instant: someone darted across the path and stepped into the bushes. Another figure followed a moment after.

"Oh, God," he said. "They've found us."

Grabbing her hand, he began to run. He didn't have to drag her along—she came willingly. "Hold on tight," he said. "If I lose you in this I might never find you."

She clenched his hand tighter.

He didn't see the first Bagger until he was inches from his face, the black veins in his eyes burning. The monster stepped out in front of him; Michael was moving too fast to stop. He slammed into it, knocking their foreheads together and falling down into a heap, dragging Clementine along with him. His face ended up right against the Bagger's mouth, and he could smell the stench of tooth decay. Letting go of Clementine's hand, he shoved upward, trying to get far away from the crazy man.

The Bagger grabbed his arm. "What's your hurry?" he snapped.

Clementine darted in from the right, kicking the man hard, and he fell, loosening his grip on Michael enough for him to pull free. Too much time was wasted. The other Baggers emerged from the woods. There were at least five of them, each as poorly dressed and unprepared for the cold as them.

"Come on," Michael said. Reaching out for Clementine, he realized he couldn't see her anymore. She'd simply disappeared into the whirling snow. He backed up several feet, losing track of the Baggers and stepping unexpectedly off the road. Falling, he stumbled into the bushes and tripped over a root, his already numb hands plunging into half a foot of icy snow.

He wanted to scream out for her, but he knew it would only alert the Baggers to his location.

From a distance he could make out the shapes of people moving in more than one direction. But which one was Clementine? It reminded him of one of those game shows where you had to pick the right box in order to win the million dollars. Moving toward the closest shadow, he hesitated.

Even if he found her now they couldn't run. There was nowhere left to run to. One couldn't outrun a blizzard. They'd only get lost in the woods and freeze to death.

Changing his mind, he started walking in one direction, hoping that might work, but he was all turned around and pretty sure he was only going in circles no matter how straight he tried to travel. He came across footprints in the snow, quickly being filled by the falling flakes. He couldn't tell if they were his own or someone else's.

He didn't even see the cabin until he stepped right into the stairs, smashing his leg on the wooden railing.

Scrambling up on all fours, he yanked open the screen door and checked the dead bolt. Locked. Without even pausing, he glanced around until he spotted the woodpile in the corner. Picking up the biggest log, he hurled it into the door's small window. Reaching his hand through the hole, he unlocked the door and stepped into the living room.

She's still out there.

He didn't care if the house was empty or not—he'd worry about that later. Running straight through to the kitchen, he pulled the drawers out, scattering kitchen supplies until his numb fingers closed over a sharp paring knife. His knuckles were bleeding; he must have cut them on the glass, but it didn't matter.

He returned to the front door and paused. If he went back out into the blizzard, he might not be able to find the house again. It was sheer dumb luck he'd found it in the first place.

He needed help.

Back in the kitchen, he tore through the cupboards again, fully aware that every single second counted. The longer he waited, the farther away Clementine could be. Had the Baggers found her yet? He didn't want to think about it. Finally he came across the ball of twine. This would work. Grabbing it, he didn't even hesitate. Ran straight back out into the cold.

If he could get this one thing right, he might be able to put his guilt behind him.

The storm seemed to have worsened in the few precious minutes wasted indoors. He took the twine and fastened one end to the stairwell. Clenching the rest of the ball tightly, he ventured back out into the whiteness.

He unraveled the string as he moved along, his fingers progressively freezing with each step. Twice he dropped the roll in the snow, and the second time he was forced down on knees to search the growing drifts.

The wind whipped his hair around, catching it on branches and in his mouth. His eyes watered, teardrops crawling and freezing on his cheeks. He thought he spotted a moving shadow but it turned out to be nothing but a tree.

Running out of time. If he didn't find her soon he'd have to retreat back to the house.

Run away all over again.

Run, you coward.

Something reached out and pulled on his jacket.

Screaming, he spun around, numb fingers clutching the knife, ready to stab the Bagger.

"Michael."

He threw his arms around her, dropping both the knife and the string, and pulled her into an awkward hug. She returned the favor, crying and laughing at the same time.

"Come on," he said. "I've found shelter."

Grabbing the twine once more, he got her to take hold of his arm and he began the daunting task of reeling them both back to the cabin.

"I thought I lost you," she said.

"You found me."

"I was so scared. I didn't want to die that way. One of the Baggers attacked me. Tried to claw my eyes out. I hit her in the head with a rock. I think I killed her."

"Good for you."

"She wasn't the first."

They found the steps and he led her up into the cabin. Once inside, he locked the door, but that wouldn't be enough.

In the living room, thankfully only about five feet from the entrance, was an antique china cabinet filled with wineglasses and fancy-looking dinnerware.

"Come on, help me," he said.

They pushed the heavy furniture, dishes and glasses spilling out and breaking on the floor. It took several minutes, but eventually they got it into place. No one would be coming through the door anytime soon. Together they went around to the kitchen and checked the back door. It was locked.

"Should we put something in front of it?" Clementine asked.

"No, we might need it for a quick exit."

"Good point."

Back to the living room they went, and Michael saw the fireplace. Beside it was a neat stack of logs and kindling. Kneeling down in front of the hearth, he began to stack the wood to make a fire. He'd had a lot of experience from camping with his dad, and it didn't take long before the flames caught and a little bit of heat spread throughout the room.

Clementine peeled off her wet jacket and sat in the middle of the floor, shivering while she tried to untie the laces on her shoes.

"I can't feel my toes," she said.

Michael went over to join her. He removed her socks and examined her feet. They were solid white, but at least there were no signs of frostbite. Taking hold of her left foot, he placed a hand on each side and started rubbing it furiously.

"My father used to do this to me after hockey practice," he said. "It works really well. You'll be warm in no time." When he finished with her first foot, he started in on the second. The color began to return to her chilled skin.

"What if they see the fire?" she asked. "Shouldn't we draw the blinds?"

"Yeah, probably a good idea."

They got up and went over to the windows. Peering out into the blizzard, Michael could see only snow. Even the trees were hard to spot. He shut the blinds just in case.

"Will they notice the smoke from the chimney?"

He shook his head. "I doubt it. Not in this storm. We'll have to be more careful once it lets up."

She moved back over toward the fireplace and he noticed she was limping. He wasn't surprised. Her sneakers were of the summer variety, and her wet socks were as thin as nylons. Ignoring his own pain, he headed to the closet by the front door. Inside he found a big woolly scarf and matching hat.

"Here," he said. Taking the hat, he pulled it down over her head. It was too big, but it would keep her warm. Next he wrapped the scarf around her neck.

"I'm gonna go upstairs and take a look," he said. "Maybe I can find some sweaters."

"Okay."

Trying to ignore the feeling of déjà vu, he wandered off, fully aware of what happened the last time he went upstairs to take a look. The last thing he wanted to find again was death.

In the second bedroom he found some winter sweaters and socks. Piling them in his arms, he hurried back to find her wrapped up in a thick blanket.

"It was behind the couch," she said.

They changed into the warmer clothes and sat down next to the fire. There was nothing to do now but wait.

"Are you hungry?" he asked.

She shook her head. "My stomach's too freaked out to eat. You?"

"Yeah, me too."

They sat together for a while, the fire crackling and spitting sparks.

"Last time I had a fire was Christmas," she said. "It was our first holiday without Heath."

Michael went over to the fire and threw another log onto the pile. "You're very close with your brother. You're lucky. I have a sister somewhere, but I never see her. She's with my mom, or she used to be with her."

"Don't talk like that. You don't know for sure."

"You're right."

"Yeah, Heath and I are close," Clementine said. "We used to hang out lots. It sucked when he went to Seattle. I wanted to go and visit, but you get busy with things? School. Cheerleading practice. Craig Strathmore. Now all those things seem unimportant. I can't remember why I cared so much about them."

"I played football and I was also in a band," Michael said. "We were terrible. Our singer always sang off-key. But I agree with you. It seemed so important. Now I don't really care if I never pick up a guitar again."

Clementine shook her head. "Don't say that. We should find you a guitar. Music is one of those things we're going to need. I think that's wonderful."

There was a lag in the conversation while the two of them stared distractedly into the fire. Finally Clementine laughed. "This is so weird."

"What? The conversation?"

"Yeah. We're trapped in this house and those monsters might break down the door any second, but we're talking about cheerleading and guitars."

Michael nodded. "Maybe it's good for us, though. Helps get our minds off stuff."

"I wish I could shut my brain down for a bit. Some days I'd give anything to stop thinking."

"Yeah, me too."

"Why?" Clementine asked after another long silence.

"I don't know."

"Do you think we deserved it? Humans aren't exactly the best things for the planet. Maybe we went too far. Did too much damage."

"I don't believe that."

"Do you believe in God?"

"No. You?"

She paused. "I'm not sure. Maybe. If there is a God, I don't think He's the one doing this."

"Could be a disease."

"Maybe."

"Which means anyone could catch it."

"That would make us immune," she said. "If we were infected, we'd surely be Baggers by now."

"Thinking about it makes my head hurt," he said. "Some things you're just better off accepting. I don't understand, but I know I want to survive. That's all I need, I guess."

She nodded, dropping back into silence.

It was the longest night of his life. Every time the house creaked, his heart pounded at his rib cage. When the wind slammed against the windows, it took all his strength not to jump up and run. He imagined he could hear the Baggers climbing up the steps to the door. He visualized them breaking the windows and climbing in to get them, their eyes distorted in rage.

But nothing happened.

Around two, Clementine drifted off, curled up on the couch closest to the fireplace. Michael grew tired, but he forced himself to stay awake. He kept busy stirring the fire around with a poker for a while. He tried reading one of the books he found on the shelf, but he couldn't concentrate. After reading the same paragraph five times he gave up and put it back. He looked through the DVD collection by the flat screen and decided the owner had terrible taste in movies.

Eventually he sat down in one of the chairs and closed his eyes.

It didn't take long till he fell asleep.

He awoke with a start several hours later. The fire was nothing but a mess of burning embers. Clementine was still on the couch, curled up into a tiny ball, only half her face showing under the winter hat.

He got up and threw a few logs on the fire, coaxing it back to life. The living room was toasty. Once the flames were active again, he looked out the window. The blizzard had ended during the night and the morning sun was beginning to rise over the treetops. The ground was a blanket of rich snow.

He couldn't see any footprints. A good sign.

He'd give the fire ten minutes or so before extinguishing it. The smoke was still too risky, even more so now.

Leaving Clementine to sleep, he wandered over to the kitchen and poked through the cupboards and studied the fancy espresso machine. He missed coffee. The way it used to be so convenient. All he had to do was go into a shop and order up a large or venti or jumbo or whatever fancy word was being used and receive a steaming hot beverage of his choice. Latte. Mocha. Caramel macchiato.

Now coffee was pretty much impossible unless they had the option of fire. Luckily for him that morning, they did. In the bottom cupboard he found a big pot, and he filled it with bottled water found in the pantry. Using the fireplace poker, he held the water over the fire until it boiled. Pouring a generous amount of coffee into the water, he stirred it around with a spoon until it looked good enough to drink.

The coffee was bitter, and the grounds got in his mouth when he reached the bottom of the cup, but it still tasted wonderful. He poured a second and then a third. By then Clementine had started to stir.

"Is it over?" she asked, stretching out on the couch and knocking half the blanket onto the floor. "Has it stopped snowing?"

"Yep." He handed her a mug. "It kinda tastes like sludge, but it's better than nothing."

She took a sip. "It's wonderful."

"We shouldn't stay long. Maybe just take a look around and see if we can get any clothing. They might still be out there, and it'll be easier to find without the storm."

"I was thinking the same thing," she said. "At least now I can feel my toes again."

One hour later they were ready to go. In the garage they found the ultimate item. A monster-sized SUV with four-wheel drive and a full tank of gas.

"We won't get far if we come across a traffic jam," he said. "But at least it'll get us a little farther down the road at a much faster speed. And we can bring some blankets this way. Might not use them, but at least we'll be better prepared."

"Okay, but I drive," she said.

"I'd better wear my seat belt."

She laughed and swatted at him. Ducking, he went around to the front of the car and manually opened the garage door.

They both saw the body at the same time.

Lying facedown, half buried in the snow, it was inches from the garage, one hand reaching out as if trying to grab the air.

"Is it one of them?" she asked.

Michael moved in closer. "I think so," he said.

"Don't touch it!"

He ignored her, pushing the body with his boot, wanting to make sure the person was dead. He'd have to move it out of the way in order to get the SUV out of the garage. He grabbed the body by the shoulders and started dragging it to the side. Clementine came to help.

The frozen body was female. Her mouth was open and filled with ice. "That's the women who tried to claw out my eyes," Clementine said. "She almost found us."

Michael shivered. What would have happened if she'd managed to make it a few more steps before collapsing? Both of them had fallen asleep. They would have been sitting ducks. Mice in a cage. Game over.

"There's another one," she said, and she pointed. Fifty feet away, a body was slouched against a tree wearing a bright red jacket.

"I think we need to leave," he said.

She nodded.

The SUV roared to life on the first try. If they were lucky the vehicle might take them all the way into Seattle.

If they were lucky.

MASON

In Revelstoke they found a working moped. There was only one helmet, which Mason insisted Chickadee wear the entire time, and she put it on without complaint.

She wasn't looking good. Paul's departure hit her hard and she'd lost a lot of the light that seemed to follow her around. She still talked lots, but the cheerful banter was gone. Now her voice had a certain sorrow to it. Sometimes she grew irritated and would snap at him, only to completely break down and apologize. It made Mason uncomfortable. He didn't know what to do to make things better.

"Are you sure you're okay?" he asked for the hundredth time.

"Just tired," she replied.

"Exhausted" was the better word choice. There were black bags under her eyes, and sometimes she seemed to have trouble focusing. Whenever they stopped, she fell asleep, sometimes even sitting up. Her head would nod and soon she'd be breathing softly, her chin resting on her chest.

Mason grew scared. He knew something was happening, and he was completely at a loss over what to do. Every time he tried to bring anything up in conversation, she'd insist she was all right and then change the subject.

He asked her if she wanted to stop in Kamloops. She said no. He asked her again in Merritt. She said no.

"I want to make it to Vancouver," she said. "I want to see the ocean. It's been forever since I last saw it. I'll bet it's beautiful. I want to walk out into the waves and feel the sand squish beneath my toes. It's the greatest feeling in the world, don't you think?"

"I don't remember," Mason said. "I was really young."

"Really? Then we've got another reason to get there fast. It'll be like you're seeing it again for the first time. I want to be the person you're with when that happens. You're gonna just die of happiness."

They made it as far as Hope.

Both of them were on the moped. Mason steered while Chickadee wrapped her arms around his waist. One second her grip was fine; the next moment her fingers loosened and she slipped away, crashing onto the pavement.

"Chee!"

He slammed the brakes. It had been raining earlier, and the back tires fishtailed behind him, forcing him into a half turn, half skid. The bike slid out from underneath him, bringing him down.

Thankfully they weren't going very fast. His leg got caught under the moped, but it didn't do much damage aside from tearing his jeans. As soon as he came to a stop he pulled himself up off the ground and ran to where Chickadee lay in the middle of the open road. She was on her back, her brown eyes staring up at the sky without blinking.

"That was really stupid of me," she whispered.

"Are you okay?" he asked. "Can you move?"

"Yeah, help me up, will you?" She reached out her hand to him and he took it. Gently, he guided her into a sitting position and helped her with the helmet. Her face was pale; she was obviously as shaken as him. "I don't know what happened. One minute I was fine, and then the world went all blurry."

"We've got to . . ." He paused, the words "take you to a doctor" froze on his tongue. The idea seemed so ridiculous; he was annoyed that he'd even thought about it for a second.

"Not really an option anymore," she said, second-guessing him. "I wish there still were doctors. Or artists. Even teachers. They're all gone, aren't they? But you're still here. I'm glad you care about me, Mason."

He picked her up. She'd lost a lot of weight since he first met her; now she was light in his arms. Without saying a word, he started back in the direction of town. If he couldn't take her to a doctor, at least he could find a motel where she could rest for a bit. He wasn't sure if it would help her, but it certainly couldn't hurt.

She wrapped her arms around him as they moved down the hill and under the overpass. Her body pressed tightly against him, she felt both cold and hot at the same time. She leaned her head into his chest and he looked down at her, inhaling the scent of her hair and kissing the top of her head.

"I must smell so bad," she said. "I can't actually remember the last time I showered."

"No," he said. "You don't."

She laughed. "Liar."

"No worse than me," he admitted.

"Then I really stink," she said.

When this whole thing started, after his mother and his friends died, he told himself he was done caring. For weeks he'd kept the numbness inside, a hollow feeling that constantly gnawed at the corner of his mind. He focused instead on being angry, growing to embrace his thoughts of rage. It kept him strong. But Chickadee had somehow managed to get through his barriers and chase the emptiness away. She'd helped him move on. He hadn't even realized how much.

Now the numbness started to creep back into his mind.

There was a group of people on the edge of town fighting over something too small to see. Mason ducked behind a car, pulling Chickadee down to the ground beside him. He had no idea who the people were, but history had taught him that no one was safe, especially those making that much noise in the middle of the afternoon. If they were to spot him now, he wouldn't be able to protect Chickadee. Instead they had to wait till the group moved farther down toward the river before attempting to sneak into a motel that offered free wireless to all its customers. Mason carried her into the main office, where he snagged a set of keys for a room that faced the back.

"Will they come back?" Chickadee asked.

"I don't know."

"What if they're staying in the motel? What will we do then?"

"I don't know."

"Why are you so upset with me?"

"I'm not."

"You sound like you are."

He ignored her. What could he say? He didn't have any answers.

Once in the room, he helped her down on the bed, double locked the door, and drew the blinds. Chickadee started coughing, and he opened up her backpack and pulled out a bottle of water.

"Please don't be mad at me," she said.

"I'm not." He reached out and brushed a few strands of hair off her face. Her skin was warm to the touch, but she didn't seem feverish. Her eyes were bright and wide, and she stared at him like he was the only person left in the world.

"I think I need to rest," she said.

Pulling the blankets off the spare bed, he drew them over her and fluffed up the pillows in a dramatic fashion to try and get her to laugh. Afterward, he sat down in a chair by the window and waited. He couldn't admit this to Chickadee, but he was terrified. He knew she wasn't feeling well—he'd known for several days. She kept insisting she was fine, and he tried to believe she really was just tired. But it was more than that and both of them knew it. The problem was he didn't know what to do. If Chickadee knew the cause of her sickness, she wasn't sharing. He listened to her breathing. It was slow and steady; she had fallen asleep. Good. Hopefully the rest would help her.

Night fell and he continued to wait by the window. Every now and then he'd take a peek to make sure they were still alone. Everything was quiet. Aside from the people they'd seen earlier, the town seemed deserted. A good sign.

They were so close to Vancouver. They could have made it in a few hours if Chickadee hadn't fallen off the bike. Vancouver was a large city—there had to be a lot of people still alive. If he could just get her there, well, maybe there was the possibility he could find a doctor.

He remembered the last night at his house several weeks ago when he destroyed everything in sight. Right now he wanted to go on a rampage against the room. Pull the paintings down off the wall, punch holes in things, smash the television, and break everything in sight. So much rage was building up inside, and he had no way to relieve the tension. When did he get this angry? He never used to be this way. Once upon a time he was a nice guy. He played soccer and hung out with his friends. He'd never been the type to get into fights or do random acts of vandalism. But yet, several weeks ago he'd murdered someone in a park.

Where was this anger coming from? Worse, deep down, why did he enjoy it?

"Mason?"

He was up off the chair in seconds and over by the bed. "I'm here," he said, sitting down beside her. She held out her hand and he took it. Her eyes were wide. Scared.

"I have diabetes."

"What?"

"I'm sorry, I should have told you sooner, but I didn't want to scare you away." She started crying. Big tears fell down her cheeks. "I'm so sorry."

"It's not your fault," he said. Pulling her close, he hugged her and stroked her hair, ignoring the tightness building up inside his chest.

"I should have told you. I should have said something. I just didn't want you to leave. I was so afraid you'd leave me."

"I'm here. I'm not leaving."

"Really?"

"Promise."

He held her. Was it enough? Shouldn't he be doing more? Chickadee continued to cry herself out, and he kept his arms wrapped tightly around her body. There were so many questions he wanted to ask, but he didn't know how to start. He knew nothing about diabetes, except maybe that she needed insulin to survive. When he was in grade school there was a kid who had to inject himself with a needle every day. Did this mean she was going to die? People survived with diabetes all the time. They had normal, long lives. Didn't they?

"There's a drugstore in town," he finally said. "Can I go get something to help?"

She shook her head against his chest. "It's too late. I've been checking the pharmacies all this time, and most of them have been looted. Remember? You caught me looking and thought I was a druggie." She tried to laugh, but it came out more like a choked sob. "It wasn't too hard the first few weeks, but then the electricity went out. Insulin has a shelf date and has to be kept cold. Even if I manage to find some, it will have expired. I've been really careful up until now. Trying to monitor my sugar intake. But it's not helping anymore."

"You told me you weren't sick."

"I'm not. I have a disease. That's a whole lot different than a cold."

"So you kept it from me? I thought we were friends. I thought we were . . ." He couldn't bring himself to suggest something different. What if he was wrong and she laughed? "You should have told me. I would have tried to help."

"I screwed up," she said. "You're right. I should have said something. But I was afraid. Look at what Paul did. He's known me his entire life. But he still left me. I was so scared you'd leave too."

"I'm not Paul."

"No, you're not."

They sat together on the bed for a while in silence. Neither of them knew what to say. Finally Mason couldn't hold back the one question he needed to ask.

"So what does this mean?"

He didn't want to know the answer. He didn't want to know the answer. He didn't want to know the answer.

"Mason?"

"Yeah?"

"Whatever happens, I want you to promise me something. Promise me you'll continue on to Vancouver and feel the ocean. Don't just stand there and look at it. Feel it."

"I don't care about the ocean."

"I do. Consider it my dying wish."

"Stop talking like that. You're not going to die. You'll be fine after some more rest. Maybe I should go check out the pharmacy, just in case."

"Can you stay with me instead? I don't want you to leave."

He hugged her tightly to his chest. "Okay."

"But promise me you'll go."

"Why? That doesn't matter anymore." How could she even think about such trivial things when she didn't even have the strength to sit up?

"It matters to me."

He decided to humor her. "Okay. I promise."

"Mean it."

He should have known she'd see through his empty promise. Nothing ever got past her. She'd known Paul was leaving the night he told his story. That's why she'd been so upset. She wasn't going to give up on this, either. He could tell by the look on her face that she desperately wanted him to go, and he knew her well enough by now to know that she always got what she wanted when she was determined enough.

"I give you my word." And this time he meant it.

She nodded slightly. They sat together in the darkness for a while. In the distance, he heard the haunting, lonely sound of a loon.

"Look on the bright side," Chickadee said after a while.

"What's that?"

"It's not the end of the world."

"Been there, done that," he said with a forced chuckle.

"You know, I'm really glad I met you, Mason Dowell," she said. "Maybe if things had been different, you could have been my boyfriend. There's something special about you. It wouldn't have taken me long to fall in love with you. I would have liked that."

"Me too."

Around two, she slipped into a coma. He pressed his fingers against her wrist and felt the rapid pulsations of her heartbeat. Her body broke out into a sweat, and several times he held her carefully as she twitched and convulsed. He continued to rock her in his arms, whispering softly into her ear, hoping she could still hear.

Sometime in the morning, just as the sun was beginning to peek over the treetops, Chickadee took her last breath.

He didn't try to revive her. All he could think about was his promise. The ocean would be nothing but salt water without her by his side.

The hardest part was letting go of her hand.

Carefully he worked his way out from underneath her body and went to the window. Opening the blinds, he blinked a few times as the sunlight hit his face.

What a beautiful day. The sun was shining and there wasn't a single cloud to be found. On the mountains the pine trees were bright and green. Their branches sparkled with morning dew. Birds chirped happily in the bushes, and a squirrel ran across the motel garden searching for breakfast.

A good day to die.

He went outside and walked around the complex without thinking. He watched a deer grazing before his presence spooked it back into the bushes. A spider spun a web from the top of a rusty swing set. A forgotten shirt hung lazily on a clothesline. He paused to look at everything that caught his interest, but afterward he couldn't remember a thing. Finally he stopped in front of a garden shed, where he found a shovel. At the tree line out the back of the motel, he began to dig.

The sun beat down and his shirt became soaked with perspiration. His lower back ached as the mound of dirt beside him grew and his hole deepened. Blisters formed on the palms of his hands, brutally stinging when they broke and mixed with his body sweat. Twice in frustration and anger he flung the shovel into the woods, listening for the satisfying sound as metal hit tree trunk.

It was hard work. Mechanical. He didn't have to think while he did it. Good. He didn't want to remember. He'd bury his pain along with her body.

Eventually he realized he wasn't alone.

A short, skinny man with a terrible overbite and a dirty baseball cap had come over to watch. When Mason glanced at him, he gave him the thumbs-up gesture.

"What do you want?" Mason asked, pressing his foot down hard on the shovel, cutting deeper into the earth. He wasn't scared of this little man in the slightest. Fear was a feeling, and the angry numbness trumped everything.

"Don't want nothing," the man said. "Just came to see whatchoo doing."

"Go away."

"Not very friendly, are you?"

Scooping some dirt up from the hole, he tossed it in the direction of the man. "Nope."

"You need to learn your manners."

"I'm not looking for a fight." He figured the man wouldn't

want to attack him either. Mason had a weapon, and shovels could really hurt if used properly.

"Why do you think I'd be wanting to fight you?"

"Isn't that what your kind does? Kill anything that moves?" How had Twiggy once put it? Destroy humanity?

"Some of us, yah. But I ain't one of those kind. I ain't looking to kill anything without purpose. I prefer to show the truth."

Mason tossed the shovel into the hole and stood straight. "You know. I keep hearing about these monsters who attack without saying a word. Psychotic nut jobs and all that. But I'm always meeting ones like you who just won't shut up. At this point I'm beginning to wish for one of the crazy ones so I can get some quiet."

The man chuckled and spat on the ground. "So it's peace ya wanting?"

"Yes. So please shut up and go away." Turning his back, he reached for the shovel and started digging again.

But the man didn't go away.

"Aren'tcha wasting your time with this hole?" he said. "I'm assuming it's for that little girl you brought down wit'cha last night. I ain't surprised. I suppose I would have killed her too if I had the chance. But why bother burying her? Leave her in the woods. I'm sure the wolves would like a feast."

Mason froze. "You'd better stop talking right now. You don't have a clue what you're saying."

"What's that? You got her, right? That is why you're digging, right?"

"If you're pushing for a fight, you're gonna get one." His fingers clenched the shovel tightly, ignoring the screams from his palms as his blisters popped and bled.

"Why would I want to do that? I don't fight my kind."

Mason paused. "What the hell are you talking about?"

The man brayed in laughter, doubling over for a few seconds. When he regained his composure, he still continued to chuckle. Mason's temper was on the verge of exploding. He began to picture what it would look like when he smashed the shovel into the monster's smiling face. Imagined him crumpling to the ground the way the man at Diefenbaker Park had.

"You really don't know, do you?" the man finally said. "You ain't figured it out yet."

"What?"

"You belong on our side, boy. You're just the kind of human they like."

In a matter of seconds, Mason closed the distance between them. Grabbing the man by the front of his shirt, he shoved him backward. He stared straight into his black-veined eyes. "You're lying." Pushed him again. "Take it back." Once more.

The look of amusement disappeared, and anger flashed through the strange man's eyes. "You watch yourself, boy. Alls I have to do is scream and they'll come a running. You ain't gonna be so tough against all of us."

"Take it back."

"Take what back? You look in a mirror lately? 'Cause you've got the face." The man wrestled himself free and out of Mason's reach. When he was far enough away, he turned and started walking back toward the main road. "But maybe I am lying. There's a very good chance. Or maybe not. If you're desirable, they'll come for you."

Mason turned and hurled the shovel as hard as he could. It bounced off a tree and fell to the ground several feet away. The hole was deep enough.

Back in the room he went straight for the bathroom. He didn't want to touch Chickadee when he was this filthy.

Stripping off all his clothes, he poured some bottled water into the sink and unwrapped one of the mini soaps. Grabbing a white cloth, he began to wash away the sweat and dirt.

Halfway through it dawned on him that he hadn't looked at himself in the mirror. He paused, the soapy cloth against his chest, and stared blankly at the sink.

What's wrong, Mason? Why won't you look at yourself?

He was just spooked, he told himself. The guy outside tried to freak him out because he was too tiny to take Mason on. It was his only form of action, his way of hurting Mason, because he was too cowardly to do anything else. The guy was probably collecting his friends now, aiming to bring them back to the motel to finish Mason off. And to guarantee Mason would stick around, the monster had tried to scare him into going back to the room and spending a bunch of time in the mirror.

So if that was the case, then why couldn't he bring his face up to look in the glass?

This was stupid. There was no logical reason for him to be scared. He hadn't done anything wrong and he certainly wasn't about to go on a killing rampage. Sure, he was angry, but it was justifiable. Who wouldn't harbor a lot of hate when everyone and everything he cared for was taken away?

"One." He began his countdown. "Two." Grabbing hold of the sink with both hands, he clung tightly until his knuckles were as white as the ceramic.

"Three."

He brought his eyes upward and straight into the mirror. His own face glared back at him, looking both surprised and frustrated at the same time. Sweaty brown hair stuck wetly to his forehead. Blue eyes were tired and bloodshot. What was he supposed to be looking for? Horns? Bloody tears gushing down his hollow cheeks? How about fangs? Nope. The answer was (D) None of the above.

His expression gave him a relieved grin. Suddenly the entire thing seemed ridiculous. Rolling his eyes, he returned to trying to clean the blisters on his hands. He'd have to put some bandages on them before he went back to bury Chickadee. The last thing he needed was an infection.

Grabbing the towel off the rack, he began to dry his body. Caught his full reflection in the mirror. He should be eating more. He'd obviously lost some weight over the past few weeks. Kinda hard to be healthy when the only edible food came in cans or packages.

Pulling a fresh shirt out of his backpack, he dressed quickly. There was a good chance that the lying guy was still out there waiting for him or was on his way over. He needed to get out of here. Get some fresh air. Calm down. Once he cooled off he'd be able to think more clearly.

But he wouldn't leave Chickadee. He'd take care of her first.

He carried her outside and tenderly lowered her body into the grave. Even though he'd wrapped her in the sheets, he could still see how small and fragile her body was. When he tossed the first shovelful of dirt over the clean white cotton, the tears began to flow freely. He ignored them, concentrating on the job instead. He kept thinking he should say something out loud, anything, to celebrate her life and the time they'd shared. But his mind remained blank. There were no words good enough to describe her, anyway.

When it was over, he turned and walked away. He didn't go back into the room to grab his backpack. He no longer wanted it. The road was the only important item he needed.

He'd allow himself to worry about all the other details later while he headed to Vancouver. He had a long road ahead of him and plenty of time to consider his options.

He still had an ocean to feel.

CLEMENTINE

They walked into Seattle. There were no more roads to lead the way. The intricate spiderweb of highways, overpasses, and tunnels were gone, leaving nothing but piles of asphalt and abandoned vehicles where they once were. Glass was everywhere. The city was covered in it. The buildings above were nothing but hollowed-out rebar and ghostly shells. The smell of smoke was strong. Several buildings were still on fire, presumably from where looters had been at work.

Dear Heath, I'm almost there. Have you waited for me? I hope you were somewhere safe when all this happened. Did they teach you earthquake safety when you got here? Remember how Mom used to warn us about what to do if a tornado ever came? I'd be both terrified and excited at the idea of one actually happening. I'm babbling now. Remember how you used to tease me and call me Empty-Head Barbie? Seattle really looks trashed. I've never seen such a mess. I'll be there in a few hours. I hope you get this message somehow. I'll send all the good vibes I have your way. Maybe you'll feel them the way Mom felt us. Either way, hang on tight. I'm coming.

Everything was quiet. Eerily quiet. Dead bodies were everywhere. Some were obviously victims of the earthquake, rotting and stinking from weeks of decomposition. Others were more recent, Bagger prey, still bloody and fresh. In places, they'd been tossed into piles, some of which had been burned. Clementine looked away when they came across the first bonfire. By the time they reached the eighth or ninth she stopped counting, and sometime after that it stopped making her nauseous.

What a strange thing to grow accustomed to.

"Smart," Michael whispered. The smell of decay was strong, almost overpowering, and both of them had their shirts pulled up over their faces. "They're cleaning the place up. They may be crazy, but I guess even Baggers worry about hygiene."

"Why would they do that?" she asked.

"Lots of reasons," he said. "If they plan on sticking around, they'll want to fix things. Get rid of the smell. I've heard that some of them are still pretty smart. They're not all random killing nut jobs."

"I guess that makes sense," she said.

Michael shrugged. "Maybe they're planning on rebuilding civilization. I'm not complaining about a little maid service. I've seen enough dead bodies to last a lifetime. If they want to clean them up, that's fine by me. Maybe they'll fix the roads next. Start up the power. Would be nice to have electricity again. Heat too. It'll be cold soon."

"You make them sound human."

"Aren't they? A lot of monsters are human."

She couldn't argue with that.

They turned the corner cautiously and came across an entire city block demolished by the earthquake. It reminded her of pictures they showed in history class of war-torn Europe after World War II. Such destruction. Hard to believe Mother Nature did that.

"I wonder how many died during the earthquakes," she said. Strange, she'd almost forgotten about the natural disaster. But in a way, the quakes started it all. That's when the killings began.

"Probably a lot here," he said. "I've never seen a city so shattered before. Look at all that glass. I wouldn't want to be underneath it when it fell from the buildings."

She shuddered. People would have been cut in half. Fortunately the Baggers had tidied up this area.

"Any idea how far the university is from here?" he asked.

She pulled out the map she'd taken from a gas station a few hours back. Opening it, they spread it out against the hood of a car, and Clementine tried to figure out where they were while Michael kept watch. They ended up having to walk several blocks until they discovered a street sign. Most of them had been destroyed or had gone missing. Once they established their location, they found the University of Washington on the map.

"Not bad at all," Michael said. "We should be able to get there in a few hours as long as we remain Baggerless."

They didn't reach the campus until nightfall. Not because of the Baggers but because many of the roads were no longer passable. Several times they had to backtrack and find new routes when they came across entire skyscrapers brought down by the quake. The city was now mountains of rubble.

Things got a little better once they reached I-5. There weren't as many buildings and they were able to pick up the pace.

When they finally reached the university, they stopped to look at the gigantic campus map.

"What dorm is he staying in again?" Michael asked.

"Mercer Hall," she said. In the corner of her pocket she still had his address written on a piece of paper. She'd looked at it so many times over the course of the past few weeks; the paper was worn thin from being constantly refolded. She'd ripped the page from Mom's address book, and she often pulled it out when she was depressed and lonely. It was the last thing she had of her mother's. Her only family heirloom.

"There it is," he said, pointing to the northwest corner of the map. "We can either go straight through, or be more careful and stick to the edge and go around."

"Let's go straight," she said. "It's dark enough and I'm tired of walking."

"Your call," Michael said.

As they moved into the campus, Clementine noticed that the damage wasn't nearly as bad as earlier in the streets. Hope rose in her thoughts, and she tried to shove it back into the corner of her mind.

Dear Heath, I'm trying hard not to get too excited. You may not be here. You may be dead. I'm almost at the end of my journey. I'm not sure what I'm going to do if you're gone. I haven't given things any thought past finding you. Where will I go from here? What will happen if I no longer have you to talk with? You've been so helpful to me along the way, even if you don't know it. Please don't be dead.

When they arrived at Mercer Hall she almost turned and ran back in the other direction. Her heartbeat was off the charts, and her palms were sweaty. She hadn't felt this way since a year ago when she waited for Craig Strathmore to pick her up for their first school dance.

"You look like you're going to throw up," Michael said. "Do you want to wait for a bit? We don't have to go in right away. Probably smarter if we sit back for a few hours and scope the place out. Anyone could be in there."

"No," she said. "I have to go now or I'll lose my courage. You're welcome to stay out here if you think it's unsafe."

"I never said I wasn't game," he said, giving her a reassuring grin.

The walkway was surrounded by trees and bushes. Mercer Hall was old and made of brick; it stood against the night, quiet and foreboding. Together they made their way up to the front. The wood-and-glass door was smashed and held open by a battered chair. Not a good sign.

Clementine gently stepped around the seat, wincing as the door squeaked and a piece of glass fell from the frame. Nothing came running around the corner to attack. No voices shouted out at them. She turned on her flashlight, and a circle of pale light struck the floor.

Inside, the vending machines were pried open by crowbars. Change littered the floor along with dented cans of pop. A few candy bars, stepped on and squished, and some empty wrappers. Michael picked up a can of Coke and opened it, taking a drink.

The elevator was jammed open, and she could see the wires leading down into the darkened shaft. They found the stairs and headed up to the third floor. Dried bloody palm prints covered the fire door as if someone had attempted some abstract art.

They could hear music when they reached the top, faint, coming from one of the far back rooms on the right side of the hall. It wasn't a good sign. Michael put one of his fingers up to his lips, and she nodded, almost offended that he thought she might start calling out her brother's name. She wasn't *that* stupid.

There were a lot of overturned chairs in the hallway. Piles of clothing and other sorts of personal items were tossed haphazardly in piles on the floor. Some of the doors were open. They walked farther inside, turning left and away from the music, Clementine counting the door numbers until they came across Heath's room.

The door was wide-open.

Her heart instantly dropped into her stomach. But she'd come this far. She would check out his room, even if it meant finding his body.

Michael reached out and took her hand. His fingers were warm and soft and she instantly felt a little stronger. Holding her breath, she closed her eyes tightly and stepped into the room.

When she found the courage to take a peek, she saw the room was empty. She immediately spotted the Glenmore High sweatshirt lying on the bed. Next to it was the brown sweater that Mom had bought Heath last Christmas.

Picking up the sweatshirt, she touched the fabric with her fingers. Her vision grew blurry as she fought back the tears. It wouldn't do her any good to cry. She still didn't know anything.

You're not dead yet. Not a memory while there's still hope. I won't believe it until I see your dead body.

She scanned the room; it was hard to take everything in at once, especially since the place had been obviously ransacked. The drawers were open on all the cupboards, and clothing was strewn across the floor and bunk beds. A computer monitor had been smashed against the wall. Something green and extremely moldy sat under the desk. There were socks everywhere. She looked for anything of value. A clue.

A note.

Someone walked right past the door, a guy with a towel wrapped around his head. He froze the moment he realized he wasn't alone. Turning carefully, he stared at them apprehensively. Wearing a pair of boxer shorts and a Batman shirt, he hardly looked threatening.

Clementine immediately knew he wasn't a Bagger. There was no way he could be faking that kind of fear. She held up her hands carefully, reassuringly—letting him know they weren't a threat either.

"Um . . . can I help you?"

"The guy who lives here," she said. "Heath White. Have you seen him?"

The towel dropped to the floor. "Heath? Yeah, he's gone, man. He split."

"Do you know where he went?"

"Him and his roommate took off somewhere. No idea. They asked me along, but I wouldn't go. I ain't leaving this place. It's much safer than being out there."

"You keep playing music like that and it won't be," Michael said.

"Nah," the guy said. "They've come and gone. Cleaned out the building. And I've got a good hiding spot."

"What if we were Baggers?" Michael said. "You'd be dead."

The guy looked puzzled. "Baggers? Is that what you're calling them, or is that what they call themselves?"

"What does it matter?" Michael said. "Their name or ours, you'd still be dead."

The guy shook his head and shrugged. "They said I wasn't worth it. They came and left and said I wasn't good enough to die. They took Stebbins and killed a bunch of others, but they left me alone. I doubt they'll come back."

"Why would they do that?" Clementine asked. "Why not kill everyone?"

"I dunno. Maybe they thought they were useful? They went after the tech students. Computer programming. Could be they want to get all the computers working again. How the hell should I know? I think there were some chemistry and premed guys, too."

"Rebuilding," Michael said softly. "By force."

"Who did they kill?" she asked.

The guy ignored the question. He was too busy studying Clementine. "Are you Heath's little sister? He talked about you sometimes."

She nodded. "Did he leave a message? Did he give you anything for me?"

"Nope." The guy picked his towel up off the floor. "Hey, do you want to go out with me sometime? You're seventeen, right?"

"You do realize you're not wearing any pants, *right*?"

"Whatever." The guy scratched at a pimple on his neck. "But I think he left a note somewhere. Maybe. I can't remember. If it's okay with you, I'm gonna go back to my room and check out my hiding spot. With my luck you probably led them right back here. Baggers. What a stupid name."

The guy turned and disappeared down the hall. Clementine and Michael exchanged looks, trying very hard not to laugh before the weird little guy was out of earshot.

She turned and started examining the room. It didn't take her long to find what she was looking for.

There on the desk, weighted down by a ring, Heath's school ring to be exact. The blue stone looked black in the darkness.

She picked up the paper and opened it.

Oct. 15

Dear Mom, Dad, and Clementine,

I don't know if you'll ever see this letter, but I pray that you're alive and well. We've been hiding out at the school for the past few weeks, and Aaron and I have decided to go someplace safer. There are attacks at night. People have been searching the dorms and killing the survivors. Most of the students on my floor are already dead. I've been lucky.

We're going to head north to Vancouver, Canada. We heard some people transmitting on the CB radio. They said it's supposed to be safe there. No monsters. The university is taking thousands of refugees from America. I don't believe it, but Aaron wants to try. Safety in numbers, right?

I hope you're well, and if you find this, I wish I could offer more. I wish I could head east, but I don't believe I'd make it alive. And the others won't come with me. I already asked. Please don't think I'm a coward, but I can't make that trip alone. So I'll head north with them.

Clementine, stay safe. Stay well. Sometimes I feel like you're here with me, whispering in my ear. Call me crazy, but I think some of Mom's intuition is rubbing off on me. I'll keep that faith that you're alive and well deep inside my heart.

Love, Heath

The tears were so bad she almost couldn't finish reading the letter. When it was over, she handed it to Michael and picked up Heath's sweatshirt again to dry her face. It wouldn't do her any good to cry. According to the date, Heath had written the letter a little more than a week ago. He'd survived the earthquakes and the initial attack. He might still be alive. She didn't have to mourn him yet.

She just had to find him.

Michael handed back the letter, and she read it again before folding it and putting it in her pocket. Picking up Heath's ring, she placed it on her middle finger. It was a little too big, but she didn't think it would fall off.

Then she pulled on Heath's shirt. Go Goblins!

"I'm going to Vancouver," she said.

"I thought you might say that." Michael smiled.

"You don't have to come."

"I have this far. Do you really think I'd leave you now? I'd probably get lost trying to find my way back home. You're stuck with me."

NOTHING

We all die alone.

No matter how many friends we think we have. No matter how many toys we own. No matter how many lies we tell each other.

We all fall down.

We've all been silenced. There are no more stories to tell, no people to listen. I could send this message in a bottle in the hopes that one day someone might find it, though. I wouldn't even have to write a story; all I need is six numbers.

There are six different types of killers in the world.

1. Those who kill quickly. Efficiently.
2. Those who enjoy making each murderous moment last forever.
3. Those who kill the soul and leave their victims alive.
4. Those who kill accidentally or in self-defense.
5. Those who hunt to feed.
6. Those who hunt for the game.

The Baggers fall into all categories. I'd like to believe I'm a one or a four, but I'm really more of a six. It all depends on the day.

Game begins.

Game ends.

So quick.

Would you like to play a game of hearts?

The evil that infects us has always been around. Since the dawn of time, before names could be named, before words were written down—they have always existed. There are no records because they leave behind no trace. How do you chronicle something you cannot see?

Once upon a time an ancient civilization grew. It prospered. The people were happy and intelligent. They created cities and erected great monuments. But something always happened. They grew greedy, perhaps, or maybe they took more than the earth was willing to offer.

And that's when their downfall began. The darkness that lies beneath started to stir.

It always notices. They always come.

They kill.

There are ruins all over the world, testaments of the atrocities, and burial chambers of the lost souls. But the facts are always misinterpreted. History is inaccurate.

Things are different today. We are all connected in one form or another. We build things in China and pay for them in America. When our computers break, we talk to people halfway around the world to get them running again. On one continent millions of people go hungry while on another they grow fat.

Because of these connections, now they will destroy us all.

We are all together in this game.

I'm talking in riddles again. I'm sorry. It happens sometimes. My brain is broken and I don't know how to fix it.

When it's time for me to die, promise you'll be the one to stop me. No mercy. Let me die alone.

ARIES

She was wrong. She'd figured it out before she got halfway back to the apartment block. She never should have allowed Daniel to talk her into leaving. But even though she knew she was wrong, she didn't turn around.

Instead she went for reinforcements. But that turned out to be more difficult than she imagined.

"We have to go back."

She stood in the middle of the room; surrounded by all the people she'd risked her life protecting. They had followed her from the very beginning, but this time around they wanted to stay put.

"Think about what you're saying," Jack remonstrated. "They're in the store and you want us to go there? That's like asking to die. We're not fighters, Aries, we can't take them on."

Joy nodded. "They'll kill us."

"I don't want to die," Eve said. Nathan put his arm around her and pulled her close.

"But it's the right thing to do," Aries said. "And we have weapons now. We've got all those baseball bats. I'd do it if it were one of you."

"That's the problem," Jack said. He paused for a few moments, as if trying to figure out the right words. "Daniel's not one of us. We don't know him."

Aries stared out at the faces of her friends. "He still helped me," she pointed out. "I'd be dead without him."

They all avoided her gaze except Colin, and he was smirking.

"Fine," she said. "Then I'll go myself."

Turning, she fled the room, trying very hard to control her temper. How could they do this to her? To Daniel? Just let someone die like that, it wasn't right. Sure, it wouldn't be easy, but her father used to say that no good job comes easy.

The problem was that she knew they were right. It would be a death trap going back to the store. They'd managed to stay alive this long because they avoided conflict. They hid in the shadows and did their best to remain invisible. Not a single one of them actually knew how to fight.

Including her.

She was fooling herself. Even with a weapon at her disposal she didn't think she could use it. The biggest thing she'd ever killed before was a horsefly, and that was after it took a big chunk out of her leg. And yet they had to start fighting back, didn't they? Otherwise the monsters would win.

In the kitchen she grabbed a package of chocolate chip cookies, then silently snuck up to the third floor where she could be alone. No one ever went into the far corner room, because they considered it too dangerous. Closing the door behind her, she turned and inched her way along the side of the room toward the section where the building had caved in. Sitting down, she dangled her feet over the edge and leaned against the wall. She liked sitting here. If she closed her eyes and only allowed herself to feel the breeze against her skin, she could pretend she was sitting on the edge of a mountaintop with nothing but valleys of trees and raging rivers below.

Ten minutes later Jack came and found her. He inched along the wall until he was close enough to sit down. It was a big move for him; Aries knew he didn't like heights and it was making him nervous sitting at the edge.

"I guess you think we're all a bunch of monsters," he said.

Aries handed him the bag of cookies and he took one. "As opposed to what? All the other monsters?"

Jack made a face. "Okay, we deserve that. But we're scared. I'm terrified. It's one thing to go out looking for supplies. But to go straight into the lion's den is another story."

They sat together on the edge of the building, eating cookies. Outside, the sky was cloudy. It was threatening to rain again. Good, because there were still a few fires downtown that could use a little extinguishing.

"I'm not disagreeing with you," she said after a while. "I'm fully aware that it's suicidal. Why do you think I'm still here?"

"Something finally got through that thick head of yours?"

She laughed through a mouthful of cookie.

"I'll tell you what," Jack said. "Let's get up at dawn and go take a peek. We'll scope out the building from a distance. If it's safe, we'll go in and check up on your Daniel. Besides, the shirt you picked out for me is too tight. I can't trust a gal to do my shopping. What's this world coming to?"

She laughed again and offered up the bag of cookies a second time. But Jack wasn't paying any attention. Peering out into the darkness, his eyes narrowed in concern.

"What do you see?" She tried to follow his gaze. The road below was nothing but shadows.

One of the shadows moved.

And then another.

A third farther down the street—a shadowy person stepped from a doorway and moved behind a parked car.

Aries turned her head slightly and checked in the other direction. She could see more of them moving, sticking close to the edge of buildings, trying to maintain secrecy. But she saw them.

And a whole lot of them were coming.

"We need to get back inside," Jack whispered in her ear.

She nodded. As quietly as possible, they moved away from the crumbled edge and back toward the hallway.

They found us, she thought. *We all knew something like this would eventually happen. We couldn't stay hidden forever. It was only a matter of time.*

They raced along the hall and down to the apartment they'd been using, where they found the rest of the group in the kitchen.

"Change of plans," Jack said. "There's a whole lot of them outside. They know we're here."

Everyone started talking at once.

"They can't get in, right?" Eve said. "They can't break through the door. It's solid metal."

"How many?" Joy asked.

"Where?" Nathan immediately got up and went to the window.

Colin didn't say a word. He backed into the wall behind him, his face instantly pale.

The time to not panic was ten minutes ago. All eyes turned toward Aries. Why her? Why not Jack? He was much better at this sort of thing. Why did they expect her to have all the answers?

"At least twenty," Aries said. "Maybe more. And no, I don't think they can break down the door. And unless they have a ladder they can't reach the windows."

"That's the least of our problems," Jack said, joining Nathan at the window. "One of them is carrying gasoline. I saw a jerrican."

"What does that mean?" Eve asked. Her voice grew higher and more breathy with each word.

"They're going to burn us out," Joy cried, just as a flaming bottle crashed through the window, sending glass, gasoline, and fire across the room. Eve screamed. Nathan bolted into action, jumping straight into the flames and stomping on them with his boots. Aries grabbed a blanket and joined him.

Another bottle sailed through the air, hitting the wall this time. Glass and fire rained down onto a couch. More flames instantly sprang to life.

The sounds of bottles breaking came from other rooms in the building. They were attacking from all sides. The room grew thick with smoke as the fire spread too quickly for them to control. Aries's eyes watered, and she couldn't see more than a few feet in front of her face.

"We've got to get out of here," Jack screamed as he beat at the flames with an old pillow.

"Downstairs," Aries said. "Come on. Let's go! Stay away from the windows."

She waited at the door until everyone ran past. Jack was the last; he grabbed her arm and pulled her along.

"Ready to try out our emergency plan?" he asked.

She nodded.

It was time to leave. They'd planned for this, knew where to meet one another in case they got separated. But in all their careful preparation, neither of them ever thought it would be this sudden. She never expected they'd be driven out with such force.

"They'll kill us," she said, coughing harshly. "The second

we open the door. They're waiting to peg us off one by one."

"Then we'll have to outsmart them," Jack rasped.

"If we run at once, they might not be able to catch us all."

"Not much of a plan," he said.

"Do we have a choice?"

He shook his head. "It's not like we can distract them with ice cream and cookies. We're flat out!"

She gave him a sad smile. It was typical of Jack, always trying to lighten the moment with humor.

They regrouped in the hallway. Even in the dark she could make out the terrified expressions on their faces. The smoke wasn't as bad there, but already they could hear the crackle of flames getting closer. If they didn't move quickly, the entire building could collapse down on them.

"We're gonna make a run for it," she said. "We don't have a choice. If we stay here we'll die. If we go outside, there's a good chance that we'll make it. Nathan, Jack, and I will go first. We'll try and create a diversion. We've got four radios between us. If we work together we should be able to stay in contact. We'll meet at Second Beach like we planned."

"I want my own radio," Colin said.

"Fine," Aries said. She wasn't going to disagree with him. Not when there was so much at stake and such little time. "Everyone grab a baseball bat and nothing else. No need to weigh ourselves down."

"I should be going first, too," Joy said. "I may be the shortest, but I can run the fastest. If I can get them chasing me, it might work."

"I'll stick with Eve and we'll follow after," Nathan said. "We'll share a radio."

"I'm with team Jack," Aries said. "Colin and Joy can each have their own radio, then. Everyone okay with that?"

They all nodded.

"Let's get going, then." She turned and ran down the hallway to the second floor apartment where they were storing the radios and the rest of the supplies. Jack and Nathan followed.

She tried hard not to think about what would happen next. There were at least twenty monsters outside, quite possibly more. The odds of all of them getting out alive were slim. When she looked over at Nathan and Jack, she knew they were thinking the exact same thing.

How was she going to bear it if one of them died? They were her new family, even Colin with all his faults.

The answer, she realized, was already there. She would just live. The same way she'd been surviving all this time. Although she'd kept hope alive, she knew deep inside that her parents were most likely dead, along with almost everybody she'd ever known. Sara was dead, and she'd loved her more than anyone else on earth. So were Ms. Darcy, Becka, and Amanda.

And she'd coped. She'd survived.

No matter how much of a leader she didn't think she was, she'd get them through this. Leaders had to make tough decisions. She was making one now. She'd deal with the consequences later.

In the apartment, she gathered the radios and handed them over to Nathan, keeping one for her and Jack. From outside the window, she could hear the crowd of human monsters. They were getting excited.

No more than five minutes had passed since they set the building on fire. Funny, it already felt like hours.

"You're not going to believe this," Jack said suddenly. He was over by the window, looking down at the street. "Some guy just ran straight into the group. He's fighting them. Stupid nut's gonna get himself killed."

Aries's heart jumped into her throat.

Daniel?

MASON

Mason found the motorcycle on the side of the road just outside of Chilliwack. He was so close now to Vancouver and his promise to Chickadee. For the next few hours he drove the bike at top speed, twisting in and out of stalled traffic, rarely using the brakes, and even jumping into the ditch in some places. Several times the bike wobbled beneath him, threatening to spin out.

It was a miracle he didn't crash. No, that wasn't the right word. It was a curse.

Vancouver was a ghost town.

The bike ran out of gas right in the middle of the intersection at Main and Hastings. He got off it, letting it drop to the ground, and staggered down the street in the direction that felt right.

Everyone he cared about was dead and he felt cheated. He should have died in the school explosion along with his friends, his body under tons of concrete. The only reason he lived was because his mother got into that stupid car accident.

He didn't deserve to live. His mother's sacrifice was all in vain.

The guy back in Hope was right about him. He was a monster. A good person would have done a better job. He would have made the doctors help his mom in the hospital. He would have noticed that Chickadee needed medication, maybe even as early as Banff when she first checked the pharmacy. He never should have accused her of doing drugs. Why hadn't he picked up on it and done whatever it took to get her the medication she needed? Instead he'd ignored the signs, even when he knew something was wrong.

He should have figured out that Paul was acting weird when he told the story back in the hotel. If he'd convinced Paul to stay behind, Chickadee wouldn't have felt so betrayed. She might have been more honest with him and told him sooner. But instead she had been afraid he'd leave her too. He should have done something to make her understand that he never would have gone. That he'd be with her to the very end. He kept his promise, didn't he? He'd come to Vancouver.

He could have saved her.

Several blocks in the distance he could see the beginning of downtown Vancouver. Huge buildings graced the skyline, many of them still standing, although most of the windows had been shattered. He knew Stanley Park was on the other side. There wasn't much farther to go now.

East Hastings was a mess of looted buildings and trashed cars. Garbage was heaped in doorways, and the streets were scattered with bottles and useless retail goods. The whole place smelled like urine and desperation. He deserved to be there.

The smoke reached his nose before he saw the flames. A block later, he came across the ambush. A group of monsters disguised as humans circled around a building, carrying Molotov cocktails. They were tossing the bottles through the windows one by one.

How many people were trapped inside?

Now the group of crazies gathered by the back doors, obviously waiting for the moment when the trapped people tried to make a run for it. Some of them brandished baseball bats and one or two were holding knives.

These monsters didn't deserve to live. Trapping people like mice. It was a mob mentality, cowardly at best.

He didn't deserve to live either. The one good person who truly deserved to walk the earth was buried back in a shallow grave in a town falsely named Hope.

At least he'd be able to take a few of them down with him.

And he'd never see the ocean. Or feel it. It bothered him slightly that he'd be breaking his promise. Hopefully Chickadee would understand this was the only way he could truly punish himself for his wrongdoings.

He didn't think. Instead he ran straight at the crowd.

ARIES

Aries didn't stop to think. Grabbing one of the baseball bats, she took the stairs two at a time, her sneakers barely touching the concrete. Behind her she could hear Jack and Nathan struggling to keep up. At the bottom, she unlatched the lock, shoved open the metal door, and stepped out onto the street.

When she saw his face, she knew the stranger wasn't Daniel. But who was he? And why was he doing something so bloody suicidal? Stopping just beyond the door, she watched the stranger attack. He was in the middle of the monsters, lashing out as the crowd swarmed him. Punching blindly, he still managed to hit targets—she saw someone's nose connect with his fist, blood spurting onto the street. Another one took a kick to the side, collapsing, only to get trampled as the others closed in on the hunt.

"Come on," she heard Jack say from behind. "Get out of here while they're distracted."

It was the opportunity of all opportunities. Silently, her friends poured out of the building and split in different directions. Nathan grabbed Eve and they disappeared into the alley. Colin and Joy headed off behind the building toward Crab

Park. The monsters were so distracted by the stranger, they didn't even notice. She turned to Jack, surprised to realize that he was the only one left. The others had vanished into the night.

"We have to help him," she said.

"We owe him that much," Jack agreed.

But what could they do?

From out of nowhere, another figure slammed his way into the group. This time it *was* Daniel. She recognized his black hair and slender frame. He obviously had a weapon of some sort in his hand, and two of the monsters crumpled to the ground. One of the mob members got behind him, raising a baseball bat in the air.

She didn't think about it. She charged the group, aiming for the guy with the bat, and using her own weapon to slam him hard in the side. Someone tried to grab her by the hair and knocked the bat out of her hands, so she twisted her body around, tightened her fingers into a fist, and planted a punch right into his jaw. Her knuckles popped and cracked, and pain flared up her hand, but it was one of the most fantastic feelings she'd ever experienced in her life. She'd never punched someone before. Who knew it could be so amazing? A female got right in her face—black-veined eyes wide, teeth bared—and practically bit her nose off. Aries pulled her arm back again, felt the crazy woman's nose break under her knuckles. Only this time it hurt a lot more.

Professional fighters and movies made it look easy.

She turned around to see hands coming straight for her throat, but Jack stepped in front of her, tackling the body to the ground. They were all involved now, a fight to the finish.

The crowd started to go crazy. They were too close together. The stranger ducked a blow, forcing a monster to punch another. Soon a bunch of them were fighting among themselves, a full-blown mob of crazies, and no one seemed to know what was happening anymore.

Daniel reached for her through the mob, grabbed her by the elbow, and pulled her back. "Are you nuts?" he shouted. "What the hell are you doing? You're gonna get yourself killed. Get out of here. Go join your friends."

"I'm not leaving you," she said. "And I'm not leaving that other guy, either. He just saved everyone's lives."

Daniel pulled her farther back from the crowd and pushed her behind a parked car. "Stay there. I'll get him."

MASON

A sharp punch to the stomach and all the air was sucked out of his body. As he tripped over someone's head, Mason's knees went in opposite directions, bending in ways nature never intended. Hitting the ground hard, he felt someone kicked him twice in the side, and he instinctively curled up into the fetal position to try and withstand the blows. A boot pressed down on his fingers and he felt them snap, and his teeth clenched down tightly to keep him from screaming.

All he needed now was a good strong kick to the head and it would be over. He would not close his eyes. He'd face death head-on.

A hand reached out through the cluster of bodies. A face appeared along with it. A guy around the same age as him grabbed hold of his arm and yanked him forward.

"Come on," the guy said. "What the hell do you think you're doing? Trying to kill yourself? There are better ways to die, my friend."

"Get lost," Mason wheezed. He breathed deeply, the air beginning to return to his lungs.

"This isn't an option," the guy said. He dodged a blow and

kicked out, sending the assailant flying through the crowd. "Whatever you think you did, well, get over it. You don't deserve to die."

"What do you know." It wasn't a question.

The guy pulled Mason closer until their noses were practically touching. "I happen to know a hell of a lot. Now get your ass up off this ground and follow me. I've got a girl over there and she's gonna be pretty pissed if you don't come back with me."

Something in his eyes made Mason believe it was true. This wasn't the time or place to be dying. He allowed the stranger to help him to his feet. Together they fought their way out of the crowd and over to where a girl and guy were waiting.

"Come on," the girl said. "We don't have much time. They're gonna notice they're just fighting each other soon." She turned to the guy beside him. "You're coming too, Daniel, don't you dare think you're gonna just run off right now."

The stranger named Daniel gave a coy smile. "I wouldn't dream of it," he answered.

He's lying.

But the girl bought into it and the four of them headed off around the corner of the building. They ran for a few blocks without stopping.

Mason tried to keep up, but he'd been hit too many times. His throat and lungs burned and a stitch in his side threatened to tear his entire body into strips. After the fourth block, he stumbled and fell to his knees. He hadn't eaten the entire day and it was a good thing. If there had been food in his stomach it would now be leaving his throat and hitting the sidewalk. He stayed there a few moments, his palms flat on the pavement, his head hovering close to the ground while he coughed his lungs out.

"Go on without me," he said. "I'm seriously screwed."

"That'll teach you to take them on by yourself," the girl panted. "Whatever possessed you to try and be a hero, anyway?"

"I'm no hero."

"You saved our lives," she said.

Mason looked up at her, and for the first time noticed how big and green her eyes were. The expression on her face was concern, and for a moment he actually believed that she cared, even if she didn't know a single thing about him.

"I'm Aries," she said. She nodded to the guy beside her. "He's Jack. And the guy over there is Daniel."

"And are you?"

"Huh?"

"Are you—an Aries?"

She laughed. "No, I'm a Gemini." She held out her hand to him and he took it, allowing her to carefully help him to his feet and into the shadows of a darkened doorway. Once he was standing, the pain in his lungs started to disappear, and soon his breathing returned to normal.

"I'm Mason."

The three of them stood squashed awkwardly for a few moments while Daniel continued to watch down the street. Finally he turned around and faced the group.

"I hate to break up this happy get-together, but they've noticed we're gone. I think it's time to start moving."

Mason could hear shouting in the distance. Sure enough, shadowy figures were moving in their direction from a few blocks away.

"Can you run again?" Aries asked him.

"I'll manage," he said. "Where are we going?"

"The ocean," she said. "That's where we're meeting the others. But we'd better lose this crowd first."

He didn't believe in fate or destiny or any of that crap they talked about in the movies. But when Aries mentioned the ocean, he couldn't help but wonder if Chickadee had somehow found a way to bring him to this girl.

CLEMENTINE

She heard the pounding footsteps but didn't actually expect the guy to run right into her. She and Michael had rounded the corner, about to check out the four-leveled parking lot to see if they could find a way to get inside the Bay department store. It was late and they were looking for a place to crash for the night.

The moment her feet stepped around the building, a guy with disheveled black hair ran straight into her. Knocking her head against his chin, she fell backward into Michael, who just managed to catch her.

She saw stars, but before she had time to count them, the guy grabbed hold of her hand.

"I'd follow if I were you," he said. "They're right behind us."

"Baggers," Michael said.

Clementine looked over the stranger's shoulder, and sure enough, off in the distance, at least twenty or thirty of them were closing the gap.

"We need to hide," a girl with long auburn hair said, joining them. Beside her were two other guys, both of whom looked extremely winded. One of them was pretty battered, too. He was holding his mangled hand against his chest.

"We were heading to the parking lot," Michael said. "Just right there. Thought maybe we could get inside the Bay."

The girl and short-haired guy exchanged looks.

"We'll be trapped," she said.

"It's a good hiding spot," he said. "We can't outrun them forever."

"But how do we know they're cool?" the battered guy said as he eyed Michael warily.

"How do we know *you're* cool?" Clementine snapped.

"We are running away from them, in case you didn't notice."

"We don't have time for this," the black-haired guy said. "We'll just have to take our chances."

The girl turned to Clementine. "Let's do it."

They ran straight across the street and into the lot. Beside the ticket booth was a tiny concrete stairwell that led straight up. Above their heads was a skywalk. If they could reach it, they might be able to gain access to the store.

The skywalk was three flights up, and by the time they reached the top, everyone was breathing heavily. The girl introduced herself as Aries in a whispered, breathy voice. She then gave out everyone else's names.

"I'm Clementine," she whispered back. "And that's Michael."

"Are we done with introductions?" Daniel asked. "I'm getting really tired of all these new faces. How many others am I going to have to endure tonight?"

"Don't worry," Aries shot back. "As soon as we're safe you can go find another hole to crawl into."

Michael and Clementine exchanged glances. What sort of fight had they literally crashed into?

Down in the street below they could hear shouting as the

Baggers spread out to search. It was only a matter of time before they found the stairwell.

"We're boned."

Clementine didn't know what Daniel meant until she glanced over at the skywalk. It was in shambles, the windows broken, the floorboards uprooted and cracked. In the middle was a hole big enough to fall through. The structure seemed to be barely holding on by a thread.

"That's not gonna take our weight," Jack said. "That wouldn't even hold a baby."

"Maybe if we go one at a time?" Aries suggested.

"It was such a good idea," Clementine said. "I forgot about the earthquake."

"You couldn't tell it was damaged from below?" Daniel said. "Why didn't you just look up then?"

"Hey, don't snap at her," Michael said. "It's not her fault."

"I think we can do it," Mason said. He didn't even hesitate. Clementine held her breath as she watched him walk briskly straight out onto the skywalk, keeping to the middle where the supports might be the strongest. When he reached the hole, he simply stepped over it as if it was a pothole in the road instead of a three-story drop to the street below. Once safely across, he waved at the others to join him.

"Show-off," Daniel muttered.

Jack went next, then Aries, followed by Daniel. Jack had the most difficulty, freezing by the hole for a good thirty seconds before his legs started working again.

"Your turn," Michael said.

She stepped out onto the skywalk, immediately feeling the breeze through the broken windows against her face. The platform seemed to move beneath her, but she tried to convince herself that it was all in her head. The metal creaked under her weight, but it held. When she saw the hole, her legs began to quiver.

Dear Heath, I think I'm going to throw up.

The thought almost brought her to hysterics. But it also gave her strength. When she found her brother, they'd look back on this and he'd be proud of her for having the guts to pull off such a dangerous stunt.

She cleared the skywalk, and Michael followed without incident.

"Store's open," Mason said.

"There could be more of them in there," Jack said.

"We'll have to take our chances," Clementine said. "They're on the stairs. I can hear them."

They ran along the hallway, past the flower shop, and into the store.

The Bay was full of light.

"What the . . ." Clementine paused, her hand on her flashlight. Fluorescent lights glowed above her head, the entire store laid out in front of them like a brilliant shopping paradise.

"Generator," Aries said. "It has to be. The power's been out for weeks. But who did this? The crazies?"

"Maybe," Daniel said. "Hard to tell. The only windows are on the first floor. You could stare at the store all day and not see anything. Could be others hiding."

"But why here?" Jack said. "Why the Bay? There's no food here? Kinda pointless. Are they planning on getting their Christmas shopping done early?"

"And it's not even Halloween yet," Michael said.

"This isn't good," Daniel said. "I've got a bad feeling. Let's find the Granville Street entrance. I think we should have left ten minutes ago."

"Agreed," Aries said. "This is too creepy."

They headed for the middle of the floor, where the escalators were. As they ran past the activewear, Clementine knocked over a bunch of mannequins, sending hat-covered heads and tank tops flying. A badminton racket sailed through the air and a plastic arm bounced down the escalator steps.

"I'll say this much," Jack said as they raced downward. "I'm never gonna look at another mannequin the same way. Those things are spooky. Even the ones dressed in bras."

They made it only to the second floor before they were spotted. At the bottom of the escalator, someone screamed, a female Bagger wearing a bloodstained sundress.

"Change of plans," Michael yelled.

"Follow me," Aries said. "We'll take the stairs."

They ran off toward the women's purses. It wasn't until they reached the hosiery department that everyone stopped dead in their tracks. Jack raised his baseball bat up in the air.

"What the hell?" Mason said it best.

The area had been completely cleaned out. Hundreds of sleeping bags lined the floor, pressed tightly together like sardines. Empty cans, packaged food, and discarded bloody clothing covered the space. In the corner, piles of uneaten groceries and survival goods were stockpiled. Without thinking, Clementine reached down and picked up a discarded rag doll. Dried blood was smeared across its rosy cheeks.

"That is one big slumber party," Michael muttered. He kicked at a pile of discarded laundry.

"That explains the generator," Mason said. "They're living here. And we just walked right into their nest."

From behind them, back at the escalators, the scuttling noise of several people running echoed across the store.

"The Baggers are in the building," Clementine muttered.

"I'd ask you why you call them that, but I don't think we

have time for a chat," Jack said. "I think the proper thing to do in this situation is run."

There were no disagreements.

They headed toward a glowing exit sign and found the stairs. There was only one more flight to go before they reached the main floor. Then they raced toward the makeup and perfume counters. Clementine had always avoided these areas in the past. She had allergies to perfume and hated the way all the scents mixed together. Even now, weeks since the store saw its last real customer, the heavy smells assaulted her nose. Suppressing an intense urge to sneeze, she ran straight for the doors, pressing hard against the latch to try and get it open. It didn't budge.

"Door's locked," she said.

"Same here," Michael said, pressing both his hands against the glass in frustration. "We need something big to break it."

"I think we need another exit," Daniel said. "Look."

She hadn't seen it at first because it was dark outside and still in the light. But looking out onto Granville Street, she saw that the pavement was lined with Baggers. Dozens of them, maybe even a hundred. They stood quietly, waiting, watching the store.

"That's it," Mason said quietly. "Game over."

"No," Clementine said. "There has to be another way out." She turned to look back at the perfume counters, but the Baggers were already there. Walking down the rows, at least twenty of them were spreading out across the floor, grinning.

"We're surrounded," Aries said.

"It's been a good fight," Michael said.

"It's not over," Clementine snapped. "There's gotta be another way." She looked back over her shoulder to see that more Baggers were appearing in the street.

Michael reached out and took her hand.

"No!" she screamed. "I'm not dying this way."

One of the Baggers leaped toward her, fingers reaching for her face. She felt Michael's hand tugging her back, but he wasn't fast enough. Just as the monster reached for her, Mason shoved her out of the way and tackled the Bagger head-on, knocking him to the ground.

It was the sign the monsters were waiting for. They began to surge forward toward the group. Behind her, Clementine could hear the sounds of them banging against the doors. Glass shattered and a burst of cold wind hit her neck.

MASON

He'd seen the guy coming and managed to get Clementine out of the way before he took the hit. The pain in his wounded hand was horrible, but he clenched his teeth tightly and fought back the nausea welling up inside his stomach. The Bagger dropped to the floor, smashing its head and knocking itself unconscious. Not that it mattered. One down, several hundred more to go.

Behind them, the glass shattered. Before he had a chance to turn, one of them slammed into his back, knocking him straight onto his knees. Someone grabbed him by the hair, jerking his neck back at an awkward angle before Jack stepped in, punching the Bagger hard enough that it let go.

He nodded at Jack; there was no time for more thanks as the Baggers swarmed the store through the broken doors.

Mason started throwing punches with his good hand. He saw Clementine and Michael picking up perfume bottles and hurling them at the monsters. Daniel went down in a sea of crazies, clothing and skin blurring as they toppled over one another to get close enough for the kill. Jack and Aries stood together, the baseball bat high above his head, as the crowd closed in.

This was it.

A female Bagger circled Mason from behind, and a brief flash of metal appeared in the corner of his eye as she raised a knife toward his face. She screamed like a banshee, filthy hair whipping around her shoulders. Mason dodged her, kicking at her legs and bringing her to the ground. With his good hand, he punched another attacker in the nose, working his way through the crowd to where Aries and Jack battled their own group of monsters.

He got to them too late; saw the baseball bat driving down into the back of Jack's skull. The sound of aluminum meeting bone, and Aries screamed. Jack's knees trembled, his entire body collapsing against a display of beauty products.

Mason dived down and managed to catch Jack before he hit the ground. As he held Jack tightly, Aries was beside him in an instant, pushing his arms away so she could take the wounded guy in her arms.

Jack's eyes were closed.

"Oh, God," she whispered. "Oh, God. Jack. No."

The same Bagger grabbed Mason's hair, yanking him backward. He fought his way free, picking up a discarded perfume bottle and smashing it over the Bagger's head. He stumbled back to Aries. Jack was motionless in her arms, blood matting his hair and slowly staining her shirt a dark red.

There was no way to sugarcoat the words that came next.

"Put him down," Mason said. "We need you. Care for him when we're done."

Aries ignored him, her eyes filled with tears. Mason reached out, touching her cheek, forcing her to look at him.

"He's not dead," Mason said. "He's breathing. Don't be stupid and give up now. He's going to die if you don't fight to save him."

Aries blinked several times as the words reached her ears. Finally she nodded and carefully placed Jack's head gently on the ground. She picked up his bloody baseball bat as she stood and immediately swung it, hitting a Bagger in the shoulder.

"You're right," she said, swinging it again. "He's not going to die. I won't let him."

Mason gave her a crooked grin. The girl had guts.

Then suddenly the store groaned, rebar stretched, more windows shattered, and the floor heaved upward as if the ground had opened its mouth and taken one gigantic burp.

"Earthquake!"

The building started shaking, makeup and perfume bottles were knocked off counters, and the sickening smell of a thousand different scents filled the air.

The Baggers stopped fighting. Many of them dropped to the ground, rolling around on the floor and muttering words no one understood. Some of them screamed in unison, a creepy, high-pitched noise coming from deep within their throats. Above them, pieces of the ceiling broke apart, plaster dropping down onto the group.

"It's gonna collapse," Michael screamed. "Everyone, outside!"

Aries and Michael grabbed Jack, pulling the unconscious kid into their arms, and carried him through the broken window.

Mason ran toward the doors, jumping over the fallen Baggers and pushing through the broken glass and onto the sidewalk. Granville Street was heaving: concrete cracked and split apart while large holes opened up to swallow street lamps and abandoned cars. A fire hydrant exploded, sending a fountain of water straight up into the air.

They staggered toward the intersection of Georgia Street, while the Bay department store gave one final shudder before collapsing into itself.

The sky opened up and rain started to fall, a few quick drops that quickly changed into a heavy shower.

There were still several Baggers on the street, but the majority of them had been trapped inside the store. Those that were outside were mostly on the ground, still writhing around, doing their strange chicken dance.

As quick as it started, it ended. The earth stopped moving. In the distance, car alarms sounded and Mason could hear a dog barking. The rain continued to hit the pavement; his hair and clothing were already soaked.

"They're moving," Clementine said. Sure enough, several of the Baggers climbed to their feet, bewildered expressions on their dirt-covered faces.

"We should split up," Aries said. "We're supposed to meet the others at Second Beach in Stanley Park. You know where that is, right?"

He could feel the picture in his back pocket the second she spoke the words. *Mom and Mason—enjoying the sun.* It took willpower to keep from yanking it out and babbling about destiny.

"I've heard about it," he finally said. "I know it's somewhere in the downtown core. We must be close. But I'm not sure where to go."

"Us neither," Clementine said.

"Then I guess we stay together."

"I've got a better idea," Daniel said. "There's no way we can outrun all of them, even with their numbers down. Aries, take your friends and head for Second Beach. Tourist Boy and I are gonna stay behind and create a diversion."

"No," Aries said. "You're not leaving me again."

Tourist Boy? Mason disliked this guy more and more by the minute. But still, the creep had a point. A diversion was exactly what they needed, and he could give it to them.

"I'm in," he said.

"Then it's settled," Daniel said. Moving toward Aries, he put his hand up to her chin. "I gave you my word, and I will keep it this time. I'll meet you on the beach."

She started to protest, but Jack weakly called out her name. Clementine and Michael were holding on to him, trying to keep him on his feet. Aries leaned in toward him, and he whispered a few words in her ear. It must have worked; she nodded, crossing her arms over her chest.

"You'd better be there," she said. She tried to hand over her baseball bat, but Daniel wouldn't take it.

"Keep that, you're going to need it."

Aries went back to the others. Michael was in charge of Jack now; he'd picked him up piggyback-style. His face was flushed under the extra weight, but he looked strong enough to carry him for a good ways. Jack was semiconscious and clinging weakly to Michael's shoulders. There was no way he'd be able to walk two feet on his own.

He hoped they'd be able to make it.

Mason watched them as they headed off down Granville Street. He knew this was the right thing to do, so why did he feel so apprehensive?

Daniel turned toward him, holding out a roll of black electrical tape. "Give me your hand."

Mason held out his broken fingers. Daniel examined them briefly.

"This is gonna hurt," he warned. Pulling gently, he straightened the bone.

Mason clenched his teeth, trying hard to ignore the pain. A wave of nausea filled his stomach.

"Let's get one thing straight," Daniel said as he began to tape two of Mason's fingers together. "I picked you for a reason. The Baggers, or whatever you want to call them, are coming. They're not going to play nice. There's only one way to deal with them."

"Yeah, I get it," Mason said. "No need to be an ass about it."

Daniel finished with the tape and tossed it on the ground. "That should hold for now." He pulled something out of his pocket. The metal gleamed against the moonlight. He held the knife out to Mason.

"I'm not a kil—" But he was, wasn't he?

"I know you can do it. That's why I picked you. You're stronger than the rest of them. You've felt the darkness."

Mason took the knife in his hands. The blade was heavier than he expected.

"Feels good, doesn't it?"

"No."

"Liar."

Mason's face grew hot. "Just what are you implying? You say a lot of stuff, but none of it makes much sense. I'm not like those monsters. I'm not into killing. I don't give a damn what you think." It took him a moment to realize he was trying to convince himself as much as Daniel.

Daniel smiled. "You're right. You're not one of them. But you've got potential. I can see it inside of you. You're walking a thin line right now; it's just a matter of time till something tilts you over to either side. You need to decide, Mason, who you want to be. You can fight here for a good cause and go join your new friends and start a life that's gonna keep you clean, or you can give in to those voices that whisper about all the bad things you've done. Make your choice. I suggest you get over it. Suck it up. Whatever you did, it's not nearly as bad as you think."

Mason stepped backward, his body pressing up against the wall behind him. "Who are you? How the hell do you know these things?"

"I'm just a guy who sees a lot, and you're like an open book, my friend." Daniel pulled a second knife from his pocket. "Now, are you a warrior or are you just some monstrosity? Follow your own road."

The words hung in the air between them.

"I'm in."

ARIES

The roaring waves washed against the shore. She stood a few feet away, staring out into the darkened water. The sound was loud but strangely soothing. Her eyes grew heavy and her heartbeat relaxed to the most normal pace she'd encountered all evening. It was impossible to stare out at the ocean and not feel peaceful.

Behind her in the east, the sun was beginning to peek through the trees. Soon it would be light and they'd have to go. It wasn't safe wandering around in the day. They all knew this.

All that energy spent on running and hiding. So much had happened in the past month. She'd almost forgotten what it used to be like before all this started. Wasted days hanging at the mall with Sara, hundreds of hours spent giggling over silly things. Wouldn't it be nice if she could turn back the clock?

Time was precious. There never was enough of it to spare.

Were her parents still out there? Would she ever get the chance to go home and see for herself?

They'd made it to the beach, where they'd found the others waiting for them. Joy, Nathan, Eve, and even Colin—she was overjoyed to see them all alive. Now that Michael and Clementine had joined them, they were growing stronger.

Jack was still alive, but he couldn't see. Something had happened to his brain when the Bagger hit him. His eyes perceived nothing but blackness.

"This is bad," he'd said earlier when she helped him down onto the sand.

"We'll get through it."

"I'm only going to hold you back," he said. "This complicates things."

"You're never going to complicate anything," she said. "You're the one person who helps make all this easier. I can't do it without you, Jack."

She smiled and it hurt her to know he didn't realize just how much she cared.

But he was alive. She didn't know if his blindness was permanent, but they'd deal with it.

They would be a family and she would keep them together. She'd keep them alive.

They just had to wait for Mason and Daniel to show, and they could head out to find a new home. She believed him when he said he'd come. There had been something different in his voice. Something truthful.

She went back over to Jack, putting her arm around him carefully as a good friend would do. She curled up against him, feeling the warmth of his body. Michael had torn up his shirt to make a bandage. Jack's head looked like he was wearing a flattened plaid hat.

"How do you feel?" she asked.

"I've got a splitting headache," he said. "And I'm blind, did I mention that? Aside from that, not bad."

She choked back a laugh.

"We have to go soon," he said.

"I know. But we can wait a few more minutes."

"Any idea where we're gonna go?"

"Wouldn't it be nice if we could stay here?" she said. "We could become beachcombers and just spend our days digging clams out of the sand."

"Sounds heavenly," he said. "But I'm allergic to shellfish."

She giggled.

"Eve suggested Shaughnessy," she said. "Over by the university. We could get one of those big mansions with a pool. That would rock."

"I'm in," Jack said. "I always knew I was destined to live somewhere rich."

In the distance a heron dove straight for the water, catching a fish in its beak. Seagulls floated lazily, completely oblivious to the shattered world around them.

"We need to start searching for other survivors," she said. "Get organized."

"Maybe we can find my brother." Clementine had come over and joined them. "He was supposed to be in Seattle, but he came here. Left me a message. Said there were survivors at the University of British Columbia."

"It's possible," Jack said. "It's just across the water. Over there to your right. At least I think it's your right. Can't tell for sure. Look for all the trees. That's Jericho Beach. UBC isn't far from there. We were just talking about finding a new hideout in Shaughnessy."

The girls looked out across the water. On the other side of English Bay, the shoreline was visible.

"Hey!" Eve's voice carried toward them. "They're here."

Aries turned around. Mason and Daniel were climbing down the stairs to the beach. She grabbed Jack's hand and gave it a squeeze. "I'll be right back." She followed Clementine over to join the group.

Everyone was happy. She realized this was the first time in weeks she'd seen people smiling and laughing all at once. It was a nice feeling. If only it would last.

There would be more hard times ahead of them. She had no reservations about it. But they would deal. They had each other and they would find a way to get through it all.

They were a group.

She reached Daniel and Mason first. Their clothes were covered in dark stains and the smell of rust overpowered the scent of salt water.

"Don't ask," Daniel said. "Because I'm not telling."

"I'm glad you're here," she said. She meant it for both of them.

"We should get going, then," Nathan said. "If we're heading to rich man's land, we've got a lot of ground to cover. Maybe we should find a shop to hole up in for the day and set out again once it gets dark. I'll carry Jack. I don't mind."

"Oooh, there's a Blenz not too far from here," Eve said. "Maybe we can figure out a way to get some coffee. I'd kill for an espresso."

"Yeah, and I'm sure we can all spend the day munching on month-old vegan brownies," Nathan said. "Seriously, wouldn't a Seven-Eleven make more sense?"

"What about Safeway?" Mason said. "We passed two on the way here."

The group continued to discuss their plans. Aries couldn't help but listen with a grin on her face. But then Daniel pressed his hand against her arm and beckoned her away.

She walked with him up the beach a ways. He was silent. She knew what was coming.

"Don't tell me." She sat down on a huge log, her feet barely touching the ground. "You're leaving."

"You know me too well." Daniel sat down beside her, their knees touching as they leaned into each other.

"Will I see you again?"

"I think so, yes."

"Good."

He smiled. "You're not going to protest?"

She glanced out over the water where the heron was still enjoying its early breakfast. "You're not going to change. I'm accepting it."

"You're going to do well, Aries," he said. "People will remember you."

"I hope so," she said. "I'm trying. We all want to make our mark in life, right? It doesn't have to be big. Sometimes we just want people to remember we were here."

"You could write your name in the sand."

She laughed. "That's not even a dent."

He reached out, his fingers pressing against her cheek. "You'll move mountains."

She stopped breathing. His eyes found hers, and he looked straight into her soul as if searching for something he'd lost. Her skin tingled as he moved his hand slightly, tilting her head to the side. The entire world slowly vanished until there was nothing to look at except him.

Lips pressed against hers. She closed her eyes, but it ended too quickly. When she opened them, he was staring back at her. She wanted to smile at him but her face was frozen. How could someone's eyes be both bright and dark at the same time?

He slid off the log and pulled a knife out of his pocket. "Then let's make a dent." Kneeling down in front of the log, he used the knife to carve her name into the wood. Then he carved his own name. By the time he finished, the others had joined them. Even Jack, who was being supported by Michael and Clementine.

They didn't even ask. Instead they lined up and each took a turn carving their names into the wood.

ARIES

DANIEL

JACK

CLEMENTINE

COLIN

JOY

NATHAN

EVE

MICHAEL

MASON

When it was over, they all stepped back to admire their work.

"It's official," Daniel said. "We exist."

Something caught Aries's eye. From across the bay, she could see tiny figures moving between the trees of Jericho Park.

She stood up and moved closer to the shore. "What is that?"

"Here." Clementine reached into her pocket and pulled

out pocket binoculars. "They're cracked, but they work. Michael gave them to me."

Aries took the binoculars and brought them up to her eyes. It took a second before her eyes got adjusted and she managed to focus on the park across the bay. From the tree line, several people were coming out onto the beach. Men and women—there were even some children.

"It's a group of people," she said.

"Baggers?"

"No, I don't think so." She watched as one of them used their own set of binoculars, staring back at her. The strangers on the beach crowded around him as he waved at her.

Aries laughed and waved back. "They see us too."

"They're still a million miles away," Michael said.

"But close enough that we can find them," she said. "And others. There will be others."

"Let me look?" Clementine asked, and Aries passed over the binoculars.

"He's not there," she said after a few minutes. "But I'm going to find him."

"I'll help you," Michael assured her.

"We'll all help you," Aries said.

They watched until the people retreated back into the woods. It didn't matter that they left. Aries knew they were there. They'd find them.

"We should go," Nathan finally said.

She nodded. Turning back to her friends, she noticed immediately that Daniel was gone. It wasn't a surprise. It was just a matter of time before he'd return, though. She was certain of that, too.

MASON

He sat down in the sand and took off his shoes and socks. Tried rolling his jeans up but couldn't get them past his calves. Not that it really mattered.

The others were still back at the log, talking among themselves, when he slipped over to the shoreline. Just as well, he kinda wanted to do this on his own. He stood up, and the sand was cool and squishy between his toes.

The ocean was before him. So gigantic. In the distance he could see an island and a few tanker boats. He wondered if anyone was on them.

The wind whipped at his hair and roared in his ears. The tangy smell of salt water and seaweed filled his nose. Bits of sand stuck to his skin, cool and wonderful.

He didn't even bother to test the water with his toe. He walked right in, the icy cold assaulting his tired feet and closing in around his ankles. Breathing rapidly, he moved farther until his jeans began to soak up the water and his knees submerged.

Closing his eyes, he felt the ocean.

NOTHING

We carved our names in the fallen tree. Our tiny mark. Our proof that we still desired life. We would not go gently into that great night.

We were leaders, followers, warriors, even cowards. Some of us were betrayers.

There are no winners in this game.

But there is tomorrow.

JEYN'S LOGIC OF EVIL

I love ideas of free will versus predetermination, and I want this to be an underlying theme throughout this series. What would happen if most of the world had free will while another smaller part had no choice but to do harm? Who would win? How many people would make bad decisions? Would those with free will willingly join sides with the Baggers for their own preservation? Or would they stand up and fight instead?

QUESTIONS

1. Is there a deeper logic? Is it more than just that humans are bad and the really bad ones are targeted to turn?

There's a meshing of science and the supernatural, you might say. Throughout history populations have disappeared or destroyed themselves. Look at the dinosaurs, the Mayans, even the Romans. Often the reasons are hard to get at—but it's as if the Earth decided it was time to start again. And that's what's going on here—humanity has done colossal damage to the planet and it's time for everything to implode. This is the moment!

There's something within the brains of those who become Baggers. It's hard to diagnose, like schizophrenia is tough to diagnose. But it's a genetic predisposition—a mutation, if you like—and it is triggered now by these earthquakes (electromagnetic impulses, plus it is just "time" for this to happen, as if it's hardwired into the condition). There's also something Darwinian about it—the survival of the strongest. There's a real sign on the door at Santa Monica College—AN EARTHQUAKE IS THE WAY THE EARTH RELIEVES ITS STRESS, BY TRANSFERRING IT TO THE PEOPLE WHO LIVE ON IT. I like this idea. There have been other earthquakes in the past, obviously, but this one is the trigger to the neurological condition within those who are Baggers.

In fact, the Baggers are a minority of the population, though of course their violence spreads their impact, and fear of them, far and wide. If you don't have this predisposition you can't simply turn into a Bagger, though of course people don't know that at the outset, and there will be fear until the truth is understood. Also, some people are just bad—and might have reasons to be bad at this time.

So it's a kind of coming together of the barely understood "supernatural" of the Earth's natural balance, and something almost genetically "implanted" or seeded into the population by that same Mother Nature. Like a natural means of population control. We (i.e. humans) believe we can control *everything*, but nature always shows us that we can't.

I also love the idea that there would be some conspiracy theorists on the road ("The Government knew this was going to happen and it was a cover-up!") as well as doomsday prophets ("The end is nigh!"). It's an interesting juxtaposition of responses to the same event, and you would see both in this situation.

2. Is there a "higher power" controlling everything?

I see this as a kind of deranged Mother Nature. Something has woken up, but in a way that blurs the edges of science and supernatural. We're not talking about a "goddess" here, except in a more metaphorical sense. It has seen the damage people have done and it's angry. It has more control over us than we realize. It's managed to get inside some of us and now it's sending its army to clean up our mess. It's done this before, e.g., back when Rome fell and when the Mayans destroyed their land and cut down their trees. The remains of its destruction are present on Easter Island and even in the museums of Rwanda. One could even say it was here in the beginning when dinosaurs exceeded their population limit. It likes to watch humans get out of control.

On the road there will be some individuals who contribute to this understanding for our characters.

3. And how do our main characters resist turning?

Either you are a Bagger or you aren't. However, those unaffected don't know this. One of the driving plots is that Mason believes he might become a Bagger. He's struggling with his inner demons, wondering if he's suddenly going to change. He has dark thoughts. He's numb on the inside. He thinks there's something wrong with him.

As is the case with most "rules" and natural laws, there are exceptions. Daniel is that exception. He has the genetic flaw but there is also something in his mind that allows him to fight against it. He's able to go in and out of consciousness, completely aware of the bad things he's doing.

The Baggers only make up about 10 percent of the population. The earthquake was a trigger point, bringing their darkness to the surface. They were able to organize their attacks all at once, targeting as many humans as possible. They disrupted all forms of communication so that they would have a stronger position. So although they still don't outnumber normal humans, they have the advantage because they are organized and they have no qualms when it comes to killing. Killing is what they *have* to do to bring about this new world order they are driven to seek.

There are two types of Baggers. One type still maintains a higher level of functioning. This type has great ideas of reconstructing society in such a way that they will make all the rules. This new society will be created from the destruction of the old civilization, just as has been done many times before.

The other type of Bagger has no reasoning. They are out-of-control monsters, killing and destroying everything in sight. They were powerful allies in the beginning but now they will be hunted down and destroyed by the upper-level Baggers.

There are still a few ideas I'm toying with. The Baggers hear voices but I'm not sure if it's just a by-product of their disorder or if there really is an element of them being "controlled." They have the ability to sense if someone is a Bagger or not. But can they communicate with each other across the world? Probably not, but there is this natural impulse to bring about change at this time.

THE MAN

He liked the basement. It was quiet down there. So quiet.

It made the voices that much easier to hear.

When they first started speaking to him, he tried to ignore them. He'd seen stuff on television about people who went plumb crazy. Hearing voices wasn't a good sign. He tried silencing them. Drinking heavily and popping sleeping pills. But the voices wouldn't go away. If anything, the drinking made them that much worse. They said terrible things. They whispered into his head about what was coming. They talked about the future. Earthquakes. Death. Chaos. They talked about how important he was. He didn't want to believe it.

But as time went on, the voices started to make sense.

His role was explained to him in great detail. He grew excited when they told him what he needed to do. He would play a part in this new world. He was necessary.

The basement had always been his space. Unfinished, it was cold and dark, and his wife didn't like to go down there because she thought the place was ugly. Ugly. Her word. She much preferred her lacy curtains and bed filled with dozens of pillows that he wasn't allowed to sleep on unless he showered first.

He kept most of his tools down here. There was a shelf in the back that was covered with all sorts of wonderful things. A power drill. A chain saw. Dozens of plastic boxes filled with nails, screws, and other bits and pieces he'd convinced her he needed. He liked to do all the handy work and she couldn't complain because he often did a good job. He enjoyed working with his hands.

In the middle was his worktable, and he sat at it now. In front of him was a device, a wonderful contraption he'd built all by himself. He found most of the information on the Internet; it was amazing what sort of stuff people could find on websites these days. Before the voices came, he mostly just checked his e-mail and the occasional dirty site his wife would never have approved of.

None of that mattered anymore.

She'd been dead since the morning.

He was vaguely disappointed about this. He had known he'd be the one to kill her, but he'd hoped to do it when he wasn't so pressed for time. He'd wanted to savor the kill, enjoy the moment, make her pay for all the annoying things she'd done over the years. But she'd surprised him earlier. Come downstairs into his work haven for some odd reason or another. Her eyes had widened when she saw his handiwork. She couldn't stop looking at the dynamite.

When she saw his eyes, she screamed. He had to silence her.

Now her body was lying in the corner. He didn't even think about trying to get rid of it. He wouldn't be in this house much longer. The earthquakes were coming and after that he'd go wherever the voices told him to. They would have more work for him to do and he'd have to travel to another city first.

When he was finished here, the entire town would be dead.

Upstairs, he could hear his children arriving home from school. Three children. One boy and two girls. Twelve, ten, and seven. Cursing, he looked at his watch, wondering how the entire day had gotten away from him so quickly.

"Mom? Dad?" his oldest son was hollering, loud enough to wake the dead.

"I'll be up in a minute," he said, pleased at how calm his voice sounded.

He picked the gun up off the table and double-checked to make sure it was loaded. Standing up, he winced a bit as his knees popped. He turned and headed for the stairs. The voices whispered away at him, a soft seduction wrapping around his brain. They knew what to do and everything they said made so much sense.

There would be no remorse.

Just another job to do.

DANIEL

"Hello, Daniel."

He didn't look up. Instead he kept his gaze on the walls. Someone had washed them recently. He could see smears of dirt from where they'd tried to wipe it away. Cracks. Something had smashed up against it. Black cracks on white wall. Odd. Somehow he'd expected this place to be spotless, but it wasn't. The tiled flooring was worn and he could see tracks in the dust from where someone had moved the desk chair a few inches closer to the window. There were scuff marks on the door, and the window blinds were bent and crooked. The janitorial staff must be slacking off.

The woman in front of him didn't wear a white lab jacket with a stethoscope around her neck. She wore a business suit, beige, and had on running shoes. Her hair hung loose around her shoulders and she didn't wear glasses.

She looked very normal.

"I'm Dr. Coats," she continued when he didn't answer or acknowledge her smiling face. "As you know, I'm here to talk with you for a bit."

He crossed his arms and then changed his mind. He'd

read about that in psychology. It was considered a defensive position. It made him look like he had something to hide. Guilty. Instead he shoved his hands in his jeans pockets and tapped his foot against the desk. His shoelaces were dirty.

"Daniel?"

His eyes flickered over toward her. She was holding a clipboard and a pen but she hadn't started writing. She was waiting for him to talk. To spill his guts. So she could take notes and make decisions.

He didn't have anything to say.

"Daniel, do you know why you're here?"

Don't say a word. They can't do anything anyway. It'll be over soon.

But he had to say something. He didn't want to spend the next hour just gazing at the scuffed walls. Why did people always feel the need to cover stillness with sound? Even at home his mother had the television on almost twenty-four/ seven. She said it calmed her nerves but she never paid any attention to it.

The problem was he didn't know where to begin. A lot was riding on this conversation. There were countless words he could use, too many versions of everything going around in his head these days. How did he begin a conversation with such variables, each of which might lead to a different outcome?

"Daniel?"

"He started it." There. First words. Not the best choice. He should have said something else. Inwardly, he cringed.

Dr. Coats's lips curled upward. "So you can talk. I was beginning to think you were a mute."

Daniel shrugged.

"Excellent beginning. But no, we're not here because he

started it." She moved over toward the side of her desk and sat down on the edge. Daniel could smell the shampoo in her hair. Or maybe it was her hand lotion. Coconut.

There was a long silence in the room while Dr. Coats waited for him to speak again. He knew he should say something, but what? There wasn't any point in talking about it as far as he was concerned. It happened. He couldn't change the past.

There was no taking it back.

He wanted to take it back.

No, you don't. You want to do it again. Don't deny it. You hated Chuck Steinberg. Hated him. He treated you like dirt every single day of your life. What about the time he kicked the stray dog you were feeding? Then he told your mother you did it. What happened then? No, he deserved it.

"You told the police you don't remember doing it." She pulled the cap off the pen and waited. "So how do you know he started it?"

"I remember that much."

She wrote a few things down before continuing. "Would you like to tell me about it? The parts you do remember?"

You're dead meat, pretty boy. I'm gonna mess you up good.

He'd spent too much of his life being invisible to most adults. Now everyone knew him. In a few short minutes he'd gone from average nobody student to the one everyone talked about in the teachers' lounge and PTA meetings. Hell, this even made the newspaper. No one came near him anymore. Students actually went out of their way to avoid his locker. The group of girls who used to giggle when he walked past now turned and looked the other way. The last part he didn't mind so much. He preferred being alone.

Safer that way.

It'll be over soon.

"Daniel?" Dr. Coats tapped her fingernails on the clipboard, staring directly at his face. "Remember, everything you say in here is confidential. But I'll also remind you, we're here to talk. I can't help you if you don't help me."

He really wished she'd stop repeating his name. No one liked being reminded they existed.

He sighed. "He came up to me after class. Slammed me into the lockers. Said I'd side swiped his car with my bike. I hadn't been anywhere near his car. I don't even know what it looks like. When I denied it, he punched me twice."

The room was quiet except for the sound of Dr. Coats's pen as it scraped the paper. She wrote for a few minutes before looking back at Daniel. He didn't continue. The phone in his pocket began to ring. He'd forgotten to turn it off. Quickly he pulled it out. The Ryan Adams song grew insanely loud as the guitars seemed to bounce off the walls. He turned it off.

Suddenly his cheeks flushed and he felt like he'd done something terribly embarrassing. It was as if he'd shown up for this appointment wearing nothing but a raincoat and a pair of wet shoes. He glanced up at the doctor for a second and noticed how she was studying him intently.

"What else do you remember, Daniel?"

His mouth was dry and he couldn't swallow. What did he remember? They told him that he'd gone crazy. Grabbed Chuck by the shirt and punched him several times in the face. Once Chuck dropped to the floor, he'd kicked him repeatedly in the head until the math and biology teachers managed to drag him away. Chuck had to go to the hospital and get treated for a concussion. The doctors had to take X-rays because they were afraid Daniel had cracked the bigger boy's skull. Afterward Daniel discovered that the blood had soaked through his sneakers, and his white socks were stained red.

But he didn't remember.

He only knew what they told him.

"I don't know," he said. "That's pretty much it."

The doctor lowered her clipboard. "That's all you can recall?"

"Yes."

"Has this ever happened to you before? Not being able to recollect certain events?"

He hesitated and then shook his head. Lied. Waited while she made more notes on her clipboard.

"Head injuries?"

"No. Maybe when I was little. Nothing major, though. Basic kid stuff. I think I fell off the couch once. Had to go to the emergency room."

"So nothing recent, then?"

He shook his head.

"Any other fights?"

"Nope." At least none that he'd admit to.

"What about aggressive tendencies? Have you had thoughts about hurting people?"

He'd never considered himself violent before. He was the quiet guy who went to school each day and hung out with a few good friends. The semipopular boy who was always reading during lunch period and playing guitar on the front lawn when the weather was good. He was a lover, not a fighter. There were a few girls who would agree with that. He was the guy everyone assumed would go on to college, get a liberal arts degree, and end up being some obscenely successful writer. Even his yearbook picture said he was the guy "most likely to win a Pulitzer Prize in literature."

But violent? No, that wasn't his style. At least that's what he thought. What he kept telling himself.

Make them suffer. They will all die.

Daniel grabbed his jacket. "I've got to go."

Dr. Coats looked up at him in surprise. "We've still got forty-five minutes. I'll have to report this if you leave now. You know this isn't voluntary."

It doesn't matter. None of this matters.

"I'm sorry," Daniel said. "I don't want to talk anymore. I've got to go."

He grabbed the handle and was out the door before she had a chance to say anything more.

Outside it was raining and he pulled his hood up over his head and stuffed his hands in the pockets of his jacket. Turning around, he looked back at the hospital, half expecting to see big, burly orderlies running out the door to hunt him down. But no one came after him, only an older guy in a wheelchair, his pencil-thin legs sticking out from under his hospital gown as he tried to open a can of Pepsi.

A cold trickle of water worked its way into his shoes, soaking his feet. Looking down, he realized he was standing in the middle of a large puddle. He stared at the water, mesmerized as the raindrops pelted a steady beat into the ground.

It made him want to go swimming. Maybe he could catch a bus out to Buntzen Lake and go for a swim. It wasn't that cold yet. It would be nice to float with the rain tickling his face as the mountains loomed over him. Maybe he could get a diving mask so he could hold his breath and watch the fish swim beneath his feet.

The car honking its horn from behind pulled him out of his trance. Daniel stepped over to the curb, shaking his head slightly to try and clear it. Swimming? Now? Man, he needed to get his priorities straight. There were far more important things to worry about.

Looking back at the hospital, he knew he was going to get in trouble for leaving early. Part of his probation was the weekly visits to work on his anger issues.

But all of that seemed so insignificant.

He didn't know what it was but only that it was coming. Soon.

None of this would matter.